EVERY OTHER DAY

Also by Jennifer Lynn Barnes

RAISED BY WOLVES

TRIAL BY FIRE

Coming soon

TAKEN BY STORM

EVERY OTHER DAY

Jennifer Lynn Barnes

Quercus

First published in Great Britain in 2012 by

Quercus
55 Baker Street
7th Floor, South Block
London
W1U 8EW

First published in the US by
Egmont USA, 443 Park Avenue South,
Suite 806, New York, NY 10016

Copyright © 2012 Jennifer Lynn Barnes

...er.

...e

ISBN 978 0 85738 970 1

1 3 5 7 9 10 8 6 4 2

TO THE BSG-ERS:
MARK, CHRIS, ALIA, AND KELLY,
MY PARTNERS IN SCI-FI CRIME

The decision to make hellhounds an endangered species was beyond asinine, but I expected nothing less from a government that had bankrolled not one, but *two*, endowed chairs in preternatural biology (one of them my father's) at the University That Shall Not Be Named. The same government that thought you could train a horde of zombies just as easily as Pavlov's dogs.

When I ring the bell, you will cease tearing the flesh from my bones.

Yeah, right.

I was fairly certain that the world would have been better off if the vast majority of it—and *all* politicians, scientists, and talk show hosts—had remained in the dark about hellhounds, zombies, and everything else that went bump in the night. Sadly, however, that ship had sailed about two hundred years before I was even born.

Thanks, Darwin. Thanks a lot.

Taking my ire out on the blade in my hand, I ran it roughly over the edge of my sharpening stone—diamond with a hint of steel.

Tomorrow, I'd probably see things differently. I might even feel bad for sending the poor, endangered pups to a bloody,

bloody death. But today wasn't tomorrow. It was today, and the power was thrumming through my veins, the need to hunt, to kill, to *win*, building up inside of me, all-consuming and impossible to deny.

I pressed my knife to the stone and leaned forward, waiting for the worst of it to pass. I liked to imagine that in the olden days, before "logic" and "reason" took over, I would have had a trainer to teach me how to keep my head above water, but these days, people didn't believe in meditation or magic or anything other than s-c-i-e-n-c-e.

They didn't even believe in me.

That meant that I was on my own with the hunt-lust. I was on my own in every way that mattered.

"Kali?"

My father always said my name with a question mark, like he couldn't remember for sure how to pronounce it and wouldn't have laid money on whether or not I was actually his. I would have just as soon not been.

"Down here," I called, sheathing my knife under the leg of my boot-cut jeans and pushing the stone back under the workbench, where it belonged.

"Oh, there you are."

My father had a tendency to make statements like that as if they were revelations to everyone in the near vicinity, the object of his reference included. If a tree fell in the woods, and Professor Armand D'Angelo wasn't around to hear it, it most definitely made no sound.

"Here I am," I confirmed. I managed to keep my tone even and cool, but it cost me, and the desire to make something bleed nearly brought me to my knees.

"Was there something you wanted?" I asked, knowing that he wouldn't have sought me out if there wasn't.

"There's a faculty dinner tonight, a small get-together at Paul and Adelaide Davis's. It would be nice if you would put in an appearance."

Since my father was single and had been for years, he made a practice of using me as his "plus one." Suffice it to say, I wasn't the kind of person who enjoyed being used. Still, hunt-lust aside, I wasn't a monster, and I had a policy against being nasty when I didn't have to be.

Even with him.

"I can't make it," I said, completely straight-faced. "There's a study group, and it's my turn to do the section outline."

I'd never been to a study group in my life, and given my grades, my father had to have known that, but he just inclined his head slightly.

"I'll pass along your regrets."

This was our language: half-truths, obvious lies, accusations neither one of us would ever make. It was a system every bit as complicated as Morse code or the dancing of bees. Don't ask, don't tell, stay civil.

My burning need to hack some hellspawn to pieces surged anew.

Without another word, my father went back the way he came, and I was relegated to maybe-I-existed, maybe-I-didn't status for another week.

Most of the time, it felt like my father and I were completely different species. Possibly literally, depending on the day and whether or not I actually qualified as human at the time.

"I'm out of here," I said, more to prove that I *had* been there and that I *did* matter than to mark my exit. With a practiced motion, I popped the basement window open, pulled myself off the ground, and wormed my way through the tiny opening. The cool air hit my face first, and by the time my torso, legs, and feet had joined it, I'd already acclimated.

People like me didn't get cold.

We never lost our balance.

We didn't even have to eat.

That was, of course, assuming that there were others. Like me. Like my mother. And *that* was assuming—as I preferred to—that my condition was hereditary. Unfortunately, since good old mom had hit the road when I was three, I couldn't exactly ask her if she'd ever had the urge to hunt the way I was hunting now.

I couldn't ask her anything.

Pushing the fuzzy memory of her face—smiling, soft—out of my mind, I took off running, my feet pounding mercilessly and rhythmically into the pavement, again and again and again.

You have to find them. Hunt them. Kill them.

Kill them now.

The need pounded through my temples. It slithered its way through artery and vein, claiming the tips of my fingers, the small of my back.

Canis daemonum might have been the scientific classification for hellhounds, but the human body has over 60,000 miles of capillaries, and every one of mine was telling me that 'hounds were just demons, plain and simple. And hunting demons was what I did.

Who I was.

The purpose for which I'd been born.

Besides which, I hadn't exactly made friends at my new high school (yet), so it wasn't like I had anywhere else to be on a Sunday night.

You're getting closer. You have to find them.

Find them now.

The world blurred around me as I ran. Superspeed was not and had never been a part of the Kali package, so if anyone saw me as I streaked past them, all they would have seen was a normal girl—not quite Indian, not quite white—running at a sprint. What spectators wouldn't realize was that I could have continued running at this pace indefinitely—or at least until the sun came up the next morning.

People like me didn't get tired. We didn't wear out. Once we got a lock on our prey, we just kept coming and coming.

"Here." The word came out in a whisper, and I could almost see the way it rippled through the air. The closer I got to my quarry, the sharper my senses became.

I was very, very close.

Taking a deep breath, I slowed to a jog and then slipped effortlessly to a standstill, appraising my surroundings. Grass in severe need of cutting. Broken bottles with edges nearly as jagged as my unnaturally sharp fingernails. Abandoned lots, like this one, were the perfect hunting ground for *Canis daemonum*. My instincts had directed me to the right place.

Now, I just had to wait for the monsters to show.

In lore, hellhounds tracked down the souls of the damned and dragged them back to hell in bloody shreds. In reality, 'hounds were attracted to rotting sores, flesh marinated in dirt and grime, and certain chemical substances that found their way into the human bloodstream from time to time. They preyed on the weak, the degenerate, the homeless.

The kind of people that others ignored and forgot. The kind who weren't missed when a government-protected species mowed them down. If the worst happened here tonight, there might be an article in the paper the next day. There might not. But either way, the rest of the world would just go on living, comfortable in the belief that it couldn't happen to them, certain that the government had the monsters under control.

That they were the kind of thing that we *could* control.

Not tonight.

My heart didn't race. My gaze never wavered. And as the fetid smell of rotting blood filled my nostrils, the unbearable pressure inside my veins fell away like a sandcastle under the force of a wave. The entire world went still.

Perfect. Utter. Calm.

I crouched, reaching for my knife, feeling its weight, its balance, its edge. And then I lifted my eyes to stare directly into the blood-red irises of one beast after another as they emerged from the brush.

Three of them. Endangered, my ass.

The sound of the hellhound's growl, like a chainsaw tearing through rusted metal, was the only warning I got before it leapt for my jugular. A human would have ducked. I leapt for *its* jugular.

Our bodies collided midair, and I buried my knife up to the hilt in one blood-red eye before my opponent's superior mass and speed sent me flying backward, three hundred pounds of ugly on top of me. As my body slammed into the ground, I twisted my wrist and was rewarded with the sound of steel tearing through the hellhound's thick, sinewy flesh. From this angle, I couldn't get to the beast's heart, but I had bigger problems. Like, for example, the claws digging into my shoulders and the massive jaw that had unhinged itself like a snake's to aid and abet my prey in biting off my head.

Not so fast, Fido.

In a single, fluid motion, I jerked my dagger out of the monster's eye and thrust my other arm into its mouth. Razor-sharp teeth clamped down over the bait, cutting through the flesh of my forearm like butter and snapping the bone.

The crunching sound wasn't exactly pleasant, and the hellhound's breath was killer, but other than that, I wasn't really bothered. People like me?

We didn't feel pain.

My blood splattered everywhere, but messy eater or not, the hellhound managed to get some of my flesh in its mouth, and the moment my blood touched its tar-black tongue, the beast froze, paralyzed. I jerked what was left of my arm out of its mouth and managed to drag myself out from underneath its carcass as it fell.

Game. Set. Match.

My prey wasn't dead, not yet, but it would be soon. Even now, my blood was spreading through the hellhound's nervous system, a toxin every bit as lethal as a serpent's venom. I wasn't planning on waiting for the creature to die from the poison, though. It couldn't move. It couldn't fight back.

Might as well cut off its head.

But first, I had to deal with its friends, whom I mentally christened Thing 2 and Thing 3. Having seen their buddy's demise, Things 2 and 3 must have known what I was (which, quite frankly, probably put them several steps up on me, since I had nothing more than a string of educated guesses). But even with the instinctual knowledge that they were about to see the ugly end of the Circle of Life, the 'hounds didn't turn tail and run.

They couldn't.

My blood smelled too, too good.

Since I wasn't keen on the idea of letting either of the remaining beasts take a nibble of Kali-bits, I pressed the flat of my knife against the already-closing wounds on my left arm, coating the blade with my blood.

There was more than one way to skin a cat/decapitate a hellhound.

With my good arm, I flung my blade at Thing 3 in a practiced motion that left it buried in my target's throat. Thing 2 was not amused. With a roar of fury that sent the smell of sulfur, already thick in the air, surging, the 'hound charged. Left with nothing but my own bloody fingertips, I let out a war cry of my own, raked my nails over its face, and fought like a girl.

Breaking the beast's thick, leathery skin wasn't by any stretch of the imagination easy, even with fingernails sharper than most blades, but I managed, because the imperative—*you have to fight, you have to kill it, kill it* now—was that powerful, that insistent.

Flesh gave way under my nails, and my blood mingled with the beast's. The toxin was slower when injected, so instead of freezing immediately, Thing 2 and Thing 3 both began stumbling, their limbs gummed down by invisible weights.

"Sit," I said as they staggered and finally went down. "Roll over."

And then I smiled. "Play dead."

A quick glance at my watch (which I wore on the hand I *hadn't* fed to the hellhound) told me that I needed to hurry this along. I had three hours until my dad got home and another six before dawn—enough time to heal, but just barely.

"Knife," I whispered. I felt a twinge, a *ping* in the back of my mind that told me exactly where my knife was, exactly how to retrieve it. Being what I was meant that I had a sixth sense for weapons—once I'd laid hands on a blade, a gun, a garrote, it was mine forever. I knew exactly how to use it. I could feel its presence like eyes staring straight at the back of my head.

I'd never lost a weapon, and I never would.

"Well," I said, smiling at the blade as I tore it from Thing 3's throat, "let's get this show on the road." The fact that I was talking to a knife probably said something revealing about my character and/or mental state, but the way I saw it, my weapon and I were in this together.

We had work to do.

Three decapitations later, my own blood wasn't the only decoration on my body. Hellhound bits had splattered everywhere, coating me in gore. Another outfit down the drain.

Story of my life.

Glancing around to make sure I hadn't been seen, I stripped down to my sports bra and jeans and rolled the bloody shirt into a small ball. It was dark enough out that stains on denim wouldn't be visible from afar, and I had no intention of letting anyone get close enough to notice that I'd been Up to No Good.

Luckily, people like me?

We're surprisingly good at fading into the background.

"Be aggressive! Be, be aggressive!"

My head was throbbing. My arm ached like I'd spent the entire night doing push-ups, and I was exhausted. So, of course, Heritage High was having a pep rally. A loud, crowded, too-early-in-the-morning, I'm-not-even-sure-what-sport-season-we're-in pep rally.

With cheerleaders.

"Go Krakens!"

High school was, without question, the ninth circle of you-know-what.

As I slumped down in the bleachers, the sea of faces around me blurred, and I found myself longing for the University School, where at least the unidentified blur of my classmates would have been a familiar blur. I'd spent the first twelve years of my academic existence, from pre-K to grade ten, at the gifted program run by my father's university. But halfway through my first semester junior year, Father Dearest had decided that such a "small environment" wasn't good for my "developing social skills," a decision that I deeply suspected had less to do with my ability to make friends and influence people and more to do with the fact that Paul Davis, the new head of my father's department, had chosen to send his seventeen-year-old daughter, Bethany, to public school.

Bethany Davis was a cheerleader.

I was not.

Leaning back against the gymnasium wall, I did my best to disappear into the bleachers. It would have been easier to lose myself in the crowd if I hadn't claimed a spot on the back row, but I hated letting people sit behind me.

Much better to keep my back to the wall.

The compulsion reminded me, as it always did, that even on my human days, I was anything but normal.

"Are you ready to beat the Trojans?" the principal asked, his voice booming from the loudspeakers as he leaned into a microphone positioned directly in the middle of the cheerleaders. To my right, some senior delinquent made a comment about "beating" and "Trojans" that I tried very hard not to hear.

"Are you ready to show them what Krakens are made of?"

A roar of assent went through the crowd, and I wondered for maybe the hundredth time how Heritage High had ended up with a giant, multiarmed sea monster as its mascot.

"Are you ready to slip your tentacles around the Trojans and crush them like the ships of yore?"

I didn't wait to hear what the dirty minds of senior boys would make of the reference to "tentacles." I really and truly did not want to know. Instead, I brought my feet up onto the bleacher, pulled my legs to my chest, and rested my chin on top of my knees. Sometimes, I felt like if I could just fold myself into a small enough ball, my body would collapse on itself like a star, and I could supernova myself into a new existence.

One that didn't involve Trojans, Krakens, tentacles, or early-morning assemblies of any kind.

With my right hand, I massaged the muscles in my left, tuning out the world around me and assessing the damage the hellhounds had wreaked the night before. There wouldn't be a scar. There wasn't so much as a scratch or a hint of redness. The only indication that muscle and bone had spent the night knitting themselves back together was the residual soreness.

If I'd had another hour before dawn this morning, even that would have taken care of itself.

Reflexively, I glanced down at my watch: twenty-one hours and seventeen minutes until my next switch. Twenty-one hours and seventeen minutes with no hunt-lust. Twenty-one hours and seventeen minutes as human as the next girl.

Twenty-one hours and seventeen minutes for the things I hunted to hunt me.

"Go Krakens!"

I was 99 percent sure this wasn't the way it was supposed to be. That if there were any other people out there with my . . . *skills*, they weren't that way one day and not the next, but ever since the puberty fairy had knocked me upside the head with her little wand, that was the way things had been for me.

Every other day, I was human. And every other day, I was . . . not.

"Kra-kens! Kra-kens! Kra-kens!"

I put my feet back down on the ground and made a half-hearted effort at clapping to the beat. I even mouthed the words to the cheers coming at me from all sides. But what I really needed wasn't a dose of school spirit; it was a glass of water, an aspirin the size of my fist, and the answers to the history exam that I hadn't studied for the night before.

"As long as I'm dreaming," I muttered, my words lost to the cacophony of the gym, "I'd also like a pony, a convertible, and a couple of friends."

"That's a tall order."

I'd known that there were people sitting next to me, but I couldn't begin to imagine how one of them had heard me. *I* hadn't even heard me.

"Would you settle for a piece of gum, an orange Tic Tac, and an introduction to the school slut?"

I tried to process the situation appropriately. The cheering had finally died down, the principal had begun dismissing us section by section to go back to class, and the girl sitting next to me—who looked all of twelve years old, but was probably closer to my age—was holding out a stick of Juicy Fruit, a lopsided grin on her pixie face.

"Gum?" she repeated.

It wasn't a giant-sized aspirin, but it would do.

"Thanks," I said, taking the gum and eyeing the box of orange Tic Tacs sticking out of her jeans pocket. Gum. Tic Tacs. Based on the power of inference and the fact that she looked like she was on the verge of introducing herself, I concluded that must make her . . .

"Skylar Hayden," the girl said, sticking out her hand. "School slut."

I shook her hand and tried to process. "The school . . ."

"Slut," Skylar chirped, the picture of perky. "Even says so, right across the front of my locker. The janitors have tried to paint over it, but the locker elves are a persistent bunch, so there it stays."

"That's awful," I said, trying to imagine myself coming face-to-face with that word scrawled across my locker each morning.

Skylar blew a wisp of white-blonde hair out of her face. "It could be worse. I mean, I could have actually had to work for the title! Seriously, some of the girls on the student council have been angling for sensual supremacy for years, and all I had to do was let Justin Thomas kiss my neck for five seconds—which, quite frankly, could have been used as a medical substitute for bloodletting in medieval times. I'm talking *total leech.*"

It took Skylar four, maybe five, seconds to rattle off this entire statement and another two to catch her breath before she plowed on. "Anyway, Justin Thomas is Kelly Masterson's boyfriend, and she's the total alpha around here—captain of the cheerleading squad, student council vice president, and so on and so forth, et cetera, et cetera—so I got to jump straight to the front of the class. It's unfair, really. A lot of people have worked really hard for the title to lose it to an upstart little dark horse like me, but c'est la vie."

I knew from the content of Skylar's speech that it must have been served with a hefty dose of sarcasm, but there wasn't so much as a hint of attitude in her tone. She did earnest and perky way too well, and the combined effect of her words and her manner took me so off guard that I actually swallowed my gum.

"You sure you don't want a Tic Tac?" Skylar asked.

Dazed and confused didn't even begin to cover my current

state of mind, so I just held out a hand and allowed her to pour a couple of orange Tic Tacs into it. I popped one into my mouth. "Thanks."

"Not a problem," she said, and then she grinned again, more pixie than not. "So what's your deal? Rumor has it you're a princess incognito."

I swallowed my Tic Tac. At this rate, I could only hope that Skylar knew the Heimlich maneuver, because sooner or later, I was going to need it.

"Rumor has it I'm a princess?" I repeated.

"Daughter of a foreign dignitary and a Hollywood Grace Kelly type," Skylar confirmed. "But I might have just made that up. You're not really on the Heritage High rumor radar yet—but don't worry. If you spend a few more minutes talking to me, you will be."

For the first time, her blue eyes took on a hint of something that wasn't pep: wariness, maybe, or an expectation that I'd take this opportunity to run far, far away and never look back. But a moment later, whatever glimmer I'd seen was gone, replaced with a steely, uncompromising optimism that must have grated on the girls trying their hardest to freeze her out.

For less than a second, I considered my options: make a friend and become a social pariah, or walk away and spend my life in comfortable obscurity.

No contest.

"I'm Kali," I said, smiling for the first time in what felt like years. "I transferred to Heritage a few weeks ago. When I'm not failing history tests, I spend my time as an insurgent superhero who lives in fear of being hunted down by monsters or bureaucrats."

Skylar didn't balk for so much as a second. "Insurgent superhero! I love it. And your delivery was even better than mine—I could totally almost believe you."

Yeah. Totally.

Time for a subject change.

"So are the girls on the cheerleading squad really out to get you?" I asked, nodding toward the gym floor as our row began to trickle out of the bleachers.

Skylar shrugged. "They've been at it for about six months. I haven't cracked yet. It's driving them nuts."

I glanced at the cheerleaders out of the corner of my eye. Down to a one, they were glaring at the girl next to me. Completely unbothered by their death stares, Skylar stood up on her tiptoes and waved at them like she was greeting her very bestest friends. The entire squad immediately averted their gazes. Apparently, it was a social no-no to acknowledge the wave of someone you'd thoroughly shunned.

"Don't you ever just get sick of it?" I asked, shivering at the enmity coming our way. Even without my powers, I would gladly have faced down hellspawn over high-school mean girls any day.

"Get sick of watching them scrambling, trying to figure out why I'm not sobbing in a puddle in the girls' room?" Skylar asked, sounding for all the world like some kind of Zen master. "Not really. I've got five older brothers. Having the tampons stolen out of my gym locker on a regular basis kind of pales next to the power of the atomic noogie."

"They steal your tampons?" I asked incredulously, when really what I was thinking was more along the lines of *define "atomic noogie."*

"It's a classic mean-girl tactic," Skylar explained, and I had to remind myself that she was talking about the tampon-stealing, not the noogie. "Wearing white is like waving a cape in front of a bull."

"Good to know."

Part of me was still waiting to wake up and find out that this whole interaction had been one incredibly offbeat dream. It probably said something about my life that I didn't doubt for a second that I'd killed three hellhounds the night before but couldn't quite believe that after three very long weeks, someone at this school was actually talking to me. Most girls my age spent no more time thinking about preternatural beasties than they did serial killers or the North American grizzly. Yes, they were out there, and no, you wouldn't want to run into one in a dark alleyway, but that was about as far as it went.

Most girls my age had friends.

"So when's your history test?" Skylar changed the subject so fast that I almost didn't notice that we'd made it out of the gym. "The one you're going to fail?"

"Fifth period," I replied, trying not to be melodramatic about it. Failing a test wasn't the end of the world. This wasn't the first time, and it probably wouldn't be the last, but I vastly preferred to reside firmly in B and C territory—not at the front of the pack and not at the rear.

"You're a junior, right?"

I nodded, not bothering to question how Skylar knew anything about me other than what I'd already told her.

"I'm a sophomore, so I'm taking European History, not US, but Mr. McCormick teaches them both, so I should have you covered. Find me at lunch, and we'll talk."

And with those words, Skylar Hayden, force of nature and self-proclaimed school slut, disappeared into a nearby class-room, leaving me in the hallway alone.

Good, I thought reflexively. *It's better that way.*

But for once, I disagreed with the part of my brain that couldn't help but think like a hunter, even on my human days.

Maybe I don't want to be alone, I thought back. *Maybe I don't want to be a freak. Did you ever think of that?*

Cover your back.

This time, I didn't resist. I'd spent too much time track-ing down monsters to believe even for a second, even in my own high school, that I was ever really safe. Angling my back toward the wall, I headed for my biology class. The only good thing about this morning's assembly was that it meant that I didn't have to listen to my bio teacher waxing poetic about the differences between natural and preternatural species.

The difference, I thought, *is that the preternatural ones are too strong, too evil, and too human-hungry to live.*

If the rest of the world would just wake up and realize that no, the things I hunted weren't just misunderstood, and that *studying* them wasn't going to make them any less lethal, my job—not to mention my life—would have been so much easier. But no. My life wasn't meant to be easy.

Nothing ever was.

My muscles ached. My stomach rumbled. I could feel a migraine coming on, and I wanted nothing more than to climb back into bed. It was always like this the day after a hunt. I felt pain. I got tired. I needed to eat.

And I was anything but invincible.

Ducking into the classroom and trudging toward my seat, I looked down at my watch for the third or fourth time since I'd gotten up that morning.

Twenty-one hours and eight minutes until my next switch. Three hours until I saw Skylar at lunch.

This is going to be a very long day.

In the three weeks I'd been attending classes at Heritage, I'd learned more about primate social behavior than I'd gleaned from a lifetime of being plunked down in front of the Discovery Channel whenever my father didn't want to deal with the fact that he had a kid. Social hierarchies, dominance displays, mating rituals . . . all of the above were present in abundance in our high school cafeteria. Up until today, I'd successfully remained invisible.

And then I'd met Skylar Hayden.

Apparently, she wasn't kidding when she said talking to her would put me on the rumor radar *like that*. Already, I could feel the stares, like bugs crawling across the surface of my skin.

Show no fear.

If there was one thing that being what I was had taught me, it was that the difference between predator and prey was the rate of your heartbeat, the sweat trickling from your temples, the urge to shiver and run.

Twelve hours earlier, I hadn't even been capable of fear. Currently, however, I was feeling it in spades—not that I was about to let anyone else see that. Standing straight and holding my head high, I tossed my dark, glossy hair over one shoulder. The deep brown color was streaked with red highlights, so dark that in the right light they could have passed for black. Even in a ponytail, my hair was the perfect length for tossing.

Play to your strengths.

Another compulsion, another rule. A good hunter knew her strengths and her weaknesses, her enemies and her prey. Right now, all I knew was that the A-list crowd liked to write derogatory things on people's lockers, that they had it out for my one and only friend at this high school, and that I was an unknown entity who had just flung herself onto their radar.

Given that the best defense was a good offense, I figured that I could at least be an unknown entity with good hair.

"Kali!"

I recognized Skylar's voice the moment I heard it. Giving the rest of the school one more second to play Assess the New Girl, I turned in her direction. There, in the very center of the cafeteria, in what even a newcomer like me recognized as prime lunchtime real estate, she was holding court at a table full of . . . guys.

Clearly, my new friend had no problems whatsoever with the idea of adding fuel to the rumor fire.

"You made it," Skylar greeted me. "And in one piece, too! Congrats. That was some impressive hair-flipping."

In other circumstances, I might have been a little frightened by just how perceptive this girl was. At the moment, however, my eyes were trained on the other occupants of her table. There were three of them, and despite the fact that they looked nothing alike, they reminded me of those Russian stacking dolls, the kind that fit perfectly inside one another, in sizes small, medium, and large. The expressions on their faces were identical: curious, but wary.

"Darryl. John Michael. Genevieve." Skylar said their names one by one, and I attempted to match the monikers to their owners. Darryl was Large. John Michael was Medium. And Genevieve was Small—and, judging by the name, female, which I hadn't realized until I took a good look at her face. Her hair was cut almost to her scalp, and she was dressed in a nondescript hoodie. I wouldn't have pegged her for a "Genevieve," but who was I to judge?

I probably didn't look like the ultimate predator. Or, for that matter, an environmental terrorist. Depending on the day and who you were talking to, I was both.

"Kali D'Angelo," I said, introducing myself before Skylar had a chance to repeat my insurgent superhero line on my behalf. Given the illegal nature of my nightly activities, I needed to lie as low as I could. "I'm new. Sort of. I've only been here a few weeks . . ."

And now, I was babbling.

"Italian?" Genevieve asked, having latched on to my last name.

I figured that I owed her for having assumed she was a guy, so I cut her some slack and answered the question she hadn't asked, which came with a "you don't look Italian" clipped to the end. "My dad's Italian. My mom was Indian. From India."

Watching people try to figure out the mix of genes that had gone into making me look so "exotic" (FYI: not my favorite word) always made me wonder why they couldn't see beneath the surface to the power, the instinct, the *difference* underneath.

Eighteen hours and twelve minutes . . .

"Kali's got a history test next period," Skylar announced, and I couldn't tell if she was deliberately changing the subject, or if she was just the type who said every thought that crossed her mind. "I told her we had her covered."

Genevieve and John Michael didn't react to this announcement at all, but a small smile worked its way onto Darryl's lips. The light behind his dark brown eyes gave him a sort of gentle-giant vibe; I wondered exactly how tall he was and why the thought of a history exam made him happy.

"Six foot seven," Skylar said helpfully. "And he's psyched, because it's not often we get to initiate someone into the code."

"The code?" I repeated.

"Darryl's a whiz with numbers," Skylar explained. "It's sort of his thing."

Darryl ducked his head, and there was something in the motion that told me more about him than I'd known the moment before. He was quiet. Bashful. And I was willing to bet a lot of money that, like me, he had parents who didn't quite get his so-called "thing." My father would have preferred a social butterfly of a daughter; Darryl's parents had probably been hoping for a football player. Instead, fate had dealt them a half-human demon slayer and an oversized mathlete, respectively.

Life's a bitch.

"You have McCormick for history, yes?" Those were the

first words John Michael had spoken since I sat down at the table. I tried to place his accent and failed miserably. It wasn't American, even though he looked every inch the Boy Next Door. He was dressed from head to toe in black, but it was all too easy to imagine him fronting a boy band or dating a Disney starlet.

Since I was willing to bet that John Michael liked being compared to tween idols about as much as I liked being called exotic, I didn't say word one about his appearance. Instead, I just nodded.

"McCormick's tests are always multiple choice," John Michael continued, the word *multiple* picking up the cadence and melody of his accent more than any of its neighbors. "Which makes you a very lucky girl."

"Because even if I guess completely randomly, I'll still probably end up getting some of the questions right?"

"No," Skylar said. "Because all multiple-choice tests are subject to . . . the code!"

I must have looked as clueless as I felt.

"It is like this," John Michael explained. "Multiple-choice tests are written by people, yes? And the people, they tend to write them in a certain way. The code is Darryl's theory about the way the tests are written. And if you know how a test is written, you can pass it, even if you do not know the answers in and of themselves."

"Seriously?" I asked.

Skylar nodded. "Darryl took the AP psychology exam last year, just for fun. He only missed two multiple-choice questions, and he never even took the class."

Okay, that was kind of impressive.

"So what's *the code*?" I couldn't help lowering my voice to a whisper as I spoke. There was a certain solemnity to this moment.

"It's pretty simple."

It took me a minute to realize that Darryl was the one speaking. His voice was low in volume, but higher in pitch than I'd expected it to be, given his size.

"McCormick's tests have four choices, A through D. One is the correct answer. Two are decoys. The fourth can be anything, except that it's not related to the first three."

I really wasn't following here.

"All you have to do is figure out which answer matches up to two different decoys," Skylar said. "So say you've got a test that asks you, I don't know . . . what the color and consistency of a zombie's tongue is."

Genevieve giggled and then popped a french fry into her mouth. Clearly, she'd never been up close and personal with the walking dead, because *ew*.

"Ahem," Skylar said, clearing her throat, but she spoiled the effect by reaching over and stealing one of Genevieve's fries. "So, anyway, what is the color and consistency of a zombie's tongue? (a) black and hardened, (b) black and rotting, (c) brown and rotting, or (d) blue and scabby?"

E, I thought, *none of the above*. Zombies didn't have tongues. Like a caterpillar eating its way through its cocoon, the first thing *Homo mortis* did upon rising was eat the flesh out of its own mouth.

"Ummm . . . D?" I guessed, because I wasn't about to share that little tidbit with the table as a whole. As far as the rest of the world knew, I didn't have any more experience with zombies than the next girl. I knew that they existed. I knew to call Preternatural Control in the unlikely event that I saw one, but that was it. I didn't know what a horde of zombies smelled like. I couldn't feel them coming from a mile away. I'd certainly never snuck into my father's lab and disemboweled twelve of them in one night.

"Wrong," Darryl said softly.

Yeah, I thought back. *Most people think what I do is very, very wrong.* But then I remembered that, unless Darryl was psychic (and really, who believed in psychics these days?), he was referring to my answer, not my hunting habits.

Darryl smiled, as if softening the blow. "If the answer was 'blue and scabby,' what would the decoys be?"

Sensing that Darryl had just about reached his word limit for continuous speech, Skylar picked up where he'd left off. "When people write multiple-choice tests, they like to give you some answers that are almost right to keep you from picking the right one. Even if the teacher tries to write the answers randomly, it's nearly impossible to do, so they end up coming up with at least a couple of alternatives that have something in common with the real answer. In this case, 'blue and scabby' is the complete oddball."

"Okay," I said slowly. "So you throw that one out and you've got three choices left."

"Right, so then you look and you find one choice that has something in common with the other two. In this case, the word *black* and the word *rotting* both appear twice."

"So the ones that have black or rotting in it are the decoys, and the one that has both words in it is the answer?" I asked. The method didn't seem foolproof to me, but it was probably better than my previous plan, which had involved playing eenie meenie miny moe.

"It does not *al*ways work," John Michael said, echoing my thoughts, "but it is a lot bett*er* than guessing random*ly*."

Again I tried to place his accent, and again I failed. Still, John Michael's words had taken my mind off zombies. And hellhounds. And the other thirty-seven species of preternatural fauna identified since Darwin had gone public with the discovery of the Galápagos hydra and mankind had started turning over stones better left unturned.

"Another one, Skylar?" The voice snapped me out of my thoughts, and without turning around I knew that the person speaking was popular, good looking, and in the process of rolling his eyes. "Seriously, Skye, you're worse about collecting strays than Vaughn is. And that's saying something, given that he's a vet."

I resisted the urge to turn around in my seat and told myself I didn't care what this holier-than-thou, cooler-than-you, condescending a-hole looked like. Even though his voice did have a way of wrapping itself around your body, heavy and warm.

"What? I'm not allowed to make friends? You afraid you'll lose your position as the most popular member of the Hayden family?"

I heard the boy's sigh a second before I felt it on the back of my neck. It was like he was standing directly behind me, even though I knew we had to be separated by at least a foot or two.

"At least it's not another guy," the boy muttered.

Skylar rolled her eyes, stood up, and practically skipped

over to the boy behind me. I refused to turn around, but a moment later, Skylar came back into view, pushing an older, larger, male version of herself toward our table.

"This is Elliot," she said. "He used to be my second-favorite brother, but he's recently been demoted to third."

I could feel Elliot's eyes on my face, but couldn't seem to bring myself to meet them.

"This is Kali," Skylar said. "Be nice."

I finally lifted my eyes and met Elliot's lighter-colored ones. He was tall – not Darryl-tall, but at least three or four inches taller than my five seven. His hair was a shade or two darker than Skylar's, but cut so short that it still looked almost white. His skin was just tan enough to make me wonder why he'd been spending so much time in the sun, and his cheek-bones were a thing of beauty.

Not that I was looking or anything.

"Elliot is one of *those guys*," Skylar said. "You know, the ones who hang out with *those girls*, even though *those girls* are constantly stealing his sister's tampons."

All of the boys, Elliot included, winced, and I made a mental note that the word *tampon* was male kryptonite.

"Hey, I told them to lay off you. And they did." Elliot turned Skylar around and searched her eyes. "They did lay off, right?"

Skylar nodded. "Course, El. You don't need to worry about me."

Elliot glanced back at the table, and it was suddenly very clear that he thought Darryl, John Michael, and Genevieve were social mistakes on his sister's part. The football legacy who chose not to play. The exchange student with a predilection for eyeliner. The quiet, intense girl who didn't look very girly.

And then, there was me. Clearly, Mr. Judgmental did not approve.

"Hi, Kali. Nice to meet you. I promise I'm not the tool I might appear." Skylar poked her brother in the side, encouraging him to parrot her words. "Go on. Say it."

Elliot flicked her in the back of the neck with his thumb. "Shut up, squirt."

"You're in serious danger of being bumped down to fourth-favorite-brother status," Skylar told him. "And Lord knows I'm not really feeling like promoting Reid, so behave."

Elliot rolled his eyes, but then he looked back at mine, and for the first time, he smiled. "Hi, Kali. It *is* nice to meet you."

I tried to make my mouth form words, but couldn't quite get it to obey, and a split second later, my moment had passed. A girl who looked vaguely familiar sidled up to Elliot, pressing her body close to his. Her hair was red, almost as dark as the streaks in mine, and offset by skin so flawless it was practically luminescent. Her white tank top looked simple and sweet, until she turned sideways to place a proprietary hand on Elliot's arm, and I realized that the top was nearly backless.

"C'mon, El," she said as my eyes were drawn to what appeared to be a tattoo on her lower back. "Everyone's waiting."

Everyone, her tone said, *who's anyone.*

I tried to work myself up to a good hair toss, but failed, because I couldn't take my eyes off the tattoo, which looked an awful lot like a serpent eating its own tail. Which meant that there was a distinct possibility that it wasn't a tattoo.

No. Couldn't be.

The girl turned again, tugging at Elliot, and this time, he allowed himself to be led away.

"Sorry about that," Skylar said. "My brothers are a little protective. Elliot doesn't understand why I'm not trying to work my way back into the popular crowd, where he can keep an eye on me. And Bethany is afraid if he spends more than five seconds talking to me, her social status might suffer. It's a girlfriend/boyfriend, brother/sister thing."

I nodded to show that I was listening, but couldn't bring myself to actually respond, because in that instant, I realized why the girl with Elliot had looked so familiar. Skylar's brother was dating Bethany Davis. The same Bethany Davis whose father was my father's new boss. The one I'd been sent to Heritage High to rub elbows with.

Staring after the golden couple, I spent a few seconds really, really hoping that Bethany Davis had a tattoo. Because if the symbol on the small of her back *wasn't* a tattoo, things were going to get very ugly, very soon.

The kind of ugly that ended with someone buried six feet under.

As much as I didn't want to consider the possibility, I had to. If the *ouroboros* on Bethany's back was real, she'd be dead by the end of the day.

And in my current state, there wasn't a thing I could do to stop it.

During World War II, what was the main source of information used by the Allies to gather intelligence from inside the opposing camp?

    (a) Human spies
    (b) Advances in technological surveillance
    (c) Chupacabra informants
    (d) Postmortem interrogation

The world was mocking me. I was sure of it. The fact that I was sitting in Mr. McCormick's fifth-period history class, taking a multiple-choice exam while Bethany Davis was out there with a death sentence inked into her flesh, would have been bad enough. That the first question on the test involved chupacabras pushed the scenario to downright ironic.

Somebody up there hates me.

Staring at the test until the question started to blur, I tried my hardest not to think about the c-word. Not about the legends that said chupacabras were the size of a large wolf, with spines decorating their backs, like some kind of mammoth porcupine or a miniature stegosaurus brought back to life. Not about the smaller, deadlier, and less fictional variety that every preternatural biologist in the world would have given their right arm to study.

Translated, *chupacabra* meant "goat-sucker." I had a few other names for them, at least one of which rhymed with the latter half of the literal translation.

Don't think about it, I told myself. *There's nothing you can do, anyway. Just answer the question.*

I took a few calming breaths and purged my mind of the unwanted mental image of a fatally still Bethany Davis, her face pale, her veins empty.

Just concentrate on the question. Use the code.

It was easy to imagine Skylar's voice in my mind, and to see Darryl's eyes light up the way they had when we'd talked about his test-taking strategy. That helped.

A little.

First, identify the oddball.

That was easy enough. "Technological surveillance" had less than nothing to do with the other three. I pressed my pencil to the page and dragged it over choice (b). I was trying so hard to stay in control of the situation that it was a miracle I didn't inadvertently snap my pencil in half.

Step two, identify the decoys.

An informant and a spy were pretty much the same thing, which meant that one of those answers was probably a decoy and one of them was probably the correct choice. Unwittingly, my gaze flickered to choice (d), which, by default, had to be the second decoy.

Postmortem interrogation.

Again with the zombies. Even if I hadn't been "initiated"

into the code, I would have been able to rule out that answer. A lack of tongue meant that zombies couldn't speak. An insatiable hunger for human flesh meant that trying to talk to one was highly inadvisable.

Postmortem interrogation. And hellhounds are just overgrown puppies. Yeah, right.

My eyes flicked back up to the other two choices, and I knew in the pit of my stomach that the correct answer was the one I least wanted to look at, let alone circle.

Informants and spies were the same thing. Chupacabras and zombies were both supernatural creatures. Ergo, the correct answer, the one with two decoys, was (c) Chupacabra informants.

Chupacabras are remarkable creatures. This time, it was my father's voice that I heard in my head. *Absolutely remarkable. At first, we thought they were little more than overgrown ticks, preternatural only in their ability to literally disappear into the creatures they feed on. But when Klaus Eigelmeier discovered that in sucking a victim's blood, chupacabras also absorb their memories . . . psychic phenomena, Kali! Bona fide psychic phenomena in a biological species!*

I'd been four or five when Klaus had proved what the Allies' strategists must have strongly suspected: *chupacabras* weren't just bloodsuckers. They were memory eaters as well.

In a different world, the idea of psychic memory transfers probably wouldn't have seemed any stranger than the fact that after Darwin's fateful voyage on the *Beagle*, the rest of the preternatural world had fallen to discovery like dominoes, with new species crawling out of the woodwork en masse. Where had they come from? Why hadn't we discovered them sooner? No one knew. But two hundred years after the fact, science had more or less gotten a handle on the limitations of preternatural ability. And psychic phenomena?

That kind of thing was unheard of, and no other species—natural or preternatural—had demonstrated any kind of psychic power, before or since. My father's enthusiasm at Eigelmeier's announcement had actually led him to look me straight in the eye. To this day, it was the most he'd ever said to me in one sitting.

Maybe that was why I could still hear him saying every word.

Maybe that was why I knew that when a chupacabra started draining its victim, the image I'd seen on Bethany's lower back—a snake eating its own tail—appeared somewhere on the victim's body.

Maybe that was why I couldn't stop picturing Bethany's eyes going vacant and empty as the chupacabra stole her memories. Her lifeblood.

And then her life.

B.

I scrawled the letter onto the page in big, defiant script, even though I knew the answer was wrong. And then, I folded my test paper in half, walked to the front of the room, handed it to the teacher, and asked to be excused.

"Excused?" Mr. McCormick gave me one of those looks that said something along the lines of *Look here, missy, I know what you're up to*, but then he seemed to realize that he did not, in fact, have any idea what my agenda was. He appeared to find this somewhat unsettling.

"If you leave now, I won't be able to let you take a makeup exam," he warned me.

I looked him straight in the eye, even though it physically hurt me to do it.

Blend in. Don't make waves. Don't look up.

That was the mantra I lived by. But not today.

"I understand," I said softly. "I just really need to go, anyway."

"You could at least guess," McCormick replied. "It's multiple choice. It wouldn't take you very long, and it would be better than a zero."

Chupacabras, I thought.

Puncture holes in perfect, luminescent skin.

Vacant, empty eyes.

"I need to be elsewhere."

That statement got me another look. This one said *I have concluded that you are on drugs.*

Clearly, I was getting nowhere fast. There was a part of me that wanted to just turn and stalk out of the room. I seriously doubted he would physically stop me, but that scenario would have inevitably ended with someone calling my father. I'd be labeled as a troublemaker.

There would be conflict.

I really didn't do conflict.

Think, Kali, I told myself, and then, all of a sudden, the answer was there, accompanied by an angelic chorus of hallelujahs.

"Tampons!"

Mr. McCormick jumped like I'd hit him with a Taser. "Excuse me?"

"Tampons," I said again.

"Ms. D'Angelo, I've been teaching for six years. I'm well aware that there may be certain . . . er . . . female issues—"

I cut him off. "Tampons." It was ridiculous. I couldn't stop saying the word, and he couldn't stop flinching. "Somebody stole mine. All of them. I need to go."

Mr. McCormick said absolutely nothing, but he handed me a bathroom pass. He seemed to know that I wouldn't be back, but accepted my absence as the price that had to be paid to keep me from saying *that dreaded word* one more time.

As I stepped into the hallway, any thrill of victory I might have felt subsided, because I couldn't deny, even for a second, what I'd known since I saw the symbol on Bethany's back.

Whether I was in class taking a test or out wandering the hallways, there wasn't anything I could do to save her. I was weak. Human. There was no instinct pounding in my temples, compelling me toward a battle I'd inevitably win. I had no idea where Bethany was, and even if I found her, what was I going to do—talk to the little parasite? Ask it to let her go? Tell the school nurse?

Who was I kidding? By the time the *ouroboros* symbol appeared on a person's skin, it was too late for medical science to intervene. The only thing that could save Bethany Davis's more-popular-than-thou, oh-so-charming personage was a trade, and even that was supposed to be pretty much impossible. But hypothetically, if the chupacabra *did* find someone it liked better, it might leave Bethany before it sucked all of the life out of her.

And if that person happened to be me . . .

I glanced down at my watch.

Seventeen hours and twelve minutes.

If I could last that long with a psychic, parasitic hellbeast sucking the blood out of my body and the thoughts out of my brain, I'd be fine, because seventeen hours and twelve minutes from now—*eleven* minutes from now—I'd change. My blood would change.

And the bloodsucker would die.

As far as plans went, it was imprecise, but at the moment, it was all I had.

† † †

"Can you tell me what class Bethany Davis is in right now?"

The secretary had her own version of Mr. McCormick's *I know what you're up to* look, and I wasn't altogether surprised to find myself on the receiving end of it. If I'd had any other choice, I wouldn't have just marched myself into the office to ask, but it was a pretty big school, and I didn't think that popping my head into every classroom, looking for Bethany, would go over much better.

"Aren't you supposed to be in class, Ms. . . ." the secretary trailed off, as she realized that she didn't know my name.

I was loathe to provide it for her, but given that there couldn't have been more than three Indian kids in the entire school, I seriously doubted she'd have trouble tracking me down if she was so inclined.

"D'Angelo," I said. "Kali. I'm new. And I really need to talk to Bethany. It's an emergency."

The secretary leaned over her nameplate, and even

though I knew she was human down to her artificial finger-nails, I got the distinct feeling she could see my soul. And that she was thinking of eating it.

"Kali D'Angelo," she repeated.

If I'd had any school-yard sins to confess, they would have come pouring out of my mouth, just listening to her say my name. But I really did try, for the most part, to be a good kid. To not cause trouble. To be left alone.

"Look, Mrs. Salinger," I said, stumbling over her name, ter-rified that I'd slip up and inadvertently address her as Mrs. Soul Eater instead, "it really is an emergency." True. "My dad works with Bethany's dad," I continued—also true. "And if I don't find her right now . . ."

My voice cracked. With a shake of her head, Mrs. Salinger handed me a tissue, assuming, I suppose, that I was on the verge of tears.

"Does this have something to do with a boy?" she asked.

Boy? I thought. *Bloodsucking menace to society? Same dif-ference, really.*

"Yes," I said seriously. "It does. Please don't eat my soul."

It took me a few seconds to realize that I'd added that last part out loud.

"Ummm . . . I mean . . ."

Mrs. Salinger held up a hand. "There's not a thing that goes on in this school that I don't know about, Kali D'Angelo. People talk. I listen. I do not, for the most part, eat souls."

"Of course not—I didn't mean to—"

My feeble apology was cut off by the sound of blood-red nails hitting a pristine keyboard. I felt like Mrs. Salinger was adding my name to the roll call in hell.

"Bethany's got drama this period," she said finally. "I believe the class is in the auditorium doing a cold read of *The Glass Menagerie.*"

"*The Glass Menagerie,*" I said, unable to keep from dumbly repeating everything the woman said.

"Go on, now."

She didn't have to tell me twice. I hightailed it out of her office and to the auditorium. I needed to find Bethany before I lost my nerve or found my common sense. Her life depended on my being simultaneously brave and stupid.

Lucky her.

As I opened the door to the auditorium, I braced myself. Every single person in the room turned and looked at me.

This time, at least, I had a cover story. "The office needs to see Bethany Davis," I said.

The drama teacher mumbled something that I couldn't decipher, but I guess he must have given Bethany permission to leave, because a moment later, she was sauntering toward me: sugar and spice and eyes that said *Did I give you leave to speak my name, lowly serf?*

I could tell already that this was going to be buckets of fun. When Bethany reached the door, she turned around and smiled, waving at the teacher in a motion that looked more like the work of a hypnotist than a teenage girl. Exactly five seconds later, the two of us were in the hallway, headed toward the office.

"Wait," I said. The word came out high and squeaky, even though my voice is normally closer to the "husky" end of the spectrum. When Bethany didn't stop, I reached out to grab her arm. She tried to shrug me off, but I tightened my grip.

"What is your problem?" she huffed. "You delivered your little message. Now, shoo."

I didn't move, and since I had a hold on her arm, neither did she.

"Oh, I know what this is about," she said, her green eyes widening in a way that made me think, for a split second, that maybe she did.

"You do?" I asked.

Her widened eyes narrowed. "You're Skylar's new little project, and you think that since I'm with Elliot, and he shares an unfortunate number of his chromosomes with Little Miss Loose Legs, you have an in."

For a few seconds, I considered letting go of her arm, turning around, and walking off. If she was retaining enough of her memories to be this much of a bitch, she clearly wasn't in that much danger.

But I couldn't make myself do it. Couldn't drop her arm. Couldn't turn around. All I could do was drop the act.

"Do you have a tattoo?"

"Excuse me?" Bethany did the ice-queen motif to perfection, but at the moment, I had bigger things to worry about than painting a giant social target on my forehead.

"It's a simple question. Yes or no—do you have a tattoo?"

Something in my voice, or maybe my eyes—which had a tendency to go nearly black when I was on a hunt—must have convinced her that I was serious, because she actually answered me.

"Not that it's any of your business, but no, I don't have a tattoo."

The desire to say *Well, then, if you want to live, come with me* was overwhelming, but I didn't see the point in being cryptic or vague.

"You have an *ouroboros* on your back." I said the words softly. I didn't want to be saying them at all.

Bethany blinked several times, and I plowed on.

"It's a symbol," I told her, "of a snake eating its own tail. It has a lot of different mythological meanings, but only one scientific one."

"You think I've been bitten," Bethany said, and something about her tone of voice reminded me that I wasn't the only one who'd grown up with a father in academia.

"I think you've been bitten. I think it burrowed inside of you. I think it's drinking your blood and absorbing your memories—"

"I know what chupacabras do." Bethany probably didn't spend her nights hunting the preternatural, but I was beginning to suspect that she knew more than I'd given her credit for and that her sole exposure to the concept of chupacabra possession wasn't some Lifetime Original Movie called *Three Days to Live*. "I know *exactly* what these things do, Kali."

She was scared enough that she'd dropped the pretense of not knowing my name. Good. Maybe that meant she'd be scared enough to listen to me, too.

"I think I can get it out of you," I said.

"Do you think I'm stupid?" she asked me, her voice equal parts vulnerability and venom. "My dad studies these things. It's all he ever even talks about. If there's an *ouroboros* on the subject's skin, there's nothing anyone can do. But at least, thanks to you, I know I'm doomed. Really appreciate that."

Each second I put off taking action, my resolve faltered.

What if I didn't last seventeen hours? What if Bethany told her father what I'd done, and he told my father, and the entire university faculty figured out that I wasn't *Homo sapiens* 24/7? What if I couldn't get the parasite to jump ship, anyway? I was human. My blood was human. There was no real reason to think that it might work.

But what if it did?

Do it. Do it now.

"Knife," I whispered, but of course, nothing happened. I wasn't a weapon whisperer. I wasn't invincible. I was just a seventeen-year-old girl who was about to do something very, very stupid.

"Close your eyes."

Bethany arched one eyebrow, opening her eyes wider. Even with mortality staring her in the face, she was still one of *those girls*.

"I might be able to help you," I said. "Close your eyes. Worst-case scenario, you lose fifteen seconds. Best-case scenario, you're not a corpse in the morning."

She closed her eyes.

I bent over and reached inside my boot. Heritage High wasn't the kind of school that invested money that could be spent on pep rallies on something as trivial as metal detectors, and I'd learned the hard way never to go anywhere unarmed.

My fingers closed over the hilt of the knife, and I stood back up, blade in hand. The weapon felt heavier than it had the night before. The balance of the blade should have comforted me, it should have been familiar, but instead, it was a reminder that I had no idea what I was doing. I was weak. I was stupid. I was alone.

Do it.

I gritted my teeth together and sliced into my own arm. For a moment, all I felt was the coolness of the knife's tip, but then the white-hot fire spread up my entire forearm, bringing tears to my eyes.

Biting down on my lip hard enough to draw blood there, too, I sheathed the knife and ran my right hand over the wound, until my fingertips were smeared with red. Taking a deep breath, I leaned forward and spread my blood across Bethany's back.

Nine hours earlier, no preternatural creature would have been able to resist the lure, but right now, I was human.

"Oh. My. God. What are you doing?"

"Keep your eyes closed." I barely recognized my own voice. I'd cut my arm deeper than I'd meant to, and the blood just kept coming and coming. I thrust my arm closer to the *ouroboros* symbol.

"Here, kitty-kitty," I said, unwilling to let the enormity of the moment sink in. "Auntie Kali has num-nums for you."

Nothing happened, and I lowered my voice in both volume and tone. The words came fast and then slow, and every single one of them sounded like it was being spoken through me more than by me.

"You want memories? I've got memories. You want blood? I've got blood. You don't want her. You want me."

Bethany stiffened. "Kali, what are you—"

"Bethany. Shut. Up." I lowered my voice to a purr. "Is this what you want? Some cheerleader? What's her best memory—getting to stand on the very top of the pyramid? Do you have any idea what I've seen? What I've done?"

Do you have any idea what I am? I wanted to say, but I didn't. My plan required me playing bait, but it also required a certain amount of discretion. If my target figured out what I was before it took the bait, this wouldn't end well for anyone.

"I know you can hear me. I know you can smell me. I know you're sucking these words out of Bethany's brain as fast as I can say them. I know that you know—you don't want her. You want me. This girl is Denny's. I'm gourmet."

This was a bad plan, bad idea. I felt that with certainty as my arm went numb. As the little stars dancing at the periphery of my vision began to turn dark and spread like inkblots across a page.

I don't want to die.

The thought came, quick and vicious, into my head, and then there was a sound like a gun going off and a smell like rotten eggs. Bethany stumbled forward and went down to her knees, and I sank into velvety nothingness. It caressed my skin, lapped at my temples, the nape of my neck. It circled me like smoke, its touch light, but all-consuming.

And just as I was about to lose consciousness, I heard the voice.

Hello, Kali. I'm Zev.

Consciousness came slowly, like the rising of the tide, my body and my mind falling gradually into sync with each other until I remembered that I was called *Kali*, that what I was feeling was known as *pain*, and that here—in this space, in this time, in this *body*—I wasn't alone.

Hello, Kali.

The voice in my head was silent, but my memory of those words was ice slipping down my spine.

Everything hurts, I thought, clinging to the pain and pushing all other sensations away. A groan escaped my throat, and my eyelids fluttered. For a second, I thought I saw a person out of the corner of my eye: broad through the shoulders, muscular and sleek and made almost entirely of shadow, but even before I'd marked its existence, it was gone.

I blinked, and the hunter in me began automatically surveying my surroundings: bright lights, a padded surface, paper that crinkled beneath me as I moved, and on the opposite wall, I could almost make out a cartoon drawing of . . .

A kraken.

This time, when I groaned, I put some oomph in it. My entire body felt like someone had taken a Weed Whacker to it, then strung me up like a piñata. Awareness of where I was and how I'd gotten there did nothing to soothe me.

Chupacabra. Blacking out. Nurse's office.

Well, crap.

I struggled to sit up, and as I did, the feeling that I wasn't alone in my body spread from my brain to my chest and from my chest out to each of my limbs. To the outside world, I probably looked no different than I had before, but whether it was my imagination or my body's reaction to being bitten, I could *feel* an alien presence in the warmth of my skin, the blush in my cheeks, the steady, but rapid beating of my heart.

A whisper in my ear.

A phantom hand on the small of my back.

I shivered and wondered if this was what it had been like for Bethany. If this was normal. And then I stopped wondering—because since when had I *ever* been normal?

Luring this thing from Bethany's body to mine wasn't normal.

Thinking that I could be bitten and survive wasn't normal.

And the way I felt now?

I forced myself to stop thinking about it and concentrated on the thing—the only thing—that mattered now.

I'm going to find you, I thought fiercely, willing my newly acquired parasite to absorb that particular thought and leave the rest alone. *I'm going to find you, and I'm going to fight you, and I'm going to win.*

Maybe it heard me. Maybe it didn't. I had no idea if these things were picky little memory eaters, or if my brain was an all-you-can-eat chupacabra buffet. I didn't know how this was supposed to work or why. For most people, it probably didn't even matter, because by the time they realized they'd been bitten, they were as good as dead.

Pushing that cheery thought out of my mind, I did a quick injury check on my organs and bones. The routine was familiar, one I paced my way through every other morning as I went from dispassionately watching my body heal to wondering if, this time, I might have pushed things too far.

Head, arms, wrists, ribs.

Feet, ankles, knees, hips.

"No broken bones." I said the words out loud, more to fill the silence and empty space before me than for the benefit of any audience. "Arm's still slashed up, though, and I feel . . ."

Awful.

Sluggish.

Violated.

Aware.

Of all of the answers on the tip of my tongue, the last one was the truest—and the most disconcerting. I'd learned the hard way to pay attention to my surroundings, but I'd never once felt so aware of my own body, like I was wearing it for the first time.

Like it was wearing me.

"Do you feel like a knife-toting freak with a hero complex? Because, no offense, but evidence would suggest that you probably should."

Despite myself, I jumped. There was enough going on inside my head that somehow, I'd neglected to realize that I wasn't the only person lying on one of these criminally uncomfortable cots.

"God, I didn't think you were ever going to wake up. I

managed to talk the nurse out of calling your dad. And mine. If anyone asks, you always get light-headed at that time of the month, and you cut your arm when you passed out."

For someone who'd been on a downward spiral toward death a half-hour before, Bethany Davis looked remarkably calm and collected as she propped herself up on both elbows, her red hair streaming down her back like she'd lifted the pose from some kind of sunscreen ad.

I processed her words and responded. "You didn't tell the nurse I'd been, I don't know, *bitten by a chupacabra*?"

I wasn't big on confrontation—at least not with humans— but Bethany must have known as well as I did that the first few hours after a person was bitten were an open window for treatment. Anyone who'd seen the travesty that was *Three Days to Live* could tell you that until the *ouroboros* appeared on a patient's body, modern science could theoretically extract and contain the chupacabra. I wasn't exactly the poster child for Fans of Modern Science, and the last thing I wanted was an overzealous doctor turning me into a case study in the *New England Journal of Preternatural Medicine*, but Bethany had no way of knowing any of that.

As far as she was concerned, I was just an ordinary girl. A knife-toting freak whose hero complex had just saved *her* life. The least she could have done was make an attempt at saving mine.

"Kali." Bethany's voice was quiet, her tone soft, and she caught her pink lips between pearly white teeth, like the motion would keep the words she was about to say inside her mouth, keep them from being true. "Sweetie, look at your stomach."

I knew what I was going to see before I glanced down at the bit of midriff peeking out over the band of my dark-wash jeans. A member of the cheerleading squad had just called me "sweetie."

This could not possibly be good.

"A snake. Eating its own tail." I said the words out loud to make them matter less. The symbol that had appeared as black ink on the small of Bethany's back was golden against the gentle bronze of my own skin. Even though I could only see the tip of the *ouroboros*, I could suddenly *feel* the full measure of the symbol, like someone was tracing a fingernail lightly around its edge.

"I would have told them." Bethany met my gaze and held it. "As soon as I woke up, I would have told them to get you to a hospital or my dad's lab ASAP if I'd thought it would do any good, but I saw the *ouroboros*, and I knew that it wouldn't."

I couldn't tear my eyes from the mark, couldn't come up with a reasonable explanation for the fact that it had appeared only moments after I'd been bitten, when the incubation period was supposed to last hours or days.

This wasn't normal. This wasn't how it was supposed to happen.

"So what's the plan?" Bethany asked.

"The plan?"

She gave me a look. "Kali, please. No messiah complex in the world is going to make someone like you take on a death sentence for someone like me. You deeply suspected the chupacabra would take the trade—even though that's supposed to be *impossible*—and you had some kind of fail-safe in place for when it did. So again, I ask, what's the plan?"

I ignored her question and hoped she'd take the message. Whatever my "plan"—and I was using the term fairly loosely— entailed, having Bethany Davis along for the ride was not a part of it.

"Has anyone else seen this?" I asked, nodding toward my stomach and then tugging on the edge of my shirt to cover the incriminating mark as best I could.

"The nurse might have." Bethany turned to sit cross-legged on her cot. "She didn't say anything, but I'm a pretty good judge of people, and there was a distinctly sketchy air about her when she agreed not to call our parents. Either I'm *really* convincing, or she's the worst school nurse *ever*, or something is up. Worst-case scenario, she called the CDC."

"The CDC," I repeated, unable to imagine why the nurse would agree not to call our parents but feel compelled to dial up the CDC.

"The Centers for Disease Control?" Bethany gave an impatient roll of her eyes. "To whom all contagious and preter-natural illnesses must be reported? Ringing any bells?"

Great.

As if dealing with my father, the legions of hell, and a variety of environmental protection agencies on a regular basis wasn't bad enough.

"Where *is* the nurse?" I asked. What I really meant was something more along the lines of *If I try to leave, will she try to stop me?*

"No idea," Bethany replied. "She bandaged your arm, gave me some orange juice, and lit out of here like the two of us had sprouted horns." She paused for a brief second. "I'm *not* going to sprout horns, am I?"

If the situation hadn't been so incredibly dire, it might have been funny. Who knew how much blood I'd lost from the cut in my arm? It was shallow, but long, and now a blood-sucker was mining me from the inside. There were memories I didn't want to lose—my mother's face, my best friend from kindergarten, the first time I'd sprayed a will-o'-the-wisp with liquid nitrogen—and thoughts that I couldn't risk *it* getting a hold of. I had bigger things to worry about than Bethany's fear of growing horns.

"Bethany, you'll be fine. Just forget this ever happened and go back to life as usual."

That was the nicest way I could think of to say *Leave me alone*. All things considered, it should have worked. I'd always excelled at being the kind of girl other people left behind.

But Bethany didn't take the bait. "So, what? You save my life, and in exchange, you expect me to abandon you to the geek squad at the CDC, so they can chop you into pieces and stuff you in neatly labeled test tubes? Or maybe I'm supposed to pretend like if we don't find a way to get that thing out of you, you won't die, or that I totally won't care at all if you do."

Actually, yes. She was the kind of person who referred to her boyfriend's baby sister as "Little Miss Loose Legs." Leaving and never giving me another thought was exactly what I expected a girl like Bethany to do.

"Seriously, Kali? I'm shallow, not a sociopath. There's a dif-ference, and I am not leaving you here alone, so suck it up and deal me in."

My mouth dropped open in abject shock, and Bethany

began speaking very slowly, as if I were a small child or a very dense jock.

"What. Is. The. Plan?" She narrowed her eyes. "I'd offer to call my dad, but he'd just put you in quarantine. And call the CDC. *And* you'd still die. Whatever your plan is, it has to be better than that."

I have a plan, and I don't need your help.

For once, my mouth and brain were in complete and total accord, so I said exactly what I was thinking. Bethany blinked several times, but before she could reply, a familiar blonde head peeked over the edge of the doorframe, and Bethany's nonsociopathic tendencies flew right out the door.

"Can I help you?" she asked, every inch the ice queen.

Skylar shook her head, sending wisps of blonde hair flying. "No, you can't help me, but I think I can help you. Both of you." Skylar paused for a breath, and that was my first clue she was on the verge of a truly epic babble. "I can't tell you why, and I can't tell you how I know, but the two of you need to get out of here in the next two minutes and forty-five seconds, or something really, really bad is going to happen to one and/or both of you, and it's going to make someone with a soul the color and consistency of bubbling tar very, very happy."

The end of Skylar's run-on sentence was punctuated by a moment of absolute silence.

Listen to her.

This time, the voice in my head *wasn't* mine, and I felt the words in the pit of my stomach, and all the way down to the soles of my feet. I wanted to argue or disobey on principle, but even to human eyes, the world looks different in the calm before the storm. Every instinct my hunting habit had taught me said that it was time to take to higher ground.

Now.

In an instant, I was beside Skylar, and Bethany followed reluctantly on my heels. Skylar shrugged off her hoodie, handed it to Bethany, and spoke in an eerily calm and measured voice. "Put this on and pull up the hood. Then walk, don't run, toward the cafeteria. When we hit the corner, turn right."

Something about the younger girl's unnaturally even keel must have penetrated Bethany's bitch shields, because she put on Skylar's worn blue hoodie—which had probably once belonged to one of her older brothers—without batting an eye. The three of us walked to the end of the hallway, and just as we turned right, I heard the telltale tone of a single woman flirting with a slightly older man.

"They said to call you if any of the cheerleaders showed signs of anemia, and once I saw the *ouroboros*, well . . ." The school nurse let her words trail off, and I stopped breathing.

Someone knew.

Maybe not about Bethany specifically, but someone had known to be on the lookout for Heritage High cheerleaders showing signs of chupacabra possession. And if they'd known and hadn't done a thing to stop it . . .

Not good.

I didn't so much as glance back over my shoulder, but as Skylar, Bethany, and I hit the glass doors at the end of the hallway, I saw a reflection of the people rounding the corner to the nurse's office. In addition to the nurse, there were two men dressed in suits, and a woman with skin a shade darker and infinitely more flawless than my own. She wore her hair pulled into a bun at the nape of her neck, and she walked with purpose, the staccato click of heels against tile cutting through the air like gunshots.

"You did the right thing by calling us," the woman said. "We'll take care of everything now."

Her voice was soft, but I heard it, heard every word, and in that moment, I knew two things with absolute, unerring certainty: one, the suits on their way to the nurse's office weren't from the CDC, and two—whether they knew it yet or not—they weren't here for a cheerleader.

They were here for the girl with the *ouroboros*. And as of five minutes ago, that girl was me.

I didn't say a word until the three of us hit the parking lot, and even then, I only opened my mouth to ask whether either of the others had a car.

"No wheels," Skylar replied, her expression mournful. "And no driver's license. Yet. That said, my brother Nathan knows how to hot-wire, and I might have picked up a few tricks along the way."

"Take it easy, Grand Theft Auto." Bethany pulled a pair of keys out of her purse. "No one is hot-wiring anything. I have wheels *and* tinted windows, which means you can help yourself to the backseat, and as long as no one sees you get in or out, I don't have to deal with the social fallout."

The redhead didn't bother waiting for a response—she just pushed a button on her keys and flounced toward the silver BMW that lit up in response. Watching Bethany reverting to type, I thought that maybe cattiness was its own kind of invincibility, as much of a crutch for Bethany as my powers were for me.

Sixteen hours and nine minutes.

Sliding into the passenger seat of the BMW and closing

the door behind me, I shut out the constant countdown in my mind and tried to concentrate on the here and now.

Right here, right now, I was infected.

Right here, right now, I was on the run.

Right here, right now . . . I had no earthly idea what I'd gotten myself into. Without meaning to, I glanced down, and my hands began gravitating toward the bottom of my shirt.

Don't touch it, I told myself sternly. *Don't think about it. Don't give in.*

Unable to help myself, I pulled the bottom of my shirt upward and the band of my jeans down, angling my hips forward in the seat to give myself a full view of the *ouroboros* etched into my skin.

The lines were thick and looked like they'd been poured onto my body as melted gold. Tentatively, I ran my hand over the surface of my skin, expecting the symbol to be raised, but felt nothing other than the muscles in my stomach and the kind of dull heat given off by a day-old sunburn.

My flesh wasn't red.

The mark didn't hurt.

But for a split second, maybe less, the hand touching it didn't feel like mine.

I can do this. I can beat this. Knowing that the parasite was already absorbing my blood and, with it, my thoughts and memories, I cut the mental pep talk off short.

I wouldn't let myself be scared.

I wouldn't let the thing inside me know that it was winning.

I wouldn't think its name.

"Kali?" Skylar said my name, pulling me back down to earth. "Any chance you want to tell me what's going on?"

I shifted so that my shirt covered the glaring beacon of obvious on my stomach and turned the tables back on Skylar. "I was going to ask you the same thing."

Skylar was the one who'd known that someone was coming for us. She was the one who'd told us where to go and how to act, the one who'd given Bethany a hoodie to cover her trademark red locks.

"What's going on?" Skylar repeated, and then, without pausing a beat, she gave her answer. "You keep touching your stomach, Bethany has accelerated through four yellow lights, both of you know something that the other one doesn't, and I'm . . ."

She mumbled the last bit.

"You're what?" I asked. Bethany looked like she was on the verge of offering up an answer of her own to that question, but she managed to restrain herself.

Skylar cleared her throat. "I'm . . ."

"You're . . . ?"

Skylar gave me a hopeful little smile and then stopped beating around the bush. "I'm a little bit psychic."

"Psychic?" Bethany and I repeated in unison.

"Just a little bit," Skylar said, like that made her claim significantly more feasible than it would have been had she claimed to be psychic *a lot*.

"No offense," Bethany began—a surefire sign that she was getting ready to say something highly offensive—"but you two totally deserve each other. Mousy little Kali carries a hunting knife to high school, and my boyfriend's social mistake of a sister thinks she's got magical powers. If you guys can find yourselves a person who swallows swords, you can totally take this act on the road."

"Hey," I said, sounding only about half as put out as I felt. "Nobody asked you to be here."

"It's my car," Bethany retorted. "And speaking of which, where are we going?"

Skylar leaned forward from the backseat. "Turn right here," she said helpfully.

"Why?" Bethany's hands tightened almost imperceptibly over the steering wheel. In the rearview mirror, I could see Skylar shrug in response.

"I just kind of feel like you should turn right here."

Bethany shot dagger eyes at her in the mirror. "Because you're psychic."

"Just a little."

To everyone's surprise—probably even her own—Bethany did turn right, but she made up for it by rolling her eyes so hard that I had doubts about whether or not she could still make out oncoming traffic. Cast in the role of mediator between two extremes, I tried rephrasing Bethany's "no offense" statement in a way that was actually less offensive.

"Skylar, I get that maybe you have . . . really good intuition about people sometimes, but you know there's no such thing as actual psychics, right?"

That was what had made Eigelmeier's discovery of the chupacabra such an astonishing scientific find. Even with the preternatural, psychic phenomena were outside the norm. With humans, it was unheard of.

Then again, so was I.

Skylar, sensing my weakness, pressed the point. "Before Darwin, most scientists thought that kelpies and griffins weren't real, either, but anyone who's ever been to the San Francisco Zoo knows that they are."

Demonic water horses that lived to drown passers-by.

Flying lions with a nearly immortal lifespan.

Kelpies. Griffins. Hellhounds. Zombies. And . . . psychics?

"Sometimes," Skylar said solemnly, "*make-believe* is just another word for rare. Turn left at the next stop sign, Bethany."

"What am I, your chauffeur?" The question was clearly rhetorical, because Bethany didn't wait for an answer. "Tell me where we're going, or I'm pulling over, and you two are walking home."

I was severely tempted to take her up on the offer. The sooner I could convince Bethany she wanted no part of this, the better off I'd be. Unfortunately, the men in suits and the woman who'd accompanied them—the one who'd promised she'd "take care of things"—had been on the lookout for a cheerleader showing signs of chupacabra possession. Without knowing exactly what the nurse had told them, I couldn't convince myself that Bethany would be better off without me. And that meant that I couldn't just send her on her merry way, no matter how much I didn't want an entourage for the things to come.

Maybe I really do have a hero complex.

The thought engendered a response in my body: a knowing feeling, a tightening of the muscles in my throat, a yes.

"Bethany, chill. Skylar, tell us where we're going." Those sentences burst out of my mouth with all of the bite I wanted to direct to the thing inside my head, and I immediately wished I could take it back.

"I won't know where we're going until we get there." Skylar was completely unfazed by my snapping. "And once we get there, I probably won't know why until you guys tell me what's going on."

"You're the psychic," Bethany muttered. "Shouldn't you be able to figure it out for yourself?"

If anything, Skylar seemed enthused by the pointed question. "Reading your minds on command would require being significantly psychic, and I'm not. I never know when I'm going to pick up something, and it comes in pieces and feelings, not in words. So who wants to clue the sophomore in?"

Not me.

I didn't want to drag Skylar into this. There was just something about her that screamed *protect me!* Whoever the men looking for the "anemic cheerleader" were, I was fairly certain I didn't want them anywhere near the Little Optimist That Could.

Unfortunately, Bethany had no such predilection. "Sometime in the past week, I got bitten by a chupacabra. Somehow—no idea how—Kali lured it out of my body and into hers. She's already far enough gone that medical science can't do a thing to save her, and she's got some kind of plan—probably a risky, unreliable one riddled with holes—to get the bloodsucker out." Bethany blew out a long breath and then glanced back over her shoulder at Skylar. "There. You know what I know about the current situation. So, any time now, feel free to do your whole 'psychic' thing and tell me where the bedazzler we're going, or I might be forced to physically hurt you."

Skylar made a *pfft* sound with her lips. "Five brothers," she said, pointing to herself. Then she pointed to Bethany. "Only child. I could totally take you. Turn left."

Bethany slammed on the brakes. "Seriously?"

"Please?" Skylar smiled winningly, and after a long moment, Bethany turned left onto an access road that dead-ended into a large parking lot. She parked and killed the engine, and for a moment, the three of us took in the sight of a large, neon-green building shaped like a figure eight.

"Skate Haven?" I asked, reading the sign on the front of the building.

"Ice-skating?" Bethany said at the exact same time.

Skylar shrugged. "This is where we're supposed to be," she said firmly. "I'm sure there's a reason. Just . . . give me a minute."

A look of deep concentration settled over her impish features, and Skylar's eyes trailed downward from my face to my stomach. Though my shirt was covering the symbol that had appeared there, Skylar's gaze was sharp and focused, like my entire torso was laid bare.

"Just out of curiosity," she said, her voice slow and thoughtful, "how do chupacabras react to the cold?"

The moment we stepped into Skate Haven, the hairs on the back of my neck stood straight up. The change was palpable, like a needle was feeding adrenaline straight into my veins. I wasn't scared. I wasn't angry. But I was *something*, and if Skylar was right, the foreign presence inside of me was having some kind of adverse reaction to the cold.

"If ice-skating was the cure for chupacabra possession, don't you think someone would have figured that out by now?" Bethany was making an admirable attempt at *not* throwing a hissy fit, but I could tell she found the effort taxing. "People spend their entire lives fighting for the chance to study these things. You can't honestly believe that no one's ever tried to see what would happen if you put one in the freezer."

Skylar angled her palms heavenward and shrugged. "Hey, I'm just the messenger. If you have a problem with my logic, take it up with the universe at large. Now, who wants ice skates?"

Without a word to either of them, I walked toward the counter and told the guy working there my shoe size. Did I think I could just freeze out a presence that had woven itself into every fiber of my being?

No.

But unlike Bethany, I wasn't looking for a way to get rid of the chupacabra. I was looking for a way to slow it down.

Fifteen hours and thirty-seven minutes.

The boy behind the counter handed me a pair of skates. They were faded and gray, but the blades gleamed like they'd just been polished, and I thought of the way my knife blade had looked as I'd pressed the tip into my forearm.

"This may be one of your last days on earth, and you're going to spend it ice-skating?" Bethany's voice was oddly hoarse. "We have no way of knowing how much time you have left. If you don't have a plan, if we're not actively fighting this . . ."

An hour before, she'd been in my shoes. This probably wasn't the way she would have chosen to spend her last day, and I couldn't help but wonder what I'd be doing if I didn't think there was at least a chance I would survive.

I didn't have an answer. Nothing on my human days made me feel the way that hunting did when I was Other. I'd never been any good at making friends, and until today, no one at Heritage had even known my name.

I didn't have hobbies. I wasn't part of any clubs. The idea of me playing on a sports team was ridiculous (for a variety of reasons, depending on the day), and the only family I had was my dad, who probably would have been torn between mild upset and academic fascination if he'd had any idea that I'd been bitten.

"Ice-skating sounds good," I said.

Bethany had to literally bite her bottom lip to keep from arguing, and after a long moment, she turned to the boy behind the counter. He immediately melted into a pile of Skate Haven goo on the floor, but managed to pull it together long enough to give her a pair of pristine white skates and a ticket for a free hot chocolate from the snack bar.

Five minutes later, I waddled toward the ice. Out of habit, I scanned the rink's perimeter and breathed in through my nose, testing the air for even the barest hint of sulfur.

Nothing.

I breathed out, and as my breath took shape in the air, I tried to remember what it felt like to be the kind of person who didn't get cold.

Didn't feel pain.

Never lost a weapon—or her balance.

And then I promptly fell flat on my face. The ice was damp, and for a few seconds, instead of hating the cold, I loved it for the way it banished the heat from my cheeks.

Cold.

That single word was all it took for something deep and fathomless to begin snaking its way up my spine. It felt like losing my body to a black hole, like lying on a sandy beach and absorbing warmth from every individual grain of sand.

"Is it working?" Skylar asked from up above me. I reached for the wall and pulled myself unsteadily back to my feet.

"I don't know."

The beast inside of me was quiet and still, but I knew it was there, and I knew with unnatural certainty that no amount of subzero temperatures would make it leave me. It wasn't going to jump ship and take on a new victim.

The two of us were in this until one of us died.

They—called—lonely. You.

The voice in my mind was strong and velvet-smooth, but the words were broken. I found myself wanting to listen, to fill in the blanks, but after a moment, there was silence.

"Still possessed?" Bethany asked, gliding past me and circling back with the ease of an Olympic contender.

"Still possessed," I told her drily, "but I think the cold is doing something."

Goose bumps dotted the flesh on my arms, and I glanced back over my shoulder, half expecting to see someone or something standing behind me.

Lonely Ones.

The phrase was suddenly there in my mind, and it brought with it a feeling of déjà vu, like these were words that I'd always known and somewhere along the way had just forgotten.

Logically, I knew that extreme cold slowed down biological processes. Bears and yeti went into hibernation; hikers in snowstorms felt their heart rates plummet. It made sense to think that lower temperatures might delay the progression of my condition.

But that wasn't what it felt like.

My heart rate wasn't slowing. The voice in my head wasn't distant. I was on edge, and it was everything I could do to keep myself from sinking into ready position and preparing my pitifully human frame to lash out.

I had no idea why.

Feel it—taste it—help—you.

"So what now?" Bethany asked, her voice barely penetrating the heady fog in my brain—the sound of his voice, the chills on my skin. "Seriously, K., we skate, and we wait, and . . . feel free to fill in the blank at any moment."

This thing is killing you, I told myself. *The chupacabra is draining your blood and absorbing your memories, and soon, there won't be anything left of you at all.*

The cold, hard truth should have snapped me out of it, but the presence in my mind seemed to wrap itself around my physical body, my wrists and ankles, my waist, my neck.

I didn't know it would be like this.

I'd thought that I might get light-headed, that my blood pressure might plummet. I'd thought that I might have trouble remembering things, little things.

I thought I'd feel violated.

But I didn't.

"We need a plan," I said, just to be saying something, to prove to myself that I still could. That I was in charge, and that whatever I was feeling was *nothing.*

"What do you mean we *need* a plan?" Bethany asked. "Don't you already have one?" She didn't wait for me to reply. "I knew it! You're in over your head, you're scared, you're *stupid,* and we're ice-skating. That's—"

Skylar elbowed Bethany in the stomach, and the older girl amended her words.

"—that's not the most helpful thing in the world to point out, so I won't."

"I do have a plan," I said softly. "Sort of. It's just that my plan requires making it to sunrise, and right now . . ."

I couldn't swear that I'd make it.

Once I gave in to the siren call in my subconscious, I wasn't sure I'd want to.

"You'll make it." Skylar smiled and nodded, like the very act of doing so could make her words true.

"What are you going to do at sunrise?"

Somehow, I wasn't surprised that Bethany was still asking questions, just like it probably didn't surprise her when all she got from me was silence in response. Luckily, Skylar didn't leave the two of us in a standoff for long.

"In the old myths, chupacabras were a variant of the whole vampire thing, and vampires turn to ash in the sun, right? I mean, myths almost never get things entirely right, but even Darwin used them to write *The Demon's Descent*." Skylar was in full-on babble mode, and Bethany and I couldn't get a word in edgewise. "So if Kali says she has a way to get rid of a chupacabra at sunrise, I believe her."

"Then why, pray tell, didn't you just leave that thing in *me*?" The words burst angrily out of Bethany's mouth, a scowl slashing its way across her face with the brutality of a disfiguring scar. "If you could have just gotten rid of it at sunrise, why couldn't *I* have been the one who risked not living that long? When you said you could help me, I didn't know you meant like this, and by the time I did . . . I couldn't stop you. I tried, but you wouldn't let me." She advanced on me, Hell on Ice Skates, like a cobra descending on its prey.

What was I supposed to say? Unless I wanted to admit that my "plan" for sunrise involved letting my own monstrous nature take its course, I couldn't answer her questions. So I said nothing, and Bethany closed the space between us, looking like she was going to burst into tears or rip out my oesophagus in a fit of fury—I wasn't sure which.

"Did it talk to you?" I asked her, stalling for time.

"Did what talk to me?"

My arms encircled my torso, and one of my sleeves drooped down over my chilled skin. "What do you think?"

I hadn't realized that talking about this would feel like peeling back a layer of clothing, a layer of skin.

"Chupacabras don't talk, Kali. They're like psychic, preternatural ticks. They don't even have brains."

I averted my eyes, and Bethany exchanged looks with Skylar.

"Does the chupacabra talk to you?" Skylar asked, managing to keep her voice pleasantly neutral.

Yes, it does. He says his name is Zev.

Needless to say, I didn't allow those words to exit my mouth. Now I knew for sure. The things I was feeling, the voice I'd heard—none of this was normal.

"Of course the chupacabra doesn't talk to me," I said, trying to work up a good scoff. "I was just messing with Bethany."

"Hey!"

Thankful that she'd taken the bait, I asked another pointed question, one that wouldn't make the two of them think I was a total head case. "Bethany, what do you know that I don't?"

I wasn't convinced that Skylar was psychic—even just a little—but anyone who could survive being the target of the high-school hit squad for six months had to have a few cards up her sleeve. In the car, she'd said that Bethany knew something about our situation that I didn't, and as long as I was opting for distraction, I figured it couldn't hurt to ask.

"So, what?" Bethany retorted, confirming my suspicions. "You can have your secrets, but I can't have mine?"

Feel it—coming—you.

The words rolled over me, and I could feel my pupils dilating, my back arching as the desire to hear entire sentences instead of broken, scattered words surged anew.

Bethany kept her eyes fixed on mine, and I wondered what she saw when she looked at me, wondered if my face was a tell to everything hiding just underneath.

"Believe it or not, I'm not trying to be difficult," Bethany said, tracing the tip of one skate delicately across the ice. "I just . . . did you hear what the nurse said to that trio back at the school? She had orders to call them if anyone like me showed signs of being bitten, and that means that either those people knew that the cheerleading squad was at risk and did nothing to stop it, or they planned it and infected us themselves."

The second possibility hadn't even occurred to me, and I wondered why Bethany's mind had hopped straight from "chupacabra" to "conspiracy."

With a shrug, she began skating backward as she talked, her voice traveling across the ice like sound over water. "About a week ago, we had our annual drug testing. Heritage High takes its honor code very seriously – Say No to Drugs, athletes as examples and all that, which wouldn't have been strange, except that we'd *already* done the pee in a cup thing back in August. If you do it more than once a year, it's not annual, and this time, they took blood."

Blood.

An image of a needle jumped into my mind, and I wondered if the memory was mine, or Zev's . . .

Don't think his name. Don't say it. Don't even call that thing a he.

"You think someone injected you?" I couldn't even believe I was saying the words, but the image of the needle was so vivid, I could feel the syringe's razor-sharp point. "Who goes around injecting cheerleaders with bloodsucking parasites?"

Kali—you have to—look—smell.

I pushed the voice down and felt it pushing back.

"What about the other cheerleaders?" I asked through gritted teeth, steeling myself against the sound of my constant companion's voice. "Are they—"

"They're fine," Bethany said tersely. "I texted. I called. Everybody but me is fine, and the only reason I never mentioned that they might not be is that it's not *your* problem—but since evidence suggests you don't seem to understand that distinction, like, *at all*, I didn't want you and your hero complex to know."

Before I could so much as reply, Bethany took off skating in earnest, her form blurring with grace and speed as she skated away from me and toward—

I blinked my eyes, hard. There was nothing on the other side of the rink. Bethany wasn't skating toward anything, but—

Yes.

Without fully knowing why, I bent to pull my skates off, moving as quickly as I could. I tried to yell out to Bethany, but couldn't find the words.

This isn't right.

The surface of the ice rippled. It cracked and bulged and began to form itself into something else. My breath caught in my chest as frost-white scales took shape on the ice, each as reflective and sharp as the blade on my knife. Cavernous eyes stared directly into mine, and I realized that my unease since stepping on the ice had nothing to do with Zev.

Had never had anything to do with Zev.

Every other day, I was human, but I knew what was out there, better than anyone. I knew what to watch for, what to look for, and I *knew* that even humans had instincts. If a chill ran up your spine when you were walking down an alleyway, it was generally a good idea to get the heck out of the alley. If you felt eyes on the back of your head, there was a good chance someone was staring at you. And if something around you felt *off* . . .

I should have known. Even on a human day, I should have known.

Opposite me on the ice, the creature materialized and reared back, like a horse bucking its rider, and the only warning before its mammoth wings lashed out, knocking Bethany roughly to the ground, was the distinct sound of cracking ice.

Run.

I couldn't run. All I could do was stand there, an ice skate in each hand, my heart pounding and a stale breath caught in the back of my throat.

Dragon. Genus: Draco.

For most of our evolutionary history, the three most dangerous kinds of predators had been large cats, snakes, and birds of prey. The human brain was wired to fear them, and dragons—*talons, scales, slit pupils*—sent that system into overdrive. I knew what was happening, but that didn't keep me from feeling it, and the fear—such a little, stupid word— reminded me that I was human.

That I was nothing.

That I was screwed.

My hold on the makeshift blades in my hands tightened, and I saw the moments leading up to this one, shattered and interlocked, like shards of glass. From the second I'd stepped onto the ice, I'd known that something wasn't right. The thing inside me had known, too. Even now, the parasite slurping down my blood was telling me to get out, its voice low and silky, like it belonged to someone who was used to being obeyed.

Run. Now.

Why? I replied, taking a single step forward and drawing the dragon's attention from Bethany to me. *Afraid something might happen to your all-you-can-eat buffet?*

Don't—foolish. Can't—you must—*Now!*

I'm sorry, I thought, sizing up the dragon and running through my very limited options. *I'm afraid this is a bad connection. I can't quite make out what you're saying. Oh well.*

The monster opposite me leapt into the air and crashed back down onto the ice. Cracks ricocheted across the surface, and I took another step forward.

Objectively, I knew I was powerless, but I couldn't shake the memory of what it was like to be a hunter, couldn't rid my body—my fragile, *human* body—of the sense that it knew exactly what to do. Rationally, I knew better, knew that I should turn tail and run, but I couldn't—not with Bethany scrambling across the ice, close enough that the dragon could bisect her with a single slice of its talons. Not with Skylar beside me, her mouth frozen in a perfect, rounded O.

"When I move," I said softly, my voice nearly lost under the sound of the dragon's equine snorts, "back away slowly. Don't look it in the eye. Don't draw its attention. You just get outside, and then you run."

Skylar nodded almost imperceptibly, but it was enough that the dragon's liquid gaze switched from my form to hers.

I had to act fast.

"Hey, ugly! Eyes on me." I moved sideways across the ice, and the dragon whirled to follow, its mammoth tail taking out the side of the rink. Debris scattered like shrapnel, and out of the corner of my eye, I saw Skylar backing away and prayed that Bethany had the sense to do the same.

"That's right, Godzilla. I'm the threat here. *Me*."

My target reared up on its back legs, and I prepared myself for the aftershock when it slammed back down onto the ice. Smoke poured from its nostrils, and I filed that information away as calmly and rationally as I could. There were several subspecies of dragons. Some were harmless. Some ate people. Some breathed fire.

None of them were native to the area.

Based on the smoke, I was going to go out on a limb and guess this was a fire-breather. Not ideal, but on the bright side, at least I didn't have to worry about being eaten alive.

"Don't worry—I called Preternatural Control!" The boy who'd given us our skates was either very brave or very stupid. Given that he didn't seem to have armed himself with so much as a fire extinguisher, I was guessing the latter. "They should be here any sec—"

Without warning, the dragon turned its pursuit from me, and its gleaming teeth closed around the boy's middle. One second the boy was there, and the next, he was splatter.

I flinched—and hated myself for flinching, almost as much as I hated myself for not saving the boy.

It looks like we're dealing with Draco carnus, I thought, desperately clinging to the cold, hard facts and trying so hard not to care. *A man-eater*.

Dully, I told myself that at least I didn't have to worry about it breathing fire. Dragons were one or the other, not both.

Or so modern science would have had me believe.

I heard the flames before I saw them, and for a split second, I lost control of my body. I couldn't feel my arms, couldn't feel my legs, could only feel a hand on the small of my back and rage bubbling inside of me, like a long-dormant volcano getting ready to spew.

Not my hand.

Not my rage.

But somehow, my body dove out of the line of fire, just as a wall of flame sliced through the ice that had been directly under my feet.

The sensation lasted a second, maybe two, and then I was in control of my body again. I climbed unsteadily to my feet and tightened my grip on the ice skates in my hand, angling the blades outward.

Here goes nothing. I took aim and fired.

I knew it wouldn't make a dent in the dragon's armor, knew that I didn't have the aim or the power or the fearlessness I needed to take down an opponent twenty times my size, but as the skate flew through the air, the dragon tore its gleaming onyx eyes from mine and followed the blade's trajectory.

Dragons liked shiny things.

While it was distracted, I wracked my brain for a way out. Unless I could get close enough to reach the soft spot under its breastplate, I didn't stand a chance of inflicting any kind of lasting damage, and Bethany was still there, her back pressed against the side of the rink, her eyes following the dragon's every move.

I jerked my head to the side, motioning for her to go. She jerked her head, motioning for me to do the same.

If we got out of this alive, I was going to kill her.

Think, Kali, I told myself. There had to be a way out. There *had* to be. I didn't want to die like this, scared and weak and unable to even remember what it felt like to be anything else.

Fifteen hours and twenty-four minutes.

Like that did me a hell of a lot of good.

I told you to run. Don't make me tell you again.

The voice was implacable and fierce, and the fact that my enemy—who shouldn't have even been able to *talk*—was ordering me around swung the pendulum of my emotions from scared to angry and from angry to *pissed*. Before I could make use of that, however, Bethany snapped. One second she was cowering behind the dragon, and the next, she was on her feet, poised on top of the remaining exterior wall of the rink. She didn't say anything. She barely even moved. She just swayed—first her hips, then her arms.

I tried to process. The two of us were on the verge of death, and she was *belly dancing*?

Go. Now. Must—lights.

I watched as the dragon turned its head to the side, absorbing Bethany's movement whole. I could have streaked across the ice yodeling the national anthem, and it wouldn't have mattered.

The beast had marked its prey. For the moment, it seemed content just watching her, but I knew that wouldn't last. I had a minute at most, maybe less, and I did the only thing I could think of—

I ran.

Not away.

Not for safety.

To the control booth, where I found a pair of employees huddled on the floor.

"Dim the lights," I told them, out of breath and running out of time, my mind echoing with the broken instructions Zev had tried to impart.

Must—lights.

Neither of the employees moved. I glanced out at the rink. The dragon, its eyes still locked on Bethany's, began to cross the ice. Soon, it would be close enough that she would be able to smell the blood and smoke on its breath, close enough that I didn't have even a second to spare.

"Turn the lights off. Now! And if you have any kind of special effects—a light show, disco ball, whatever—turn those on, too."

One of the employees pointed a single, shaky finger to the control panel, and I scanned it, looking for the switch. Out on the ice, Bethany continued her impromptu belly dance. She swayed. The dragon swayed. She blinked. It blinked. Any moment, any second, it could snap out of it, go in for the kill—

I flipped the switch. The rink went dark. And then, a second later, a smattering of lights appeared on the ceiling, swirling steadily.

That's right, I told the dragon silently. *Swirly, shiny lights.*

Slowly, the beast stopped swaying. It tore its eyes from Bethany's, and it lay down on its front paws in the middle of the ravaged rink. Its scales—the exact color of the ice— glistened in the uneven lighting. Even from a distance, I could make out the crystalline texture of its skin.

Slowly, painfully, the dragon's breathing became even, its

mammoth chest rising and falling, its eyes fixed on the ceiling above. Then, just as suddenly as it had appeared, the creature was gone, its body melding into the ice underneath.

Unnatural, the voice in my head whispered, disturbingly clear. Even though I agreed with the sentiment, I tried to shut out the voice and did everything in my power not to think about the fact that if it hadn't been for his suggestion, I might not have thought to go for the lights.

Bethany would have been dragon bait.

And I would probably have been dead.

If I had a nickel for every time I'd almost died, I would have been driving to school in a Ferrari and flying off to Bora-Bora on the weekends. One of these days, I'd cut it too close to dawn or run into a monster that was too strong. With the way I lived, the things I hunted, death was only a matter of time.

One more brush with oblivion shouldn't have bothered me.

I shouldn't have been dwelling on the fact that the parasite that had saved my life was killing me now.

But I was.

Our standoff with Puff the Man-Eating, Fire-Breathing Creature of Doom had lasted minutes, but the police—not to mention a Preternatural Control team—had shown up before we could make ourselves scarce, and the resulting inquisition had been dragging on for over an hour. If Bethany and I had been adults, if the kids working at Skate Haven had been adults, then maybe we wouldn't have had to answer the same questions sixteen times apiece.

But we weren't adults.

We were teenagers who claimed to have had a run-in with some subspecies of dragon that could disappear into ice like a kelpie into water. And, oh yeah, it breathed fire *and* ate people, and its scales were the color of ice.

"So let me get this straight," the policewoman interviewing me said for maybe the fiftieth time. "It was some kind of . . . *ice dragon*."

I may as well have been telling her it belched gumdrops and had a weakness for Saturday-morning cartoons. Forget the fact that there was obvious damage to the rink—not to mention the remains of the boy who'd actually placed the 911 call in the first place. It didn't matter that our stories were consistent both with the damage and with one another's accounts of what had gone down. Dragons stayed away from cities. They didn't just hang out at local hot spots. And they didn't have any kind of affinity for ice.

So obviously, the teenagers were lying. Or on drugs. Or both.

This is why you don't call the police. Or Preternatural Control. No matter what. Ever.

If I'd doubted the rule—and I was fairly sure I never had—I certainly never would again. My skin itched just talking to the authorities, and it was all I could do to meet my interrogator's eyes, when what I really wanted to do was to get out of there, stat.

The police department had more than a few open cases with my name on them—figuratively, and I had no desire to make that literal. The chances that anyone would think to connect a witness in a horrific dragon mauling with the vigilante responsible for dozens of area beastie slayings was slim. It wasn't like my usual MO involved laser light shows, but still—the sooner I got out of there, the better.

"Ice dragon," I said, repeating the police officer's incredulous words.

For some reason, my voice sounded very far away: slow and gummy and like I wasn't quite speaking English. As I turned this thought over in my head, I noticed that my interrogator's face was looking less like a face and more like a sea of unrelated features, each blurring into the next.

Weird.

I blinked, and when that did me no good, I reached out for the railing to steady myself.

"Miss, are you feeling all right?" the officer asked.

Her voice sounded even farther away than mine.

"I'm fine," I said—or at least, that's what I think I said. The details are, to this day, a little unclear. "Just give me a minute."

"Ohmigosh!"

It took me a few seconds to realize that the exclamation in question had come from Skylar, who, up until that point, had wisely stayed out of the fray. I'd entertained the notion that she'd had the common sense to go home and leave Bethany and me to sort this out on our own.

Apparently not.

"You look, like, *so pale*. Did you forget to eat lunch? Please tell me you didn't forget to eat lunch!" Skylar shook her head morosely, laying on the teenage ingénue vibe so thick that I doubted that anyone—let alone Officer So What You're Telling Me Is—would buy it.

I wasn't suffering from low blood sugar.

I was—I was—it took me a minute to put the sensation into words.

Dying.

"She's hypoglycemic," Skylar said, rattling off the word like she'd cut her teeth working in emergency rooms. "Are you guys done here? Because it's almost six o'clock, and if we don't get some food in her soon, her blood sugar is going to get dangerously low."

The police officer blinked. Or maybe I did. Either way, words were exchanged and Skylar's effervescence must have won the day, because a few minutes after she'd appeared on the scene, Bethany and I were free to go.

"In retrospect," Skylar said, once we'd made it out the front door, "I'm not sure ice-skating was a good idea."

"You think?" Bethany snorted. "Maybe if you were actually psychic, you could tell us why, in the name of all that is good and holy in this world, your little instincts led us *here*."

I felt foggy and disconnected. I could barely keep up with the back and forth between the two of them, but the moment the question was out of Bethany's mouth, a second Preternatural Control team shuffled by us, a dark-haired woman leading the way.

Click. Click. Click.

The sound of heels against concrete penetrated the fog in my brain, and I froze. For a moment, I thought that the woman in heels—the one from the school, the one coming toward us now—was here for me, but she brushed past us on her way into the rink.

She never even turned around.

Click. Click. Click.

Even after she was gone, I could still hear the sound of her heels echoing through the recesses of my brain.

Who is she? Why is she here? So tired . . .

My thoughts were a jumbled mess. I could barely move. And as Bethany and Skylar practically poured me into the backseat of the BMW, I thought about what had just happened—everything that had happened—and I managed to stave off the dizziness and nausea coursing through my entire body just long enough to spare a few words for the BMW's belly-dancing owner.

"I can't believe you did that," I told Bethany, my words slurred and packing next to no heat. "You should have run."

"I was providing a distraction so you could run," Bethany retorted. "And that dragon was, I might add, totally distracted."

I tried to tell Bethany exactly what I thought of her "distraction," but somewhere between my brain and my mouth, the words got lost, and they came out in a jumble.

Bethany turned to Skylar. "What's wrong with her?"

For once, Skylar was silent, and her silence was answer enough.

"She's only been infected for four hours," Bethany said, her voice going dry. "She should be fine."

I closed my eyes, and somewhere inside of me, something shifted. I shouldn't have been able to lure the beast from Bethany's body to mine. I shouldn't have developed an *ouroboros* the moment I'd been bitten. And I certainly shouldn't have been hearing voices.

You—Promise—Fine.

I smelled wet grass, rain, honeysuckle. I saw the outline of a body, solid and sleek. I heard a voice shouting at me from a distance, but couldn't make out a single word.

This time, I didn't fight to hold on to consciousness—couldn't—and my last thought as I drifted into oblivion was that the woman in the heels reminded me of someone.

And that could not possibly be good.

† † †

I woke up staring into eyes the exact shade of my comforter at home: faded turquoise, so light that I felt like if I stared at them long enough, I'd be able to see straight through. It took a moment before the rest of the features fell into place: blond hair, suntanned skin, cheekbones sharp enough to draw blood.

Elliot.

His name came to me a second before the rest of my senses returned. I bolted straight up, realized I was in some kind of bed, and began scrambling backward on my hands and heels.

"Hey, hey—" He looked like he wanted to reach for me, but he must have had some sense of self-preservation, because he kept his hands right where they were. "It's okay. I'm not going to hurt you. You passed out, and Skylar and Beth brought you here."

It was weird to hear Bethany referred to as *Beth*—almost as weird as it was to wake up alone in a room with her boyfriend.

"Define 'here,'" I said sharply. Or, at least, I meant to say it sharply. Despite my best efforts, the words came out little and vulnerable instead.

"We're at my brother Vaughn's house," Elliot told me. "Skylar called me when Bethany went off the rails."

I decided I did not want to know what Bethany "going off the rails" entailed.

"She was really worried about you," Elliot continued. "We all were."

I felt like I'd fallen into some kind of parallel universe. For years, I'd spent every other night fighting to the death with nightmares made flesh. I came home broken and bleeding, with bones poking through my skin, and no one had ever noticed. No one had ever worried. Even when I was little, before the changes started, I could remember bumps and bruises, waking up in a cold sweat, vicious bouts of the flu—and no one had ever sat next to my bed waiting for me to wake up.

No one had *cared*.

"I'm fine," I said, pulling my knees instinctively to my chest, like shielding my body from Elliot's view might keep him from recognizing my words as a lie.

"You're not fine." His response was immediate. "You've been bitten by a chupacabra. You're anemic, your blood pressure fell through the floor, and the only reason you're not in a hospital right now is that Vaughn said you were sleeping, not unconscious. We figured you could use the rest."

I didn't know which part of what he said was the most surprising: the fact that Skylar and Bethany had told him about the chupacabra, or his proclamation that I could "use some rest."

In the past twenty-four hours, I'd taken out a pack of hell-hounds, offered myself up to a bloodsucker to save the life of a girl I barely knew, come *this close* to having my head torn off by a genetic impossibility of a dragon—and they thought I needed some *rest*?

"What time is it?" I asked, disturbed by the fact that I didn't know. "And where's everyone else?"

Bethany didn't strike me as the kind of girl who willingly left her boyfriend alone with a member of the opposite sex. I didn't know whether to be flattered that she trusted me or offended that she clearly didn't think I was a threat.

"Skylar and Vaughn went to get some painkillers. Beth's father called, and she had to go. She said to tell you that if you die while she's gone, she'll take it personally."

It was funny—all I'd wanted since I'd woken up in the nurse's office was to get Bethany out of the picture, but the fact that she'd just *left* me there didn't feel like a relief.

"Anything else she said to tell me?" I asked, trying not to sound betrayed or offended or, God forbid, hurt.

Elliot smiled—it was a lopsided expression on his otherwise symmetrical face: wry and rueful and just a tiny bit sardonic. "She said to tell you that she was going to pump her father for information about chupacabras. She's not holding her breath that he'll have any answers, but given that he's one of the foremost experts in the world, she'll probably do you more good there than here. And she also said to tell you . . ." Elliot trailed off, and I couldn't push down the impulse to look him straight in those gentle, turquoise eyes.

"What?"

"She said her best memory isn't standing on top of some cheerleading pyramid." Elliot leaned forward, resting his forearms on his knees. "She said it was hide-and-seek, when she was nine."

For some reason, my throat tightened when Elliot said

those words, and I swallowed, hard. That was playing dirty, and Bethany had to have known it. I'd saved her because I couldn't just stand by and let her die. Not because I wanted to know her, not because I wanted anything in return.

All I wanted was to go home, go to bed, and wake up cured in the morning.

As a matter of reflex, my eyes were drawn to a clock on the wall. It was a quarter past eight.

Ten hours and forty-five minutes.

"How's my patient?" A new voice—deep and baritone, so gentle that I instinctively wanted to trust its owner—snapped me from my reverie.

"She's awake," Elliot said needlessly. "I should go. Come on, Skye."

The second I heard Skylar's name, my eyes sought her out. She was standing next to a man easily three times her size, but within seconds, it was clear who was calling the shots around here, and it wasn't Elliot or the man with the soothing voice.

"Don't be ridiculous, El. I'm not going anywhere, and neither are you."

Elliot narrowed his eyes at his sister, but she just stared back and grinned. "I'm not telling you what to do," she volunteered helpfully, "I'm just telling you what you're *going* to do. There's a difference."

"Skylar," Elliot said with the thinning patience of an older sibling much abused, "you are *not* psychic."

Skylar sighed. "Elliot," she informed me, "is a *skeptic.*" From her tone of voice, you would have thought it was a dirty word.

"Elliot," the boy in question repeated, his tone mimicking hers exactly, "has common sense. If you run around sticking your nose into things that are none of your business, you're going to get yourself hurt. You're not psychic, you're not super-woman, and if Mom and Dad had any idea you skipped school and almost got yourself eaten—"

Skylar finished his sentence for him. "They'd tell me, very sternly, not to do it again."

"You want to help me out here?" Elliot asked, exasperated. At first, I thought he was talking to me, but then the man standing beside Skylar answered.

"We both know Skylar's spoiled rotten and doesn't follow directions worth a damn," he said, his tone mild, though he did raise one eyebrow at Skylar in a way that actually made her fidget. "Right now, I'm more concerned about her friend."

"Kali," Skylar supplied.

The man—who I could only assume was another one of Skylar's many brothers—smiled, but the expression didn't quite reach his eyes. "Hello, Kali," he said, his voice soft as he came to sit on the side of the bed. "I'm Vaughn, unfortunate older brother to Tweedledee and Tweedledum here. How are you feeling?"

"Fine," I replied, but Vaughn gave me the same raised-eyebrow look he'd given Skylar, and I found myself looking down and away.

Vaughn lifted a hand to the side of my face, and I flinched, but his hold was gentle as he angled my eyes back toward his. "You're not fine, Kali. There's an *ouroboros* on your stomach, and your body's working overtime, trying to replace the blood you've already lost."

I knew without Vaughn having to tell me so that *trying* was the operative word. I felt better than I had since I'd been bitten, but that didn't change anything. The creature inside me was still sucking me dry. At this rate, I might not make it to sunrise.

Some plan, I thought.

I waited for the voice in my head to gloat.

Nothing.

"I can't feel it," I said out loud, thankful that I'd managed not to refer to my would-be killer as a *him.* "Before, there was a . . . presence."

I couldn't describe it any better than that, not without making all three Haydens think I'd really gone off my metaphorical rocker.

"Based on your height and weight, it should take approximately four days for your condition to run its course." Vaughn's tone never changed, but there was no gentling news like that. "Are you sure you were bitten this afternoon?"

"I'm sure." It wasn't like smearing my blood on Bethany's back and luring her death sentence to jump ship was the kind of thing I'd forget.

Bethany. Chupacabra.

An expletive exited my mouth.

"Got something you'd like to share with the class?" Skylar asked, unperturbed.

I opened my mouth and then shut it again, unsure how much Skylar had told Elliot, let alone Vaughn.

"Everything," Skylar said, and for the first time, I realized that she had a habit of doing that—responding to things I hadn't said out loud.

"Skye?" Vaughn's voice was even and calm, and it occurred to me that her whole family was probably used to this—or as used to Skylar as any person *could* get.

"Kali?" Skylar deftly passed Vaughn's question on to me, and this time, I answered, despite the instinct screaming at me, from somewhere in my memory, that people like me kept secrets for a reason.

"I can't believe you three let Bethany walk out of here," I said. "Skylar told you about the woman at the school, didn't she? And her suit-wearing henchmen?"

Elliot rolled his eyes heavenward. "Skylar," he said crisply, "exaggerates."

"Does Bethany exaggerate, too?" I shot back.

"Bethany can take care of herself," Elliot said. "And her dad isn't exactly the kind of guy you say no to."

The expression on my face must have betrayed what I thought about that, because Elliot's voice took on a defensive tone.

"*If* there were some shady characters at the high school, and *if* they were looking for a cheerleader who'd been bitten— trust me, they won't get within a mile of Beth's house. Her dad does some of his work at home, and the place is under surveillance, twenty-four seven."

"Shady characters?" Skylar repeated incredulously. "What are you, eighty?"

"Skylar," Vaughn said softly, and to my surprise, Skylar shut her mouth. A moment later, I could understand why she'd done it, because Vaughn turned his gaze back to me, and I realized that he was the type of person who never had to raise his voice, never had to so much as narrow his eyes.

"You need to call your parents," he said, and I got the feeling that it wasn't a suggestion. "For whatever reason, you seem to be having an unusual reaction to your condition. We don't know how fast it's going to progress, and I'm out of my league when it comes to treatment."

I met Vaughn's eyes. We both knew that the problem wasn't that he was out of his league. The problem was that there was no treatment. No cure. There was nothing that Vaughn—or any medical professional—could do. If I'd been fully human, I would have been a dead girl walking, and as far as Skylar's brother knew, that's exactly what I was.

You think I'm dying. I didn't say the words out loud, but I didn't have to. I could tell just by looking at Vaughn that he knew—and that he wasn't going to back off until I called home.

"I'll call my dad," I said, "but I'm not going to tell him, not yet. Not over the phone."

I hoped Vaughn wouldn't press the issue, and he didn't. Instead, he just handed me the phone. After a pregnant pause, I dialed our home number, banking on the fact that my father rarely left work before nine. I got the answering machine and hung up.

"He's still at work," I said, handing the phone to Vaughn, who turned around and pressed it right back into my palm.

"Try his cell."

I narrowed my eyes, and Skylar snorted. "Try having *five* of them," she told me. "I can't tie my shoes without someone telling me I'm doing it wrong."

Sensing that I wasn't going to win this one, I dialed my father's cell number. I wasn't at all surprised when it went to voice mail, too.

"Hi," I said, feeling nine kinds of awkward leaving a message, when the two of us spoke so rarely face to face. "It's Kali. I'm calling because I got a little sick today, and my friend's older brother thought I should call you. I guess he's a doctor or something."

I paused, wondering why I was doing this. My dad probably wouldn't even listen to his messages.

"Anyway, I'll be home soon."

Another pause, another reminder that this was the most I'd said to my father in months.

"Bye."

I hung up the phone and handed it back to Vaughn. "He wasn't there," I explained needlessly. "I left a message."

I half expected Vaughn to hand the phone back and suggest I call my mother, but he didn't. Maybe Skylar wasn't the only person in her family with good instincts.

"Elliot can drive you home," he said instead. "He'll stay with you until your dad gets there."

Elliot looked like he was on the verge of replying, but Vaughn silenced him with another one of those looks. Before I knew what was happening, Skylar's brothers were helping me to Elliot's car, even though I could have walked on my own just fine.

Elliot opened the passenger door for me, a gesture completely at odds with the tight set of his lips and the dagger eyes he was shooting at Vaughn. I climbed in and managed to thank Vaughn for his help. As Elliot rounded to his side of the car, Skylar poked her head in my side and pressed a folded white square of paper into my hand.

"It's this thing," she said, which was, quite frankly, less

than illuminating. "I can't get it out of my head. I think it might be important."

"Thanks, Skylar." I realized as I said the words that it wasn't just the paper I was thanking her for. It was introducing herself to me at the pep rally that morning and sitting with me at lunch and coming back for me after the drama with the dragon.

I wasn't used to being the kind of person that other people came back for.

"I'll see you tomorrow," Skylar said. "I *know* I will." She tapped her forefinger against her temple and winked.

She thinks I'll live through the night.

The thought was strangely comforting, and as the door closed between us, leaving me alone with Elliot, I tightened my grip on the paper in my hand. Maybe Skylar was psychic, and maybe she wasn't. Maybe she just had really good instincts and a thousand-watt smile.

"She's not psychic," Elliot told me tersely. "There's no such thing as psychics, and I'd appreciate it if you didn't encourage her."

"I'm not."

Elliot didn't look like he believed me, but he managed a weak smile that did absolutely nothing to disguise the fact that he probably didn't want to be stuck on Kali babysitting duty until my father got home.

I could hardly blame him. Hanging out with a good-as-dead girl probably wasn't anyone's idea of a stellar time.

Nine hours and fifty-nine minutes.

This day was *never* going to end.

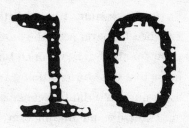

My father came home. Elliot left, and there was a moment—a single moment—when I thought my dad might look at me and see: the pallor to my skin, the dark circles under my eyes, the bruises, the swollen joints. I laid my hand over the bottom of my T-shirt, playing with the edge, flicking the bottom up and down, up and down, waiting for him to look at me.

To *see*.

"Your friend seems nice," he said absentmindedly. He might as well have backhanded me, and I couldn't even hate him for it. He meant well. He *meant* to love me.

Then again, you know what they say about the road to hell.

"Elliot's not my friend," I said, my voice as neutral and pleasant as the professor's. "He's dating Bethany Davis."

Bethany's name caught my father's attention, the way I'd known it would.

"Is he now? I had a feeling you two would hit it off."

For one horrific moment, I thought my father might reach over and pat me on the head, like a little kid. Like a dog.

"You should invite Bethany over here one day after school," he said. "Or perhaps I could talk to Paul about the four of us going out for a father–daughter dinner?"

In that instant, I hated Bethany, hated her so much that I wished I'd never seen the *ouroboros* on her back or that I'd turned a blind eye to it once I had. I knew it wasn't rational, knew that this conversation wasn't any more her fault than it was mine, but I didn't feel like being rational.

I felt like puking all over my father's dress-for-success designer shoes.

"Kali?"

I got bitten by a chupacabra, and I might not make it to morning. Just thought you should know.

I couldn't coerce my lips into saying the words. What was the point? Instead, I took the easy way out, the way I always did with him, the way he always did with me.

"I'm really tired," I said. "I'm going to bed."

Another parent might have gotten upset that I hadn't replied to his suggestion, but my father never yelled at me. The two of us never fought. I'd go on my merry way, and he'd go on his, and if I died in the middle of the night, he'd live.

He'd just have to find another way to cozy up to Paul Davis.

By some miracle, I made it upstairs without breaking down or passing out. I closed my bedroom door behind me and sank down onto the floor.

Eight hours and fifty-one minutes.

I was tired, I was light-headed, and all I wanted was to go to sleep and bring on the dawn, but I knew with sudden prescience that it wasn't going to happen. I wasn't going to be able to stop thinking about it, any of it—not about my dad, or the thing inside of me, or the fact that somewhere out there, someone was looking for me.

For Bethany.

How did I get myself into this?

I was normally good at lying low, but this was pretty much the opposite. Assuming the best happened, and I *did* survive the night, that would be a giant red flag right there—to Bethany, to Skylar and her brothers, to the woman in heels.

—Hurt—You.

With everything going on inside my head, the return of the voice was almost a relief. I was the kind of person who needed an enemy. I needed something I could fight, something I could kill.

Back again? I asked silently, disregarding the fact that according to modern science, chupacabras had the mental capacity of an amoeba. *And here I thought Elliot and Vaughn had scared you away.*

No response. Then again, what did I expect? I was talking to a parasite. I was dying. And there was a part of me that couldn't help wishing that Elliot hadn't left just so I wouldn't have to be going through this alone.

Not like you.

That was the clearest thing the little interloper had said since the ice rink—like I needed a reminder that I was different. Like I'd ever been able to forget, even for a second, that I wasn't like other girls—that I wasn't like anyone.

This wasn't how I'd pictured spending what could end up being my last night on earth: alone in my bedroom, talking to the voice in my head and feeling sorry for myself. I needed to do something.

At that moment, I would have given anything for the hunt-lust, the restlessness, the *purpose* I'd felt the night before.

Every other day, I was a demon hunter. I was powerful. I was something.

But now?

Now I was just lost and lonely and dying, and the closest thing I had to company was the creature that was killing me.

Lovely.

I could feel my throat tightening, and my eyes started to burn.

Screw this.

I may have been different, I may have been a loner, I may have been a *freak*, but I wasn't a crier. Not about this, not about anything. Determined to quell the urge, I turned my attention to the piece of paper Skylar had pressed into my palm as I was leaving Vaughn's house. I tugged it out of my pocket and unfolded it, careful not to tear the edges.

It's this thing, Skylar had said. *I can't get it out of my head. I think it might be important.*

Staring at the drawing, I had the oddest sense of déjà vu. The symbol was simple: an octagon bisected by a ribbon—or possibly a ladder, spiraling around an invisible line. The shape itself was uneven and asymmetrical, and I got the feeling that drawing was not a talent that Skylar had in any kind of abundance.

I don't know how long I sat there, staring at the sketch and waiting for the lightbulb moment when everything clicked into place, but all I managed to accomplish was giving myself a headache.

Your body's working overtime, trying to replace the blood it's lost.

Thinking back on Vaughn's diagnosis, I remembered—belatedly—that at lunch, Elliot had mentioned something about one of their brothers being a vet. I snorted.

I passed out, and Skylar took me to a vet.

The irony of the situation—that maybe I was an animal, no more human than the things I fought—did not escape me.

Not—animal.

"The bloodsucking parasite doesn't think I'm an animal," I said, my voice dry. "I feel so very comforted."

"Kali?" Belatedly, I realized that my father had stuck his head into my room, and I was torn between wondering what he wanted now and hoping that he hadn't overheard me talking to thin air.

"What do you want?" I asked, too tired to sugarcoat things and pretend that everything was okay between us, or that there was even an *us* to speak of at all.

"I . . . erm . . ." My father rarely stuttered. Eloquence was kind of his thing, so the fact that he was stumbling over his words drew my attention more than the fact that he was here. "I just wanted you to know that I didn't call Paul Davis," he said. "If you and Bethany want to get together—that is, if you decide you want to—well, it's up to you, okay?"

That was about as close as he could possibly come to apologizing, and saying okay without meeting his eyes was as close as I could come to accepting it. A few seconds passed with neither one of us saying anything else, and then he turned to leave.

"Night, Dad," I called after him. There was a chance—and I didn't know how big it was—that this might be the last conversation the two of us ever had. I owed it to him to say *something*, even if it wasn't what I wanted to be saying.

"Good night, Kali."

† † †

Around two in the morning, I finally fell asleep, but the only thing waiting for me in my dreams was more of the same: more monsters, more doubts, a nagging feeling that I was missing something, that I was screwing everything up.

I dreamed I was dreaming.

I dreamed I was dying.

I dreamed I was covered in blood.

I turned over in bed, my white sheets dyed in shades of red, and there was a man there, staring at me, drenched in shadow from head to toe. There was something beautiful about his features, something deadly, and his eyes . . .

Those eyes.

They were the color of tarnished silver, set deep in a face that wasn't human, but wasn't not.

He reached out and touched me, trailing shadows everywhere he went, and I breathed in the darkness.

Breathed it out.

I dreamed I was dreaming.

I dreamed I was dying.

I woke up covered in blood.

I woke in darkness. Before I could scream, someone pounced on me, covering my mouth with two hands. Without even thinking about it, I grabbed the person by the wrists, digging my fingers into her flesh. I would have kept squeezing as hard as my still-human hands could manage, but at some point, I came out of the fugue state my dream had left me in and recognized the person on top of me.

"Bethany?"

Half convinced I was still asleep, I stopped fighting, and Bethany pulled back to the foot of the bed, like she thought I might fly off the handle at any moment and go for her eyes.

"What is your problem?" she huffed.

"My problem?" I repeated dumbly. "You're leering over me in the middle of the night, and you want to know what *my* problem is?"

"You were having a nightmare," Bethany retorted. "I was trying to wake you up."

"By smothering me to death?" My head felt like someone had taken a chainsaw to the inside. I wasn't feeling overly charitable.

"You're bleeding, Kali." Bethany's voice was matter-of-fact.

"When I came in, you were clawing at the *ouroboros*. Your stomach's a mess."

As soon as Bethany mentioned the *ouroboros*, I felt the sharp, burning sensation of cool air assaulting raw flesh. Even through the shadow-lit room, I could see that Bethany wasn't exaggerating: I'd already bled through my shirt. Wincing as I pulled cotton away from the open wound, I sat up, trying to process.

Bethany Davis had apparently broken into my house.

I'd dreamed of something that wasn't human, something that had eyes only for me.

And while my dream-self had been making nice with Old Silver Eyes, my hands had apparently been trying to scratch their way through the chupacabra's mark.

Does not compute.

"Bethany, what are you doing in my bedroom at—"I looked at the clock on my nightstand—"five forty-four in the morning? How did you even get in?"

Bethany shrugged.

"Forget it," I said, deciding I had bigger things to worry about. "I don't want to know."

We were getting close enough to dawn that I could almost taste the coming change. The idea that I might *not* die seemed disturbingly novel, like there was a bigger part of me than I'd realized that had believed, from the moment I'd decided to save Bethany, that it was all over for me.

One hour and thirteen minutes.

"Are you even listening to me?" Bethany's pointed whisper broke into my thoughts, and I realized that I hadn't heard a word she'd said.

"We need to get out of here. Now." Bethany crossed her arms over her chest. "Come on, Kali. Chop-chop."

"Bethany, it's five forty-five in the morning. I slept maybe three hours last night, and I feel like someone's coated my entire body in wet cement." I wasn't much of a morning person to begin with—and chupacabra possession wasn't exactly helping the matter. "I just want to take a nice, long shower and forget that any of this ever happened."

"They were at my house, K." Bethany's words broke through the fog in my brain. She couldn't meet my eyes, and in an uncharacteristically nervous gesture, she worried at the end of my comforter, rubbing it back and forth between manicured fingers. "That woman from school. Her little henchmen. I woke up in the middle of the night, and they were there. At first I thought they were looking for me, but then I heard my dad—he was talking to them, and it wasn't about me."

"Okay," I said, forcing my brain to wake up and process the situation. "What were they talking about?"

Bethany angled her eyes upward, the comforter clutched in one hand. "Specimen retrieval."

Specimen.

The word alone was enough to send a chill creeping across the back of my neck. I'd been raised in academia. I knew what people would do to get their hands on grant money, private funding, elite access. I could only imagine what those same people would do if they knew there was uncharted territory out there: a species they'd never studied, an impossibility no one had quantified.

Me.

"What kind of specimen?" My throat felt like sandpaper, the words catching as I pushed them out of my mouth.

"The kind that can be injected into teenagers during random drug tests." Bethany's voice was higher and clearer than mine, and in the course of that single sentence, it went from light and wispy to diamond-hard. "I know it sounds crazy, and I don't have any proof whatsoever, but I'm telling you, Kali, I have a really bad feeling about this."

If I'd thought someone was purposely infecting teenagers with a lethal parasite, I probably would have had a really bad feeling about it, too.

"Did they actually say that was what they were doing?"

Bethany's eyes flashed at my question, and she threw down the comforter. "Yeah, Kali. The woman in charge laid out all of their most unethical and illegal activities for my benefit. There was a PowerPoint presentation, followed by a musical number, and I caught it all on tape."

I ignored the sarcasm. "What did she say—exactly?"

Bethany stood up, smoothing down her skirt and fixing me with a hundred-yard stare. "She said that one of the specimens had taken and that there were indications that it had selected a new and as yet unidentified host."

Well, that was something to be grateful for at least.

"She also reported that the situation with the MC-407 model had been contained and that they'd squelched any reports about the incident in the press." Bethany took a deep breath. "And then she asked my dad to activate the tracking system on the missing specimen."

The second I heard the words *tracking system*, my eyes went to my stomach and then to the bloody tips of my fingers.

What if I hadn't been trying to scratch through the *ouroboros*? What if I'd been trying to gouge out the tracker?

"I don't know what's going on, Kali, but once my dad gets that tracking system up and running, they'll be able to pinpoint your location. Unless you want them to know your name, too, you probably shouldn't be at home when that happens."

My brain finally kicked into high gear. Bethany was right—the last thing I wanted was for the men in suits to have my home address, especially since there was a decent chance that, if they were working with Bethany's dad, they knew who my dad was, too. I could just imagine his reaction to being asked to bring me into the lab for testing.

In fact, the whole scenario—being tracked down, caught, thrown in a tiny room with *bright lights, loud noises, white coats, needles* . . . it was all too easy to imagine. I couldn't let myself go there. I had to move.

Rolling out of bed, I stripped off my blood-soaked shirt and replaced it with a new one. Since I hadn't bothered to change into pajamas the night before, I didn't need to search for my jeans. Looping my hair into a loose ponytail, I glanced back over my shoulder at Bethany, half expecting her to have some kind of comment on my personal hygiene.

"Ready?" she asked me, not bothering to editorialize on my sense of fashion—or lack thereof. I nodded, and a second later, the two of us were creeping down the stairs and out the front door, my father fast asleep in his room and none the wiser.

The BMW was parked down the street, and without a word, the two of us made our way toward it. I knew this was a bad idea, knew that I should ditch Bethany before it was too late, but she had a car, and I didn't want to do this alone.

"Where are we going?" Bethany turned the key in the ignition, and the car purred to life.

"As far away as we can get." I hadn't thought through this plan—in fact, I didn't *have* a plan, but putting distance between the tracking device inside of me and any tie to my real life was the only option that made sense.

Fifty-nine minutes and thirteen seconds.

This close to the shift, I didn't even need to look at my watch. I just knew. I had less than an hour until my blood turned toxic, which meant that I had less than an hour to evade capture, ditch Bethany, and hole up somewhere the real world wouldn't dare to tread.

"Hit the highway."

Bethany didn't have to be told twice. The two of us fell into a loaded silence, and I couldn't help but think how different we were. I was perpetually on the outside, looking in, and she was on the inside, oblivious to the fact that there was anything else out there at all.

And yet.

She was driving my getaway car, and I couldn't help thinking that if things got ugly, maybe I could distract our pursuers long enough for her to disappear.

"Thanks," I said, and the word hung awkwardly in the air, like humidity, thick enough to drown us both.

"You're the one who saved my life," Bethany replied. The words were closer to a complaint than to gratitude—not because she'd wanted to die, but because she wasn't the kind of person who liked being indebted to anyone.

Some people were born for the spotlight, and some of us lived on the fringe. I was beginning to suspect that you could keep people at an arm's length regardless.

"We're not friends," I told Bethany, but the words came out more like a question.

"No," she agreed. "We're not."

My gaze flickered over to her speedometer, and my eyebrows skyrocketed. Bethany drove the way I hunted: like she was invincible, like death was an inevitability and a friend.

"Do you really think your dad is working with these people?"

Bethany shrugged and tapped her fingernail impatiently against the steering wheel, like going ninety miles an hour wasn't nearly fast enough. "He was sitting in his office discussing specimen retrieval, Kali. Whatever's going on, my father is in it up to his eyeballs."

"You don't sound surprised."

Bethany spared a glance for me out of the corner of her eye, then switched her gaze back to the open road. "I'm not. My dad is a brilliant academic, Kali, but brilliant academics don't suddenly up and move into multimillion-dollar houses and buy their daughters BMWs. He took the position here because the department didn't mind him dabbling in the private sector. I'm guessing the goons in the suits are Private and Sector."

"And the woman?" I found myself asking.

"As far as I can tell," Bethany said, "she's calling the shots."

Click. Click. Click.

I hadn't ever gotten a good enough look at the woman in

question to conjure up the image of her face in my mind, but I could still hear the clicking of heels against pavement.

My stomach clenched.

I'd spent enough time around academics to know that there was more money in business than there ever would be in a university setting—but that didn't make the people who funded that kind of research evil. Pharmaceutical companies had engineered countless medical advances; most new technology wasn't developed by university professors. Still, I had to wonder: what kind of money was there in preternatural studies?

Want—use—now—us.

I breathed the shadow in. I breathed it out, and I ignored the voice in my head.

Half an hour. Just half an hour, and this would all be over. The chupacabra would die, and with any luck, the tracking device would go out with it. Bethany and I could go back to not knowing each other, and whatever her father was doing in the private sector could stay there.

"You're not going to tell me your plan, are you?" More tapping of Bethany's fingertip against the steering wheel, and another glance cast at me out of the corner of her eye.

"You don't want to know." That seemed to be a safe response. "We're not friends. I don't trust you, and you don't like me, but I'm not lying when I say that I'm going to be okay. I'm not being stupid or optimistic or self-sacrificing. If you dropped me off on the side of the road right now, by the time I hitched my way home, I'd be fine."

I half expected Bethany to stop the car and let me out, but she didn't. Instead, her green eyes narrowed. The muscles in my throat tightened, and the bottom fell out of my stomach.

I knew better than to let people in. I knew better than to let them see even a fraction of what I was underneath this shell. So why had I just told Bethany that I could do the impossible? Chupacabra possession was always fatal once the *ouroboros* appeared. *Always.* My confidence in being able to cure myself had to strike her as either miraculous or bizarre.

"You're right," Bethany said, switching lanes and pressing down on the accelerator. "I don't want to know."

You also don't want to be here, I thought dully. *You don't want to know what you know about your father, and you don't want to be tangled up in this mess with me.*

I realized then that even once I was cured, this wouldn't be over for Bethany. She'd still have to go to bed at night knowing that her father was involved in something that could have killed me, something that could have killed her. She'd have to get in her BMW every single day and wonder where the money had come from.

Unable to meet her eyes, I busied my hands by reaching into my front pocket and pulling out the piece of paper Skylar had given me the day before. Catching a glimpse of it, Bethany slammed on the brakes. If I hadn't been wearing my seat belt, I would have gone straight through the windshield. As it was, I was pretty sure I'd busted an ovary or two from the impact with the seat belt itself.

"Where did you get that?" Bethany's eyes focused on the paper in my hand with an intensity that made me eye it like it might burst into flames at any moment.

"Skylar gave it to me."

Bethany made an involuntary face the second I said Skylar's name. "And what, exactly, did Miss Little Bit Psychic say when she gave it to you?" Bethany eased her foot off the brakes and began driving again, but this time, she kept to the speed limit—a surefire sign that her attention was on me and not the road.

"Skylar said she couldn't get the image out of her mind and that she thought it might be important." I felt silly even saying the words, but there was a part of me that actually believed Skylar was psychic. She'd known the men in suits were coming, she had an uncanny habit of responding to things I'd left unsaid, and her "instincts" had led us straight to the ice rink—and the man-eating, fire-breathing dragon.

And eventually, to the woman in heels.

Though, now that I thought about it, those last two weren't exactly marks in her favor.

"Did Skylar say where she'd seen it?" Bethany asked, her enunciation a shade too crisp, each word a little too sharp.

Unsure why she was asking, I shrugged. "In her mind?"

For a second, looking at Bethany was like looking at Elliot when he'd told me not to encourage his sister in her delusions of psychic grandeur. Before Bethany could say something to that effect, I preempted the effort. "Have you seen this symbol before?"

Bethany didn't reply, and that told me everything I needed to know. She had.

"Care to clue me in?"

Bethany took her eyes off mine. "Care to tell me how you're going to get rid of that chupacabra at dawn?"

This time, the silence that descended on the car wasn't so much awkward as charged. I would have laid money that wherever Bethany had seen this symbol, it had something to do with the work her father was doing for the suits. Given that she'd already told me that Daddy Dearest was involved in this up to his eyeballs, it was hard to imagine why she'd suddenly be playing things close to the vest.

You don't want to know, I reminded myself, using the exact same words I'd said to Bethany earlier. The less I knew about her, the less she knew about me, the easier this would be on all of us. I was supposed to be invisible. I was supposed to fade into the background. I was supposed to do what I did—

Alone.

Shut up, I thought back fiercely. *Just shut up.* It was bad enough dealing with my own instincts, knowing that I'd never be able to tell anyone else what I really was. I didn't need a bloodsucker reminding me that no matter what happened, at the end of the day I'd still be me, and there'd still be a glass wall separating me from the rest of the world. I wouldn't ever be human.

I could feel the shift coming, taste it on the tip of my tongue. It was a matter of minutes now. *Twenty. Fifteen. Ten.* The surface of my skin was electric. My bones itched. I became acutely aware of the blood in my veins, the length of each and every one of my limbs.

It always seemed strange to me that in the last few minutes before I became something else, I felt more human than ever. I was hungry, starving, and the wounds I'd scratched into my own stomach stung, bringing tears to my eyes. I wanted to cry, and I wanted to scream. I was tired, I was lonely, and an insane part of me wanted to stay that way. No matter how many times I went through this, I couldn't convince my brain that shifting was different than dying, that when I was Other, I was still myself. Instead, I responded to the inevitability of the change like a girl facing down her own mortality, knowing that in *nine minutes, eight minutes, seven,* her life as she knew it would come to end.

"Are you all right?" Bethany's concern cut through my haze, and I nodded.

"Can you drop me off here?" I asked, my voice quiet, my arms wrapping around my torso, like if I held on hard enough, I could stay human just that much longer.

This is what you wanted. This is what you've been waiting for. I tried to talk myself into it, but the rush of sensation all around me was deafening.

—Alone.

Alone, alone, alone. The word echoed through my body, and I had two reactions to it, each visceral and strong. Part of me said no, and part of me said yes. Part of me wanted the change, and part of me didn't want to give up being what I was now.

It was kind of ironic—I spent my human days wishing I wasn't human, but in the last moments before I made the switch, I didn't want to give that up.

"I'm not dropping you off anywhere," Bethany said. "You're really pale, and your pupils are huge. Are you shaking?"

I was. I was trembling, my body vibrating with the knowledge that in a few minutes, everything would change.

I'm going to kill you, I thought, trying to focus on the

chupacabra and not on the things I'd lose once I crossed over. *You're going to die.*

Broken.

I might have actually laughed out loud at the word. The parasite in my head was calling me broken, and he was right. Didn't mean I was any less likely to kill him dead. Didn't make the tears in my eyes sting any less.

"Kali." Bethany's voice went up in pitch. "Kali, I need you to open your eyes and look at me."

My eyelids fluttered, and I managed to look at her long enough to tell that she was dialing a cell phone—probably calling Elliot or Vaughn or someone else who didn't know me from Adam.

From Eve.

Bethany cursed under her breath and hung up the phone. "If you die on me, I will kill you."

I giggled.

She thought the chupacabra was draining me, the way it had the night before. She thought I was dying, drifting further and further away. She thought I was on the verge of going to sleep and never waking up.

The sound of the engine revving permeated my brain, and I forced myself to focus, to concentrate.

"You have to let me out now," I said, fumbling with my seat belt, wrenching it off. "I need to—have to—*go.*"

"We're being followed," Bethany said, and that snapped me out of it. My back was arching, my blood was burning its way through my veins, but for once, my mind was on something other than the coming change. I glanced in the rearview mirror and saw the SUV accelerating toward us. Morning traffic was just starting to pick up, and Bethany zoomed around the other cars like she'd had a past life driving Indy 500s. She hit the exit, flew across an intersection, and hopped back on the highway going the other way. For a few seconds, I thought we'd lost our tail, but then the SUV appeared again, and this time, I saw the passenger-side window cracking.

I saw the gun.

"Specimen retrieval," I told myself. That was what Bethany had said. They were here to retrieve me, to bring the chupacabra inside of me back to the lab. For whatever reason, to them it was worth tracking, and if it was worth tracking, it was worth taking alive.

Right?

Bethany cursed, each word punctuating the one before it, like shots coming off an automatic. The car behind us changed lanes and, without warning, swerved, sideswiping the BMW with brutal, unforgiving force.

Bethany's fingers tightened over the steering wheel, and the last thing I saw before I lost all sense of reality was her white knuckles bulging under paper-thin skin, giving her the look of a skeleton, of Death itself.

Brakes squealing. Glass breaking. Shattering. My world is turned upside down. White-hot pain.

This time, my head really did go through the windshield.

Three minutes. Two. One.

And then I died.

I'm in a tunnel, lying very still, metal all around me. It's loud and dark, and I'm so scared. My bones are shaking. I want it to be over. I want to get out.

"Hold on, baby. You're doing great."

The voice echoes through the tunnel. Mommy? *Everything is humming—it's humming so loudly I want to scream. I want to cover my ears, but I can't.*

Can't move my arms.

Can't move my legs.

I want to go home.

"The image quality is shot to hell."

"She's scared, Rena."

Daddy?

"You have to be still, Kali. Be so still."

Still as the grave.

Oxygen rushed into my lungs like water tearing its way through a dam. I gasped and bolted straight up. Glass crunched underneath me; shards flew off my body, sparkling like raindrops in the newborn sun. Slowly, the world came into focus. Bethany and the BMW were gone, the carnage around me the only evidence that they'd ever been there at all.

They left me here? They ran us off the road, I went through the windshield, and they just left?

So much for specimen retrieval.

Stiffly, I brought my right hand up to my left shoulder, popping it back into place. I pulled bits and pieces of windshield from my face, my chest, my arms. I reached my blood-soaked hands up and manually tilted my head to the side, then snapped it backward. The sound of crunching bones was unpleasant, but not overly so.

Twenty-three hours and nineteen minutes.

That was more than enough time for me to heal. Already, the surface wounds were closing, leaving nothing but smears of blood in their wake. I could hear bones knitting themselves back together, could feel my spine righting itself with nothing more than a curious pressure at the nape of my neck.

Somebody tried to kill me. I should be dead.

That realization wasn't as disturbing as it would have been on a human day. People like me weren't scared to die, and we weren't easy to kill. The scent of blood—coppery, wet—was familiar, but for some reason, this time, there were layers to the smell that I'd never inhaled before: iron, honey, sweat.

If you can smell your blood, they can smell it.

For a moment, I thought the warning was a product of my own mind, but then a glint of gold caught my eye. Under my ravaged shirt, under the blood, I could see part of an all-too-familiar symbol.

No.

I pulled at the fabric, wrenching it away from my stomach. The flesh underneath was smeared with messy streaks of blood, like someone had been finger-painting on my torso, but the red color did nothing to mask the image of a snake eating its own tail.

The *ouroboros*.

No. This couldn't be happening. This wasn't the plan. My blood was poison, and the thing inside me was supposed to be dying. It was supposed to be gone.

Kali.

I didn't want to be hearing the voice. I didn't want to still be infected, to know that come dawn, I might still be dying.

You're not dying. The human body can't handle the bite. Yours can.

In tandem with the words, the *ouroboros* on my stomach trembled and then an inklike substance began to bleed outward from its surface. Like vines climbing a wall, string-thin wisps of gold snaked their way across my skin, up my torso, around to my back.

I couldn't tear my eyes from the mark's progress. As it painted me in crisscrossing lines, the *ouroboros* glowed with an unearthly sheen. Beads of sweat gathered on the surface of my skin, and unable to resist, I dragged one bloody finger across the length of the symbol, tracing it, feeling it—

Your wounds are healing. At this rate, you'll be fine within an hour, but until then, you need to mask the smell of your blood.

There was no way I'd be completely healed in an hour. I was fast, but not that fast.

There are some advantages to getting bitten.

The voice in my head was clearer than it had ever been, like its owner was whispering the words directly into the back of my neck. My eyes focused on a point in the distance, and I saw him.

The man from my dreams.

He was a head or so taller than me, his skin lighter, his eyes silver. Shadow clung to the surface of his body, but this time I could see an unearthly light through the darkness.

He didn't belong here.

Neither do you.

I met his silver eyes, so dark I could feel myself getting lost in them, and for a moment I saw him somewhere else: cement walls, blackened floor, blood.

Kali. Focus.

The words were sharp, and it took me a minute to process the fact that the voice in my head was yelling at me.

The people who left you here will expect your body to be discovered soon. They're counting on it being ruled a hit-and-run. They'll be surprised enough when your body doesn't turn up. The last thing you need is to draw every beast in a thirty-mile radius to your side.

I hated to admit it, but the chupacabra had a point.

The second that thought crossed my mind, a low, rumbling chuckle echoed through my brain. **I'm not a Nibbler, Kali. Nibblers can't talk.**

Nibblers? *Nibblers?*

You're not a chupacabra? I asked silently, because that was what he seemed to be implying.

No. I'm not.

He sounded fairly certain, but I couldn't help asking again. *You're seriously not the chupacabra who bit me yesterday?*

I'd started hearing the voice right after I'd been bitten. The simplest explanation was usually the right one—even if it involved assuming that a parasite was capable of speech.

I'm not a Nibbler, Kali. I *have* a Nibbler.

I looked down at the symbol on my stomach, pictured one on his.

So I have a chupacabra inside my body and you have one inside of yours and that lets us play psychic telephone?

He had to realize how ridiculous that sounded.

More ridiculous than thinking that a Nibbler can talk?

After spending the past eighteen hours trying to keep Skylar, Bethany, and the whole motley crew from thinking I was insane, I really wasn't in the mood to be mocked by the voice in my head.

The voice that apparently did not belong to a chupacabra.

If you're not the thing that bit me, I said sharply, *who the hell are you?*

I knew before the response came that he would give me his name—Zev.

What the hell are you? I amended my silent question, and Zev answered with a question of his own.

What the hell are *you*?

In the distance, the man I'd seen disappeared back into the depths of my mind. My body stiff, I climbed to my feet.

What the hell was I? How many times had I asked myself that same question?

I wanted answers—lots of them—but there was no denying that Zev's suggestion that I make myself scarce was a good one: I was injured, and even with my healing abilities kicked into overdrive, I wasn't in any shape to fight off every monster that came creeping out of the woodwork. My blood was every-where. The air was thick with it. It was only a matter of time before the wind carried the scent to the wrong nostrils.

This isn't over, I told the mystery boy in my mind. *You* are *going to answer my questions.*

Silence.

Without another word—out loud or internal—I turned and walked up to the road, half naked and covered in blood, trying not to think about the mark on my stomach or the distinct feeling that life, as I knew it, was over.

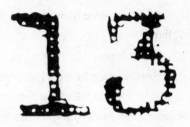

I was fairly certain that the kind of person who picked up girls on the side of the road wasn't the kind of person you wanted to be alone in a car with for any extended period of time. I suspected this was doubly true if you were covered in your own blood and wearing the shredded remains of a T-shirt that had most definitely seen better days.

Still, beggars couldn't be choosers. I needed a shower. I needed fresh clothes, and I needed to get off the side of the highway before some well-meaning passer-by called the cops. My options were severely limited, and of those, Eddie seemed like the best bet. He had a proto-beer belly and biceps that told me he liked to feel strong. I knew the second I saw him, pulling into the gas station, that he would pick me up when he pulled out, no questions asked.

I also knew he'd probably try to take a little something in return.

Don't do this, Kali.

I wasn't sure whether Zev meant those words as a warning or an order, but either way, I didn't feel particularly compelled to listen. Whoever or whatever he was, he was nothing to me, and I was used to taking care of myself.

I had a knife strapped to my calf and the instincts of a killer.

I'll be fine.

Besides, I'd already almost died once today. That really had a way of putting things in perspective. So I got into Eddie's car. I relegated Zev's voice to the back of my mind, and I bided my time. We had made it to the outskirts of town, about a mile away from the university, when Eddie pulled off onto an access road and put one hand on my shoulder.

"I'll kill you," I said conversationally. The words weren't a threat—more of an observation, really, and it disturbed me that I could be so matter-of-fact about taking human life. I'd never felt the need to hunt anyone who fell on that side of the natural/preternatural divide, but the hunt-lust was already building up inside of me, and I'd had a really bad morning.

"Excuse me?" Eddie asked, gob-smacked and so fatally stupid that I almost couldn't stand to look at him.

"Don't touch me," I clarified, the air around me pulsing with a rhythm I recognized all too well. One that wanted me to lay a trap. To hunt. To kill.

"Hey now, sweetheart. I could have called the cops when I saw you. Still could. Girl like you, looking like that—"

Eddie's hand ventured from my shoulder down my collar-bone, and something inside of me snapped. One second I was me, and the next, I'd been pushed outside of my body, and I was watching my mouth move and listening to words that weren't mine snaking their way out of my lips.

"She probably wouldn't kill you. She has a certain fond-ness for humans, thinks she's one of them."

I watched, disembodied, as a dangerous, glittering smile cut across the features of my face, and I flashed back to the moment at the ice rink when I'd lost control of my body, when something or someone else had thrown it out of the dragon's line of fire.

"What in the blazing hell are you talking about?" Eddie didn't remove his hand from my collarbone, but it didn't venture any lower, either.

"The girl won't kill you, but I will. I'll take this knife and slit you from the throat down, split your body in two along the lines of your delicate human spine."

Zev's voice was lower than mine, almost mechanical in the way it left my mouth.

I fought for control of my own body.

I can handle this!

I am handling this, Zev said calmly, and I knew by his tone of voice that he wasn't arguing with me. He was simply stating a fact.

I was beginning to wish I'd never gotten into a car with Eddie.

Eddie—who was likely coming to a similar conclusion himself—stupidly persisted in trying to make a point with the creature wearing my body.

"Now, look here, girl."

"Leave." In the span of a heartbeat, Zev had my knife in his hand, and he dragged the point gently across the surface of my assailant's Adam's apple. "Run."

Eddie froze. "You crazy bitch."

Within a second, Zev had the edge of the knife pressed to the underside of the man's chin, hard enough to draw blood.

Small red spheres beaded up on the surface of Eddie's skin, coating his stubble.

Zev licked his lips.

Or rather, he licked mine.

My tongue. My lips. My hand holding the knife.

I clung to that thought, and somehow, my mind overpowered Zev's and shoved him out.

The *ouroboros* on my stomach burned like dry ice, like fire.

"I don't think he likes it when you call me a bitch," I told Eddie drily, trying not to sound as thrown as I felt.

"He?" Eddie's Adam's apple bobbed upward, and my eyes lit on a series of tiny cuts in the surface of his skin.

Blood.

People like me didn't get hungry. We didn't even need to eat. But for a moment, a split second that rocked me to the core, I was very, very thirsty.

"I should go," I said, forcing myself to pull the knife from Eddie's throat, trying not to look at the blood beading up on its surface.

"I'm calling the cops!" Eddie seemed intent on proving that he wasn't the brightest crayon in the box. I gave him a look.

"And telling them what? That you picked up a girl covered in blood, and when you tried to put the moves on her, the demon inside of her threatened your life?" I snorted. "Good luck with that one."

I am not a demon. Zev sounded extremely put out. **Demon is a very offensive word.**

I rolled my eyes. *You would have killed him, Zev.*

Yes.

And you don't see anything wrong with that?

He would have hurt you, came the reply. **He may well hurt someone else.**

One hand on the hilt of my knife and the other on the door handle, I turned my gaze back to Eddie. The last thing I wanted was him doing this to someone else—someone who might not have a knife strapped to one leg and a would-be murderer inside her brain.

"We have your scent now," I said, sounding less than human myself. "I wouldn't recommend picking up any more teenage girls."

To hit home the point, I brought the bloodstained knife to my nose and breathed in deeply. My tongue flickered out between my lips, but I pulled the blade back before the two could touch.

"Goodbye, Eddie."

I opened the car door, hopped to the ground, and without ever turning back to look over my shoulder, walked back toward the highway and started to jog.

With my endurance, I could have run all the way home, but I was still covered in my own blood and didn't want to risk being seen any more than I had to.

I needed a shower and a change of clothing. I needed to blend, and growing up in academia, I knew college campuses the way other girls knew the layout of the local mall. The university was close enough, and it wasn't hard to find a block of dorms. Sticking to the shadows as much as possible, I found a door that had been propped open and headed to the second-floor communal bathroom.

As I'd suspected, there weren't many people up this early

in the morning. I took my hair down from its ponytail and let it hang in my face, masking the blood there and praying that my dark T-shirt—or at least, what was left of it—would hide the rest.

I made it to the bathroom without being spotted and surveyed my surroundings. One shower was already in use, and the occupant had hung her clothes on a hook outside the curtain: jeans, a tank top, a sizeable bra. Deciding the third item wouldn't fit, I gently slipped the first two off the hook and walked back out the door, up another flight of stairs, and into the third-floor bathroom. I tossed the clothes over the shower rod, pulled the curtain, and started stripping off my own.

Hot water should have felt good on my ravaged body, but it didn't. I could feel the warmth, but my muscles weren't sore and they weren't looking for relief. Mechanically, I ran my hands over my limbs, checking for injuries that hadn't yet healed. A few areas were raw and red, but as I washed the blood and dirt from my pores, decorating the drain in shades of black and red, even those areas began to fade, leaving my light brown skin creamy and smooth.

Untouched.

As I turned my attention to my hair, it occurred to me that if Zev was there, in my mind, he might be getting quite the show. I paused, searching for him, but for the first time, I felt nothing. I dug deeper, pushed harder, and the image I'd seen while I was lying on the side of the road pulsed like a strobe light in front of my eyes.

Cement walls, scorch marks on the floor, and a figure swathed in shadow, lying on one side.

As quick as a camera flash, the image was gone. The steam from the shower settled on my skin, and I could feel my mind loosening up, until an idea took shape.

Zev had said that chupacabra bites were fatal in humans, but that some people could handle being bitten. Some people benefited from it. People like me.

And when I'd asked Zev what he was, he'd thrown the question back to me, like we were the same.

I'd spent my entire life looking for answers, and now, against all odds, they were there, in my head.

I wrung the last of the bloodied water from my hair and wrenched the shower knob into the OFF position. Quickly, silently, I put on the jeans I'd stolen and slipped the tank top over my head. My boots had survived the crash mostly intact, and without even thinking, I sheathed my knife, securing it in place beneath the leg of the pilfered Sevens. My body hummed where it came in contact with the blade, and a familiar urge began to beckon to me in rhythm with my own heartbeat.

I wanted to *hunt.* I needed to *kill.* And when a human girl brushed past me and hopped into the shower stall next to mine, I caught the scent of her blood in the air.

Wet. Coppery. Honey.

Easy, Kali. The thirst isn't yours. It's the Nibbler's.

I tried to process what he was saying. Wasn't the chupacabra supposed to be draining *my* blood?

It's a part of you now. It makes you stronger. It connects us. And sooner or later, you'll have to feed it.

I had to get out of there—away from the smell of the girl in the shower, away from the suggestion that the chupacabra inside of me wanted blood. An uncomfortable idea—not to mention impossible—was taking form in my mind, and I didn't want to give life to it.

I didn't want to think about the kind of creature that could heal from any wound and thirsted for human blood.

You should burn the clothing.

I almost thanked Zev for changing the subject, but caught myself just in time. It was disturbing how natural having someone else in my head seemed, and I couldn't push down that little whisper inside of me, the one that said that people like me were meant to come in pairs.

Lonely Ones. I remembered the phrase from the ice rink, and Zev echoed it, the timbre of his voice setting his words off from my own.

You never knew, he said, half questioning, half tender. What you are, what was missing.

I walked out of the bathroom, down the stairs, and out the door.

Talk to me, Kali. I tried to explain things to you yesterday, but you couldn't hear me. The connection's so much clearer now . . .

I ignored him and set to work scrounging up a bottle of nail-polish remover and a lighter. Ducking back behind one of the dorms, I zeroed in on an empty trash can, dumped my clothes, and followed Zev's suggestion to a T.

I burned my clothes.

For a few seconds, I watched the flames. And then, unsure that it would work, I tried reaching for Zev's mind. He'd taken over my body twice now—first with the dragon, then with Eddie. Turnaround was only fair play. Tit for tat.

My breathing slowed, and I felt it—the thing inside my

body. And then, my skin tingling with unnatural charge, I felt the thing inside of Zev's.

My body. My Nibbler. His Nibbler. Him.

For a second—a split second—I saw the world through Zev's eyes, wore his body as my own.

Concrete walls. Concrete floor. A woman with ruby-red lips. Blood.

I came out of it without warning. My bloodied clothes were ashes, and the fire had burned itself out.

Where are you? I asked Zev silently. *What was that?*

The voice in my head was silent.

You wanted me to talk. I'm talking.

Still nothing. Whatever I'd seen, whatever Zev was hiding, he clearly wasn't forthcoming about it. All he wanted to talk about was *me*. What I was. What was happening to my body. How to keep predators off my trail.

Even thinking about that last one sent a whisper of discontent through my arteries and veins—I wasn't built for running away from the monsters. I wanted desperately to run toward them—track them down, kill them. Luckily, I was used to restraining myself, used to acting human even when I wasn't, and the human part of my brain reminded me that right now, preternatural beasties weren't exactly my primary concern.

Someone had made a strong attempt at killing me this morning. With any luck, between my transition from human to not and my trip through the windshield, I might have managed to knock out their tracking system, but whoever was calling the shots probably wouldn't be thrilled if and when they found out I was still alive. Worse, I was pretty sure that

Bethany had seen me fly through the windshield, and now she was missing. Had our pursuers taken her captive? Had they hurt her? What had she told them?

Was she dead?

Easy, Kali. Zev was back. My fingers curled slightly, like someone was stroking my palm. **It's not your fault.**

"It *is* my fault," I said softly, resisting the impulse to speak the words straight from my mind to his. "People like me don't have friends. We don't have enemies. We don't carpool, we don't argue, we don't let other people care."

But I had. I'd let Bethany help me, just because I'd helped her. Somehow, she'd crept under my skin. She'd seen a glimmer of the real me.

And now she was gone, possibly missing, possibly dead.

I'm going to find her, I said silently, daring Zev to argue, to try to tell me what to do when he couldn't even answer a simple question himself. *I'm going to find her, and I'm going to find out what they did to her—even if it means going straight to the belly of the beast.*

The house looked more like a coliseum than an actual home. Enormous columns lined the front door on either side; the lawn was pristine. At the moment, however, I was more concerned with the ten-foot-tall security gate that marked the property's borders on all sides.

The gate was a problem.

I could have climbed it. If there'd been a pack of hellhounds on the other side, I doubtlessly would have, but this was recon, not a confrontation. I needed to be invisible, and that meant that if I was going to scale the gate, I at the very least needed to identify the least conspicuous location from which to do so.

I moved with the absolute silence of a panther stalking its prey, light on my feet, drawn to the shadows. The tank top I'd pilfered from the dormitories was black. The jeans had a dark wash. I could do this. I could blend. I could disappear into my surroundings . . .

About a quarter of the way around the house, I made my move, sidling up to the wall. It was made of brick and topped with wrought iron. I braced my foot against the base of the wall and curled the tips of my fingers downward, poised to dig my nails into the mortar.

"I bet you were a cat in a former life."

I didn't jump. I didn't curse. My heart didn't beat any faster at the interruption, but my breath caught in my throat.

"Skylar?"

"Hiya, Kali."

For someone who gave every appearance of being Human with a capital H—physically, at least—Skylar Hayden was surprisingly stealthy.

"What are you doing here?" I asked, relaxing my hands and mimicking her posture, like I hadn't been on the verge of beginning my career in breaking and entering a few seconds before.

"No idea." Skylar grinned. "The universe works in mysterious ways."

"Uh-huh," I said. "Likely story."

"Also, when you and Bethany didn't show up for school this morning, Elliot kind of freaked. He called Bethany, and her dad answered the phone. I tried calling you, but apparently, you don't have a cell phone."

"I lost it," I said. If by "lost," you mean "used it to dismember some zombies a few nights ago." I went through cell phones almost as quickly as I went through clothes.

"In any case, I told Elliot you guys were fine, he went to class, and I came here. Speaking of, why are you here? I sense that the chocolate chips have hit the fan."

"What else do you sense?"

Skylar shrugged. "Little bit psychic," she reminded me. "I have my limitations."

She seems . . . enthusiastic.

I almost responded to Zev's words out loud, but stopped myself just in time. *That's one word for it.*

"So why are we climbing the Davises' wall?" Skylar clearly wasn't put out by the idea—just curious.

"*We* are not climbing anything," I told her. "*I* need to get inside Bethany's house. The two of us were in an accident this morning, and I think the people we saw yesterday might have taken her."

"Taken her where?"

"I don't know, Skylar. All I know is that someone ran our car off the road, I got knocked unconscious, and when I woke up, Bethany and the car were both gone." I hadn't meant to tell her that much. At this rate, I'd be confessing my deepest, darkest secrets by noon.

You seem to be somewhat attached to this human.

I ignored the running commentary in my head—and the scent of strawberries and blood, which I belatedly realized was the way Skylar smelled to the parasite inside of me. The one that connected me to Zev. The one that, according to Zev, I would eventually have to feed.

If I concentrated, I could hear Skylar's heart beating, could see the pulse of her carotid artery in her neck.

I focused on not concentrating.

"If you think someone took Bethany, why are we at her house? Shouldn't we be looking for evidence at the scene of the crime? Talking to people who might have seen where she went? Or, *ohhh*, we could check out local hospitals, and I could borrow Genevieve's police scanner, and maybe Darryl could hack the DMV."

I wasn't sure which part of that run-on statement to respond to first. "Genevieve has a police scanner?"

Skylar shrugged. "We all have hobbies."

Given what I spent my spare time doing, I wasn't exactly in a position to be throwing stones.

"This isn't a game, Skylar." My voice was serious, but when Skylar responded, her tone made mine seem like child's play.

"I know, Kali." Her blue eyes were shadowed, her mouth set into a firm line. "Trust me, I know."

Somehow, it was easy to believe that she knew the stakes, maybe even better than I did. "We shouldn't be talking here," I told her. "Someone might see us, and let's just say that the people who ran Bethany's car off the road might have reason to be looking for me."

Like the fact that I was still in possession of their "specimen."

And the fact that my body had disappeared from the side of the road.

The fact that I wasn't dead . . .

On the off-chance that Skylar *was* psychic, I stopped that line of thinking in its tracks and started talking, careful to keep the details to a bare minimum. I needed to tell Skylar enough to convince her this was dangerous, but not so much that I'd put her in *more* danger. Hitting a few key points, I ended with, "Whatever's going on, Bethany's dad is involved. She mentioned something about her dad keeping some of his equipment at home. He might have records here, too . . ."

I trailed off.

All I needed was a name. Once we knew who Bethany's father was working for, Skylar could go Nancy Drew them to her heart's content.

Know thy enemy.

Drain them dry.

"Kali?" Skylar's voice broke into my thoughts, and I realized that I'd been staring—at her throat.

"Yeah?"

"You didn't get rid of the chupacabra, did you?"

I didn't answer. Instead, I turned back to the wall. "I need to get inside."

Skylar nodded. "Go ahead. I'll work on Plan B."

More terrifying words had never been spoken, but before I could convince Skylar that there would be no Plan B, she was already off and running, and I was left with two choices: follow her or scale the wall.

I scaled the wall.

The mortar cracked under the force of my fingernails, and I flashed back to the feel of thick, leathery flesh giving way under my razor-sharp nails.

They're out there. They're waiting. They're yours.

Find them. Find them now.

It was only nine thirty in the morning, and already, I wanted to hunt so badly I could taste it on the tip of my tongue, bittersweet.

Dropping to the ground and landing in a crouch, I couldn't help turning my inner ear to the world around me. There was something close. Something old.

Something deadly.

Ignoring the hum of the preternatural at the edge of my senses, I made my way to the side of Bethany's house. The windows were closed. A camera stared down at me from overhead. I dodged its view and considered my options.

"For what it's worth, I'm going in the front door."

This time, Skylar didn't appear right next to me. Instead, she yelled the words across the lawn, from the gargantuan front porch.

How had she gotten past the gate?

"I had the guard buzz me in," Skylar called. "He's really very nice."

Even from a distance, I could tell that the expression on Skylar's face was anything but innocent. She wanted in—not just the house, but the situation. If the woman in heels was keeping track of the Davises' visitors, Skylar had just thrown herself onto her radar, and from the way she was standing there, I got the feeling that it was intentional, that she would keep doing it, again and again, until her life was on the line as much as mine.

Until she'd destroyed every reason I had for wanting to keep her out.

As I watched, horrified, Skylar stepped forward and rang the doorbell. I pressed my back against the side of the house, slipping as far into the shadows as I could. The front door opened, and Skylar grinned.

"Hey, Bethany," she said, her voice carrying. "What's up?"

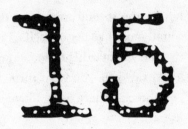

Bethany looked like a shadow of her former self. She was wearing a light yellow sundress, faded and out of season. Her pale skin was marred by bruises, and her left arm was in a sling.

Red hair hung in a limp ponytail to one side, and even from a distance, I could see a sluggish quality to the way she moved, the way she blinked.

Had they drugged her?

Without even meaning to, I stepped out from the shadows. I began moving toward the duo on the front porch, but before I'd fully crossed the lawn, Bethany marked my presence. She stared at me, like she was trying to see through some kind of fog.

She shook.

Her mouth moved, but I couldn't make out the words until I got closer.

"You're dead."

I stepped up onto the porch, careful to keep my back to the surveillance.

"I saw you. I saw you die. You're dead."

The first time she said it, Bethany's voice was monotone,

but by the second time—and the third—she was starting to sound more like her old self.

She was starting to sound pissed.

"I saw you. You went through the windshield. You broke your neck. There was blood—so much blood, and your legs . . ."

"Maybe you saw wrong," Skylar suggested.

"I know what I saw. Kali's dead, and I'm crazy. They drugged me up, and now I'm crazy. They were afraid I'd tell someone. They knew my dad couldn't keep me here forever, so they made me crazy."

"You're not crazy," I said calmly. "You must have just gotten things mixed up in the wreck. I was bleeding, but they were mostly surface cuts. When I woke up, you were gone. I was worried, so I came here."

"I think I'd know if you weren't dead," Bethany snapped. "And, no offense, but I'm pretty sure I'm more qualified to tell if I'm crazy than you are."

I couldn't tell if Bethany was on the verge of hysterics or reading me the riot act. Skylar must have been leaning toward the "hysterical" interpretation, because she wound up and smacked her, right across the face.

Bethany blinked. "Did you just hit me?" she asked, disbelief coloring her every feature.

Skylar raised both hands, palms outward. "I come in peace!"

"You do not come in peace. You hit me."

"I hit in peace!"

Sensing that this could devolve into an all-out brawl very quickly, I took matters into my own hands—literally. I stepped forward and put my right palm on Bethany's shoulder.

"I told you I'd be okay, and I'm okay," I said softly.

I could see the wheels turning in Bethany's head, see her wanting to believe me.

"Are *you* okay?" I asked her.

Bethany shrugged off my touch. "I'm fine."

"No, you're not," Skylar piped up. "Somebody drugged you, and your dad is keeping you locked up in your own home. That's not fine."

"What is she even doing here?" Bethany directed the question at me, and I took that as evidence that she was at the very least less sure that I was a hallucination than she'd been a moment before.

Skylar didn't wait for me to answer Bethany's question—she jumped right in herself. "Someone's watching you, Bethany. They're after Kali. And I can't shake the idea that this is bigger, that there's something else, *someone* else . . ." Skylar frowned. "Bad people are doing bad things. Good people are doing bad things, too. I'm supposed to be here. I'm supposed to help."

Skylar blinked, and her eyes stayed closed for a fraction of a second longer than they should have. "This is it."

She sounded . . . sad. Stubborn, determined, and sad.

"This is what?" I asked, wondering how many times I'd worn that same expression on my face and what exactly had put it on hers.

"It," Skylar said simply. "This is *it*."

Bethany snorted. "Because that really clears things up."

Skylar smiled, but the expression only took on half her face. "Give it a few days," she said, "and it will."

I had no idea what she was talking about, but for better or worse, at the moment, I had bigger fish to fry.

I'd come here as step one in a plan to track down Bethany, but it looked like I wasn't going to need steps two through four. Instead, I needed to find out what Bethany knew, what she remembered.

Besides the fact that I should have been dead.

"Can we come in?" I asked.

Bethany planted her body firmly in front of the open door. "My dad could come home any second. You shouldn't be here when he does."

"Then can we go somewhere else?" I gave her a look. "We need to talk."

"I can't leave," Bethany replied without hesitation. "They'll know if I do. My dad said everything was going to be okay. He said he'd take care of it, but I have to stay here."

There was something in her eyes when she talked about her father—not quite anger, not quite fear.

"Why didn't you go to the police?" I didn't mean for the words to come out of my mouth with an edge to them, but they did. Bethany had left me on the side of the road. Maybe she hadn't had a choice. Maybe they'd forced her to go, but she'd left me broken and bleeding on the ground and hadn't lifted a hand against the people who'd put me there.

"You were already dead!"

The vehemence of Bethany's words took me by surprise.

"You were dead, and it was my fault. I was the one driving. I was the one who got bitten. I couldn't—I can't do this again."

Again?

"There was nothing I could do for you, Kali."

"But there was something you could do for someone else." Skylar tilted her head from one side to the other and then back again, staring intently at the lines of Bethany's face. "Someone you love."

Bethany's eyes hardened, and she stepped back into the house, ready to slam the door in our faces. Unfortunately for her, I was quick.

Too quick.

Quicker than I would have been two days before.

There are some benefits to being bitten.

As Zev's words echoed in my head, I realized how very close I was standing to Bethany. How fast her heart was pounding. How hungry the thing inside me was. I was fast and strong and *more* than I'd been two days before—and the chupacabra wanted blood.

Twenty-one hours and nine minutes.

"You can't come in," Bethany snapped, bringing me back to the present.

"Evidence would suggest otherwise," Skylar commented, following my lead and stepping into the house.

"Get out."

"Nope." Skylar grinned. "I want to see Château Davis. You've been dating my brother for six months, and you've stolen my tampons twice. The least you can do is give me a tour."

"Skylar," Bethany said, her voice cracking. "Please, both of you, just get out."

"Bethany?"

I half expected to run into Bethany's father, but instead, the voice that had issued that query was clearly female.

"You guys need to go," Bethany said again, her voice low and urgent.

"Bethany, dear," the voice called from the other room, "have you seen Tyler?"

Bethany flinched. A moment later, her face was a blank canvas, flat and unreadable. She plastered on a smile and turned around, just as a woman wearing heels and a white silk bathrobe stepped into the room. She had long, wavy hair that straddled the line between blonde and red. Her eyes were wide, her smile inviting.

"Oh dear," she said. "I didn't realize Bethie had guests."

"They were just leaving," Bethany said.

"Don't be silly, sweetheart. They should at least stay for breakfast. Have you seen your brother? It's omelet day, and you know how he feels about those."

Bethany stood up a little straighter, and her face softened. "Okay, Mom. Okay."

I wasn't sure what Bethany was saying "okay" to, but it seemed to satisfy her mother, who ran a smoothing hand over the white silk robe.

"I ought to get dressed," she said absentmindedly. "Something's not right."

"Everything's fine," Bethany said. "I promise."

Her mother nodded, and a second later she was gone, leaving the three of us in the foyer, silent, the air thick with all of the things we weren't saying.

"She's the one you're helping," Skylar said. "Your mom. What did your dad say he'd do for her if you kept your mouth shut about what happened out on the highway this morning?"

In my mind, I rephrased Skylar's question—*What did he say he'd do to your mother if you didn't?*

"It's none of your business," Bethany said, her voice low and full of warning. "You never saw her. She's fine."

I couldn't shake the look in Mrs. Davis's eyes, the singsong tone to her voice. I'd seen her before, at university functions. She'd seemed fine.

Normal.

Like Bethany, only older.

What's wrong with her? I wondered, but that wasn't the kind of question you asked out loud.

So instead, I asked something else. "Who's Tyler?"

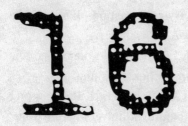

Bethany left us in the foyer. She didn't say a word, didn't respond to the question. If I'd had more practice with the whole "friend" thing, maybe I would have known what to say or do next, but I didn't.

"She'll be back," Skylar said. I wasn't so sure, but up until now, Skylar's instincts had been right on point. Unfortunately, she chose that moment to turn her focus from Bethany to me. "Bethany wasn't wrong," she said slowly. "Was she? About you going through the windshield, about your broken neck?"

Don't tell her.

This time, I didn't object to Zev weighing in or the advice he was dispensing. That was how I'd always gotten by, how I survived. By not opening my mouth. By keeping people at arm's length.

"My neck isn't broken," I said stiffly. "I'm fine."

"People only ever say they're fine when they're not." With those words, Skylar's eyes went from my face to my stomach. Even clothed in the tank top, I felt naked. I felt like she could see straight through me.

I don't know what would have happened next, if Bethany's mother hadn't interrupted our little standoff. All smiles, she came back into the room garbed in a twin set and jeans, every inch the suburban soccer mom. For a moment, I thought she was going to offer us lemonade or something, but instead, she fixed her gaze on a spot about a foot in front of Skylar and me.

"Tyler," she said, in one of those mom voices—halfway between exasperation and indulgence. "Stop pestering Bethany's friends."

It took me a moment to digest her words. I stopped breathing.

"I am so sorry, girls," Mrs. Davis continued, a smile dancing across her face, her eyes flitting back and forth, like she was tracking someone's movement, even though there wasn't anyone there.

I looked at Skylar. She looked at me. The two of us looked at the spot on the floor.

"C'mon, Ty," Mrs. Davis said. "Leave the girls alone. I've got an omelet with your name on it and a big glass of milk."

She held out her hand and beckoned. After a brief pause, she flitted away, her movements purposeful and graceful. As I watched, she reached out, like she was tousling someone's hair and then she paused.

She turned and looked back over her shoulder.

And for a split second, maybe less, it looked like she might crumble to the ground. Like she knew there wasn't anyone in this room but the three of us. Like wherever her Tyler had gone, Bethany's mother wished she could go there, too.

That split second of clarity was fleeting, and a moment later, the bright smile returned, but I was left with an aching sadness. I watched Mrs. Davis walk out of the room, murmuring gaily to nobody at all.

Beside me, Skylar wiped the back of her hand roughly across her face.

"You okay?" I asked her. After what we'd just seen, I wasn't entirely certain that *I* was okay.

Skylar shook her head. "I'll be fine," she said. "It's just— she's so sad. She's drowning."

For once, Skylar didn't elaborate, and when Bethany came back in a moment later, I struggled to hide my own emotions, to make it seem like Skylar and I hadn't just seen into the intimate depths of her mother's broken mind.

"Here," Bethany said, tersely. It took me a moment to realize that she was holding out a slip of paper. No, not paper—a brochure.

I took it from her. "Chimera Biomedical," I read, but my eyes were drawn away from the words to the image below them: an octagon bisected by a ladder, spiraling around an invisible line.

Only this time, the ladder looked less like a ladder and more like a DNA helix.

"They specialize in gene therapy," Bethany said stiffly. "Regeneration."

"Regeneration?"

Bethany stared pointedly at the tips of her toes. "Reviving brain cells. Stimulating nerve growth. Growing organs."

"Do they do stem-cell research?" Skylar asked, taking the brochure from my hand and staring intently at the symbol— the one she'd drawn for me the day before.

"Look," Bethany said. "This is what you wanted to know,

isn't it? You wanted to know what that symbol was, and I told you. You want to know who my dad is working for. Well, this is it. It has to be. It explains everything. Why he's been working so much. Why he'd do something like this. Why Skylar drew the symbol."

I processed Bethany's words, but felt like I was missing something—the reason she hadn't told me this company's name the second she'd seen the symbol; the things she was saying about her dad.

"Your mom came back in here a second ago," Skylar told her, gauging her reaction. "Looking for Tyler."

This time, Bethany didn't react to the sound of the name. She just raised one eyebrow, untouchable and cool. "So?"

I knew then, knew that Tyler wasn't a figment of her mother's imagination. Knew that he'd been real once, that he wasn't any more.

"You had a brother," I said, thinking of all the times I'd wished for a sibling, for someone in my house other than just my dad and me. "But something happened."

Bethany's chin wavered, and I realized that she was biting the inside of her cheeks—anything to keep herself from showing a hint of weakness to the two of us.

Skylar sucked in a breath, that same sad smile painting her face, like if she let her lips tilt downward, she might start crying instead. "It wasn't your fault," she said, her voice soft, her tone even.

I thought of the things Bethany had said when she realized I was alive. *You were dead, and it was my fault. I couldn't—I can't do this again.*

"The accident today wasn't your fault, either," I told her.

"It's always my fault," Bethany said, voice steady, hands shaking. "My mom. My dad. Tyler. I was supposed to be watching him. *Me*. But he wanted to go to a friend's house, and I wanted to watch something on TV, so I let him. I let him go, and he was goofing around on their diving board—it was the middle of winter. There wasn't any water in the pool, and he should have known better. I shouldn't have let him go."

Bethany shrugged, like that could make the words she was about to say matter less. "He fell."

I wondered how old she'd been at the time, how old her little brother was when he died.

"He's not dead." Skylar said the words suddenly, and I wasn't sure whether she was responding to my thoughts or if she'd seen something in that exact moment that had started her lips moving. "He fell. On concrete. Hit his head, but he didn't die."

"Coma," Bethany said flatly. "For the past four years. Once upon a time, the doctors thought he might wake up. There were some experimental treatments, but they didn't work. Now they say he's brain-dead. It doesn't matter. Either way, he's gone."

I tried to imagine what must have been going through her head at that moment, how she must feel, but I couldn't. I had my reasons for keeping people at arm's length, and she had hers. My dad and I barely even spoke. My mother had left when I was three. But Bethany—

Her brother was brain-dead.

Her mother believed he was still running around the house.

And her father was conducting illegal experiments on unwitting teenagers—Bethany included.

Suddenly, it clicked in my head: the brochure I was holding, Bethany's familiarity with Chimera Biomedical, her father's willingness to break the law for them.

"You said there were experimental treatments." I watched her reaction to my words. "You said, when Tyler first got hurt, he underwent experimental treatments."

Bethany turned her attention back to her toes. "So?"

"Whose experimental treatments were they?" I knew the answer before I asked the question. Bethany eyeballed me, and when she responded, her words were clipped.

"Who do you think?"

The brochure in my hand. The look on Bethany's face the first time she'd seen the symbol.

"Chimera Biomedical," I said, expelling a breath and giving it a moment. "Are they still treating him?"

"No," Bethany said too quickly.

"Beth—"

"Don't call me Beth," she snapped.

I didn't need overly developed people skills to see that snapping at me about her name was probably easier than admitting that if her father was working for Chimera, he hadn't just taken this job for the pay grade. He hadn't agreed to experiment on teenagers for the money.

He was looking for a cure.

"Why chupacabras?" I asked. Bethany shrugged.

"Why not?" she said. "They've tried everything else. Nothing works—nothing is ever going to work, but try telling that to the great Paul Davis. Sometimes, I'd swear he's more delusional than my mother, and as I'm sure you've gathered, that's saying something. If Chimera Biomedical told my dad that his research might jump-start Tyler's brain, there's nothing that he wouldn't do." Bethany swallowed hard. "Obviously."

The wheels in my head turned slowly as I looked down at the pamphlet, Bethany's earlier words about Chimera echoing in my head.

They specialized in regeneration: regrowing nerves, reviving dead brain cells. And right now, they were studying chupacabras.

My mind went to Zev and the things he'd told me about "Nibblers."

Any comments from the peanut gallery? I asked him. *What would a biomedical company want with a deadly preternatural parasite?*

At first, I didn't think Zev would respond, but then, he bit out four words, his voice decisive and harsh.

Leave it alone, Kali.

If anything, his words made me want to do the opposite, and the way he'd issued the command made me think that this was dangerous—and personal. I chewed on that for a moment. Chimera was studying chupacabras. Zev knew something about it, something he had no intention of telling me.

Chupacabras. Regeneration. Zev acting like pushing this was particularly dangerous for me.

An insidious possibility took root in my mind, and a moment later, it seemed less like a possibility and more like a fact. All of a sudden, I *knew* why Dr. Davis thought that injecting someone with a chupacabra might not be a death sentence, why he might believe that the preternatural held the key to waking his son up from a deep and unforgiving sleep.

People like me didn't get hungry. We never got tired. We couldn't feel pain. And when we got bitten, we didn't die.

We healed very, very quickly.

To a scientist, that would have seemed like a medical miracle. To a chupacabra expert whose son was dying, it might have seemed like a sign.

Chimera isn't just playing around with chupacabras, I realized, my mind reeling. They knew—about the effect that chupacabras had on certain people.

People like me.

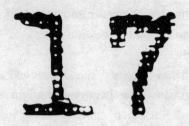

17

"Kali?"

I must have looked about as good as I felt, because Skylar said my name in a tentative, talking-a-puppy-out-from-underneath-a-car type of tone.

I shook my head to clear it of unwanted thoughts—unwanted weakness.

"It's nothing," I said.

Bethany twirled a finger through her hair, a dangerous glint in her emerald eyes. "Isn't it always?"

I didn't want to take her meaning, but she didn't leave me any other options.

"When you talked that chupacabra out of my body and into yours, it was nothing. And when you passed out at the skating rink, it was nothing. When you went through the windshield of my car and I thought you *died*—nothing. So, come on, Kali, share. What kind of nothing is it this time?"

The urge to answer her question fully and honestly took me completely by surprise. I wasn't exactly the bare-my-soul type, but Bethany had just rattled off her sordid family history like it was some kind of halftime cheer. She'd let me in, and for the first time, I actually wanted to do the same, to tell someone the truth.

That I wasn't normal.

That I wasn't human.

That even though I was used to being something else, being bitten by a chupacabra had changed things, changed me.

And that, somehow, Chimera knew—maybe not about me specifically, but about the fact that people like me existed and that being bitten by a chupacabra had a different effect on us than it had on normal people. If Bethany was right and Chimera had been infecting teens on purpose, then chances were good that they were either systematically looking for people like me—or trying to create them.

"It doesn't matter," I said out of habit, unable to make myself say anything else. Talking made me feel like I had the dry heaves, and all I wanted was to just throw up the truth and be done with it. "I'm fine."

"You're not fine." Skylar caught my gaze and held it, and even though her face still looked pixie-young and innocent, there was an alien weight to the set of her features, like she was a thousand years old instead of fifteen. "And it does matter. Everything that's happened, everything that's going to happen in the next twenty-four hours—it matters. *You* matter, and whether you want to believe this or not, you can't do this alone, Kali."

She paused and cast her eyes downward, her voice going very quiet. "You shouldn't have to."

I wanted to believe her. I wanted to tell her everything, tell *them* everything. I opened my mouth, and—nothing. I'd been keeping secrets for so long that I wasn't entirely sure I knew how to let them go.

Don't. The humans won't understand. They never do.

Somehow, I wasn't surprised that Zev was weighing in, telling me that every instinct I'd ever had to keep other people at bay was right on the mark. Then again, he'd also told me to leave Chimera Biomedical Corp. alone.

That wasn't going to happen.

The past twenty-four hours had whetted my appetite for answers, and I needed to know—what I was, what Zev was, what the men in suits and the Paul Davises of the world knew that I didn't.

Leave it, Kali. You're better off if they think you're dead.

I wondered briefly how old Zev was—because he was talking to me like I was a child.

That, as much as Skylar's vehement claim that I didn't have to do this alone, prodded me into taking a small, terrifying step toward telling the others the truth. "I think I know what Chimera is trying to do." Admitting that out loud sounded funny, even to my own ears. Deep inside me, Zev cursed in a language that I neither recognized nor understood. I ignored it—and him.

"I think I know why the Chimera scientists are playing around with chupacabras—why they'd kill to keep that kind of experiment to themselves."

Interest flickered across Bethany's face, but in the bat of an eyelash, she'd wiped her face completely clean, and it was gone. "And we're just supposed to take your word on this because the almighty Kali D'Angelo can't be bothered to deal us in?"

"I'll tell you," I said, pushing back against Zev's objections, "once I'm sure."

Making that promise—meaning it—hurt, like I'd been keeping secrets for so long that prying them loose would require the shredding of flesh—most likely mine.

"What do you need to be sure about?" Skylar asked. The question set me up to ask Bethany for something that I was 90 percent certain she wouldn't want to give, so I crossed my fingers and took the plunge.

"I need access to your dad's files."

For a moment, Beth stood very still, like there was a snake on the floor in front of her and any movement might tempt it to strike.

"Kali, they already tried to kill you once," she said finally. "The people my dad's working for don't kid around, and I'm already on their watch list. They probably know you're here, talking to me. If I let you into the lab, they'll know that, too."

"Is that a no?" Skylar asked, wide-eyed and far too innocent.

Bethany didn't dignify that question with a response.

After a few seconds of silence, I decided I'd have to give Bethany something—a tiny piece of myself, tit for tat for the secrets she'd already given me. Slowly, painfully, I brought my hands to the bottom of my stolen tank top. I pulled the fabric up, inch by inch and bit by bit, until I was standing in Bethany's foyer uncovered from the waist up, save for my chest.

I heard Skylar's sharp intake of breath, saw Bethany blink one, two, three times as she took in the sight of my stomach, my rib cage, my waist. I didn't look down, but dragged my fingertips across my flesh.

Across the *ouroboros* and the pattern—golden, intricate, overwhelming—inked into the surface of my skin.

"What is that?" Bethany asked. Somehow, she pulled off sounding unimpressed, even though her face betrayed her horror, her fascination, her awe.

"That," I said, "is why I think I know what your father's endgame is. It's why I need you to let me into his lab."

That wasn't exactly the truth, and it wasn't full disclosure, but it was something.

Skylar reached forward and ran her index finger lightly over the surface of my skin. She closed her eyes and tilted her head back, offering her face up to the ceiling. When she opened her eyes again, she seemed lighter, more sure of herself—like whatever burden she'd been carrying since she'd met me on the Davises' front lawn had been somehow lifted from her shoulders.

"I knew it," she said simply. "This is it." In typical Skylar fashion, she didn't wait for either of us to process that statement; she just plowed right on, talking and switching subjects with no warning whatsoever. "Is the lab in the basement?" she asked Bethany, who still hadn't managed to tear her eyes away from the markings on my skin. "Because I kind of feel like the lab might be in the basement."

"Would you just stop it with the feelings?" Bethany snapped. Skylar recoiled, but recovered quickly, and I wondered how many times her peppy you-can't-hurt-me facade had rebounded too quickly for the outside world to notice that she wasn't quite as bulletproof as she seemed.

"I don't care about your *feelings*, Skylar, and I don't care about Kali's questionable taste in body art." Bethany was a good liar—but not good enough. Sensing that I wasn't buying her outright dismissal of the situation, she continued, her voice softer, her face every bit as guarded as it had been a moment before. "I can't do this any more. Even if I wanted to, I couldn't."

Bethany's eyes flickered toward the kitchen, and I thought about her mother, dressed in a twin set and talking to the air.

"What exactly did your father say to keep you from calling the police?" I asked, gauging her reaction to my question and seeing the moment it hit its mark.

"Does it matter?" Bethany asked bitterly. "Either way, I can't help you. You should get out of here before he gets home."

I thought about my dad—about the painful silences and well-rehearsed lies, the fact that he knew less about me than the people in this room, neither of whom I'd known for longer than a day.

"Your dad wouldn't hurt your mom . . . would he?" Skylar sounded painfully young, and I wondered how someone with any psychic ability at all could still believe the best about the world.

In response to Skylar's question, Bethany straightened her shoulders and stared at the wall behind the younger girl's head as she answered. "My father wouldn't hit my mom. He wouldn't put a gun to her head. But would he take her to see Tyler, force her to look at him until she had a very public breakdown in close proximity to the hospital's psych ward?" Bethany shrugged. "It's hard to say, really."

The idea that Bethany's father would even think of holding something like that over her head was disgusting. As much as I wanted access to the lab in the basement, I wasn't about to press her to take that kind of risk for me. She had someone else to think about, someone to take care of. I, of all people, could understand that.

If I'd had a mother, I would have done anything to protect her.

"It's okay, Bethany." I caught her eye; she looked away. "You do what you need to do. We'll go."

Don't think this means I'm giving up, I told Zev silently as I nudged Skylar toward the door. *There's more than one way to decapitate a hellhound, and as it so happens, I know them all.*

Zev didn't respond, and something about the silence felt unnatural. Wrong. One second he was there, and the next, my mind felt . . . empty. If our chupacabras served as a two-way radio between my mind and his, it felt like he'd just hung up. A small sliver of panic rose up inside of me, and for the second time, I went looking for him.

I started the way I had before, by thinking about the parasite that had burrowed deep inside of me. I felt it, and a second later, I felt Zev's. Felt *Zev—*

And then I was in. I saw the world through his eyes.

Saw men in masks.

Saw needles, scalpels, concrete walls.

Saw blood.

I came back into my own body a second later, my skin an odd fit for my soul, like a shoe crammed onto the wrong foot or a sweater two sizes too large. Was this what Zev had felt like after he'd taken over my body in Eddie's car?

"Kali? Are we going?" Skylar was still standing next to Bethany, who'd wrapped her arms around her torso, like she'd been tasked with holding her own entrails in. "You said we should go. But then you didn't go."

"We should go," I said roughly, turning my back on them both. No matter where I looked, all I could see was the men in the masks, the concrete cell. It was clear now—too clear—how Chimera Biomedical knew that there were people out there like me, why Zev had asked me to stay out of it.

They had him.

I could talk to him and he could talk to me. I could enter his mind, and he'd spent time in mine, but physically, he was *trapped*. His body was locked up somewhere—in some kind of cell.

Some kind of cage.

Every nightmare I'd ever had about being caught, cut into pieces, studied like a rat in a maze—that was Zev's reality. Suddenly, the fact that Bethany couldn't help me didn't seem like as much of a roadblock because, come hell or high water, I was going to find a way in.

I had to.

There was one person in this world—that I knew of for sure—who was like me. *One.* A person who'd haunted my dreams, taken over my body, protected me, even when I didn't want protection.

And that person, that one person, was somebody's *specimen*.

Before, I'd wanted to know what Chimera knew. Now, I wanted them gone.

"Kali?" This time, Bethany was the one who said my name,

and the tone in her voice reminded me of the way she'd sounded talking to her mom.

She thinks I've lost it. Maybe she's right. My hands were fisted, my steely fingernails digging into the flesh of my palms. It didn't hurt. I didn't even feel it, but I could smell the beads of blood as they dribbled down the insides of my hands.

"I'm fine," I said, because that was exactly what you said when you really, really weren't. "I should go."

I was halfway past Bethany and headed for the front door when she grabbed my arm. I wrenched out of her grasp and resisted the reflex to send the heel of my palm crashing into her throat.

Throat. Blood.

Chimera had Zev, Bethany wanted to help me, but couldn't, and all I could think about was how much I wanted this all to be over and how very, very thirsty I was.

"I'm going," I said, more for Skylar's benefit than Bethany's. "Don't worry about me. Don't follow."

I didn't give them a chance to react. I just took off out the front door, darting across the lawn—

Twenty hours and forty-two minutes.

I'd find a way to take down Chimera. But first, I needed to hunt.

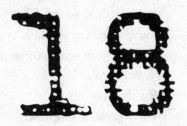

Closer. Closer. You're getting closer. This way, Kali. This way.

If the hunt-lust had been a hum under my skin before, it was a full-blown song now: sweet, melodic, unearthly.

I wanted to hunt. The thing inside me wanted to feed. No room in my mind for anything else, I wove in and out of the shadows, my inner compass set toward something that reeked of sulfur—something sleek and quiet, something wrong.

Normally, I scanned the papers for reports on preternatural activity. I liked going in knowing what brand of beastie I'd be fighting, but at the moment, I didn't care what the instinct was driving me toward.

All I cared about was making it dead.

The trail ended a mile, maybe two, away from Bethany's house, at a water park that was closed and abandoned for the winter. Getting in was easy enough, and soon, I was prowling the length of the park, surrounded by bright colors, mammoth slides, and empty, waterless pools.

On the horizon, across a sprawling parking lot, I could see the outline of a Ferris wheel—the fair coming to call and pick up the seasonal slack, while Water World stood empty, save for the shadows, the slides, and me.

I paused, tilting my head to the side, letting the sights and sounds, the smells wash over my senses, each one heightened almost to the point of pain.

Peeling paint.

Wet concrete.

A nearly inaudible hiss.

I whirled around, but saw nothing except the barest hint of shadow. I smelled something cold and wet and rotting.

I bent down to unsheathe my knife. I was close now, very close. The question was—close to what?

Beads of sweat rose on my skin, not because I was nervous—I wasn't—and not because I was hot. It was adrenaline, plain and simple, and when I caught a glimpse of myself in a fun house–style mirror—installed, no doubt, to entertain the masses while they waited in hot summer lines— my brown eyes were glowing with an unholy sheen.

You're close now. So very close.

I could almost picture myself here on a human day, standing in line for the Silver Bullet and stealing peeks at myself in the long line of mirrors, each a distortion, none an exact reflection of this body.

None of them the real me.

Somewhere, overhead, there was a creak—rusted metal, giving under the weight of something . . . something . . .

I looked up.

For a split second, there was nothing but the metal staircase, winding its way up to the top of the Silver Bullet, but then I heard the telltale sound of scales scraping against metal—a light swoosh, a tongue flickering out to taste the stale and humid air.

Whatever it was, my prey was tasting for me.

I averted my eyes a second before the creature came into view. It swung down from the rafters, its tail—the width of an oak tree, the length of my legs—wrapping around the creaking, rusted stairs.

Basilisk, I realized, a second too late. Its snakelike body gave way to a triangular head with slit nostrils, a nearly human mouth, and eyes the exact color and cut of a ruby.

Knowledge of how to kill the thing flooded my brain. I might have been failing history, but this was the kind of pop quiz I was built for. To kill a basilisk, I'd have to drive my blade into its brain—easier said than done, given that my point of entry was a soft spot inside the creature's mouth, and the fact that I'd die if I looked a basilisk straight in the eyes.

Moving swiftly, I turned my attention to the line of mirrors. In the right person's hand, anything was a weapon, and with prey I couldn't physically look at, I needed to get creative. Knife in one hand, I drove my elbow into the closest mirror as hard as I could—again and again and again.

The glass shattered, needle-sharp shards digging into the flesh of my arm. Using the tip of my knife, I pried larger shards loose from the mirror's frame—one for each hand.

I slipped my knife hilt-first into my waistband at the small of my back, then tightened my grip on my makeshift blades. The rough edges of the glass dug into the flesh of my palms. Blood ran down my wrists like rain on a windshield.

Here, snakey, snakey, snakey, I thought.

There was a hiss and then a thump as it fell onto the concrete behind me.

"That's right," I said softly, tracking its movement in the remaining mirrors. "Come to Kali."

The creature pulled back, holding itself aloft, swaying. Short arms, capped off by gray, gnarled hands, grew out of its snakelike body. It moved its fingers as it swayed, and its lips parted, revealing pearl-white fangs. I could smell the blood on them, smell this thing's last meal.

I waited. One second, two, three, four—the beast surged forward. With one last glance in the mirror, I spun, eyes closed, burying a glass shard in one glittering red eye.

The basilisk screamed—an ugly, all-too-human sound—and lashed out with its tail, knocking me back into one of the mirrors. My head hit the glass with a sickening *thunk*, but I didn't open my eyes.

Didn't wince.

I smiled.

Fangs the size of my index finger struck, burying themselves in my torso and ripping through my flesh. The venom should have burned like fire. It should have brought me to my knees—but it didn't. Blood bubbled out of the puncture holes, and I felt a light breeze against my face as the basilisk pulled back and moved to strike again.

I rolled sideways, turning my head away from the creature's lethal gaze before opening my eyes and angling the remaining glass shard in my hand to give me a better view of its motion. The serpent looked long and skinny—clownish—in this lying little piece of glass. My blood dripped off its fangs.

It wobbled, snarled, reached for me with ghastly hands—
Too slow.

"You poison me," I said, driving my arm backward, aiming

the shard at its one remaining eye. "I poison you. Karma's a bitch."

It came for me again, but I turned, driving the shard back into its skull, obliterating the eye and, with it, the basilisk's biggest weapon. Opening my own eyes, I stared it right in the bleeding face. It began shaking, bucking wildly, hissing-screaming.

I brought my hand to the small of my back, withdrew the knife. Glancing down at the puncture holes in my side, I saw that they were already healing—an angry purple-black color giving way to the pink of baby-fresh skin.

Moving impossibly fast, I was beside the basilisk in an instant. I tackled it, pinning the top half of its body to the ground, dodging its tail as it slammed down with enough force to shatter the concrete. With a final, gurgling hiss, the basilisk opened its mouth to strike again. I shoved the knife into its open mouth, ignoring the fangs and driving the blade back into its brain.

Dizzy, I pulled myself to my feet and let go of my prey. I stumbled backward. It swayed. It gargled.

It went down. Hard.

My chest rose and fell as I watched the basilisk's life fizzle out in front of me. After it stopped moving, I paced forward, examining its corpse. In the four years I'd been hunting, I'd only seen one other basilisk—and this one was easily twice its size. If I'd looked it in the eye, even once, it might have had me.

If I hadn't been so strong, so fast—if my wounds hadn't started healing, if the venom coursing through my veins even now had been as fatal to me as my blood was to it—I'd be dead.

I retrieved my knife, shoving the thing's massive head to one side. "Not today."

I waited for the release that usually came from hunting, but it didn't come. The air was thick with the smell of blood—the monster's, mine. I could feel it, taste it.

I wanted it.

That's not you, Kali. That's the Nibbler.

I barely heard Zev's words, barely registered the fact that he was back, that whatever the men in masks had been doing to him, it was over now. I was too focused on the present to process. I'd hunted. I'd killed. And now, the only thing left was a burning, incessant hunger.

Thirst.

I could feel the lines of gold on my body pulsating, re-arranging themselves. I could feel the *ouroboros* heating up. It didn't hurt—but I felt it.

I felt it everywhere.

Hungry. Thirsty. Perfect, blessed heat.

Giving into the urge, I brought my knife up, level with my face. I turned it sideways, watching the basilisk's black-red blood drip down onto the concrete, one drop at a time.

I brought the blade to my lips.

I opened my mouth.

And I fed.

† † †

Nineteen hours and twenty-nine minutes.

It was barely eleven thirty in the morning, and I was already on my third set of clothes of the day.

This time, I didn't need Zev to tell me to burn my old ones. I took another shower, too—as much to rid myself of the memory of what I'd just done as to wash my body clean of blood. Though my wounds were well on their way to healing completely, I bandaged my side before slipping on shirt number three and a pair of my own jeans.

I wondered how long it would be before someone found the basilisk and called the police—and then I wondered how exactly Water World had come to play host to a creature that was native to climates far drier and more brutal than ours.

More than that, though, I wondered if I'd ever forget the way its blood had tasted—bitter, like cocoa powder, with just a hint of sour milk.

Human blood tastes better, Zev said, right on cue.

I chose to ignore that comment, and focused instead on the fact that Zev was alive and seemingly well.

"So," I said, knowing that I didn't need to speak out loud, but doing so, anyway, because it made his presence feel less intimate, less intrusive. "Chimera Biomedical."

I couldn't say more than that without sounding flippant or sad, so I stopped.

Chimera Biomedical is not your concern, Kali. I'm more than capable of taking care of myself.

I pictured the cement cell, the men in masks.

"So you're enjoying their hospitality?"

Zev snorted. **I got stupid. They got lucky. Right now, the odds are stacked in their favor. That won't always be the case.**

I dragged my fingertips through my wet hair, combing out the tangles and trying not to think about what, exactly, Zev might do once he got the upper hand. "How long have you been there?"

There was a long pause, and I could practically feel Zev deciding whether or not to tell me the truth.

Two years.

I literally stopped breathing.

It's not such a long time, Zev said, his voice meditative and soft, *for someone like us.*

I couldn't help the way that last word echoed through my own thoughts.

There was an *us*.

I'd never had that, never known for a fact that I wasn't one of a kind.

"I'm going to get you out," I said, my throat dry and my eyes tearing up. "You know that, right? I can't just leave you there. I'm going to get you out."

That's not a good idea, he said sharply, each word more implacable than the last. *There's a lot about this place you don't know. You can't win, Kali, and you shouldn't try.*

"Wanna bet?" I asked, matching the steel in his tone with some of my own.

Zev paused, and when he finally replied, his words were deliberate, like he was used to doling out cruelty in measured doses.

You're young, Kali, and you're inexperienced, and if yesterday was any indication, you have an Achilles' heel that I do not. Don't let your Nibbler fool you into thinking you're something you are not.

Zev's words hit their target. In another twenty hours, I'd be human again—basilisk bait, breakable, a normal teenage girl. If Chimera caught me and put me in one of their little cells, I wouldn't hold up nearly as well as Zev had.

I wouldn't last two years.

I shoved my hands into the pockets of my jeans, staring myself down in the mirror. "I guess that means that whatever I'm going to do, I need to do it quick."

Zev must have sensed that arguing was useless, because he stopped trying to tell me what to do. Good. Maybe I'd actually managed to keep him from realizing exactly how hard that last comment of his had hit me.

I'd only had a couple of seconds to marvel at the fact that there was someone else out there like me before that someone else had turned around and reminded me that even to our kind—his kind—I wasn't quite right.

I was still out of place.

I was broken.

I tried not wonder if I would ever fit in anywhere—ever feel like a whole person instead of two broken, disconnected halves.

I looked away from my own reflection and picked up my toothbrush. I brushed my teeth—over and over again, until the only taste on my tongue was Aquafresh. I looped my hair back into a ponytail and then considered my options.

I'd meant what I'd said to Zev. Broken or not, outlier or not, I wasn't just going to leave him there to rot. I wasn't going to sit back and hope that Chimera wasn't going to come for me next.

I needed to know where they were keeping Zev. Who was involved. What the company knew about me. I needed proof—the kind that could be used as insurance or taken to the police.

And I only had twenty hours to get it.

I thought my way through the situation, strangely alert now that the beast inside of me had fed. So far, I only had one real lead on Chimera—Beth's father. Since Beth was watching out for her own interests—and her mother's—that left me with exactly one option for recon.

Paul Davis's place of work.

Which—as it so happened—was also my father's.

"Unlike the full spectrum of species in the animal kingdom, preternatural creatures share no common ancestry with humans—or any other natural species. Any similarities we see—say, between a dragon and a Komodo dragon, a kraken and a giant squid—appear to be the product of convergent, rather than divergent, evolution."

My dad was a different person when he lectured: his eyes sparkled, his lips turned upward, and even from the back of the lecture hall, I could feel the energy he brought to the room. The students in his Introduction to Preternatural Biology class may or may not have understood what he was saying, but most of them appeared to be paying more attention to him than to their inboxes, and I'd been hanging around college campuses long enough to know that that was something.

Come to think of it, I'd spent more mornings than I cared to remember like this growing up: hanging out at the back of a lecture hall whenever a babysitter canceled last minute, or my father forgot that we'd been given the day off from school. I'd seen him in college-professor mode enough that it shouldn't have surprised me, but it always did.

In front of a class full of students, waxing on about evolution, he seemed so present. He seemed happy.

"Think what it must have been like for Darwin, two hundred years ago. He took that voyage on the *Beagle* expecting to document the natural world, and he stumbled across something . . . impossible. A creature who could defy the laws of physics—straight out of the pages of mythology, hidden from human discovery for thousands upon thousands of years. In that one moment, the entire landscape of scientific investigation was drastically and irrevocably changed. The *impossible* became a widespread scientific reality, as omnipresent as gravity and, in some cases, nearly as hard to see."

I'd heard this lecture so often, I could have given it myself. Instead, I stuck to the shadows and moved my way toward the front of the auditorium. A couple of his students might have noticed me, but the professor went on, oblivious.

"What are the three key markers of preternatural evolution?" The question was rhetorical, and he went right into the answer—just as I went right for a chair near the front of the auditorium, where he'd left his briefcase and keys.

"It's all right there in the DNA: preternaturality is typically marked by a triple, rather than double, helix structure; the presence of base pairs that themselves appear to have distinctly unnatural properties; and the secretion of amino acids—or, as they are more commonly called, preter-proteins—that defy our most basic natural laws, and in doing so, caused a resurgent interest in the pseudoscience of alchemy for a large part of the twentieth century."

I slipped my hand into my father's blazer jacket, which he'd left on his chair when he'd taken to the stage to lecture.

As a kid, I'd completed the exact same motion searching for change for the vending machines, but this time, I was looking for something slightly less benign: his university ID card.

Got it.

My hand closed around its target, and I slipped back into the shadows and made for the exit.

"But given these differences, are preternatural creatures really unnatural? Or are they simply the product of a different kind of evolution—one with a different starting point, a different progression? Were they always here? Where did they come from? And are their fundamental and most basic natures really all that different from ours? Which leads me to . . ."

My father actually started tapping out a drumroll on his podium. A handful of students joined in. A new PowerPoint slide appeared on the projector screen, and my father's voice boomed out over the drumroll.

"Sexual Selection and Preternatural Mating Behavior! Or, if you prefer: sex and the supernatural—when demons get down and dirty."

That was my cue to leave. The one benefit of having a father who only remembered my existence every other Thursday was that we'd never had a sit-down talk about the birds and the bees. Hearing him say the word "sex" twice in one minute was more than enough for me.

As I slipped out the back of the room, and the door closed behind me, I glanced back over my shoulder, half expecting him to have snapped out of lecture mode and noticed my exit—but he didn't. I wasn't suprised. People like me were good at fading into the background, and I'd probably had more practice than most.

Mousy little Kali . . . wasn't that what Bethany had called me? I'd spent my whole human life not making waves, hiding what I was, trying not to be noticed.

Until now.

Breaking into Paul Davis's lab—for a purpose completely unrelated to hunting—wasn't exactly the work of a human chameleon. It wasn't low risk, it wasn't subtle.

Oh well.

Like Theseus working his way through the labyrinth, I wound my way through hallway after hallway, took to the stairs, and made my way to my father's lab. I swiped his ID, and the door unlocked itself. Since I'd relieved him of his last subject pool with the Great Zombie Raid of Sophomore Year, he'd been doing mostly theoretical research, but his office still backed up to his old lab space—which, in turn, was located adjacent to the space that had been given to the new head of the department.

Two more key-card swipes, and I was in a restricted-access hallway. Facial masks and foot covers sat just outside one door. The entire place reeked of plastic and human sweat, but the part of me that wasn't human could smell a hint of something animal among the antiseptic.

CAUTION, read the sign on the door. LIVE SPECIMENS.

Caution, I thought, my eyes narrowing. *Illegal biomedical experimentation.* My father's card didn't grant me direct access to the other labs, but I could still feel a light buzz of power from the blood I'd ingested.

Stronger. Faster. More invincible.

I fed the chupacabra, and it fed me. Trying not to think about what exactly I'd fed it, I made use of the increased strength and forced the door open. The lock gave way with a sickening creak, and I slipped into the room, expecting to see . . . something.

Something other than empty aquariums, empty cages. Something other than petri dishes, carefully labeled and stored away.

A clipboard on the far wall drew my attention, and I crossed the room, moving silently, so light on my toes that I might as well have been floating. Careful not to touch anything, I skimmed the top sheet, then helped myself to a pair of latex gloves.

PRINCIPAL INVESTIGATOR: PAUL DAVIS

PROTOCOL #: 85477892

GENETIC MUTATION IN THE NORTHERN CHUPACABRA.

It wasn't exactly the kind of evidence I'd hoped for, but really, what was I expecting? It wasn't like Paul Davis was going to apply for university approval for his real research program. Methodically, I made my way through the room, mentally dividing it into a grid and searching every square from ceiling to floor, wall to wall.

Whatever Dr. Davis was doing for Chimera, he wasn't doing it here.

Determined to find something, lest my latest stint as a hardened criminal be for naught, I made my way from Davis's lab to the attached office.

Filing cabinets.

Computers.

Papers covering every available surface.

Bingo.

I started with his desk and looked for anything with

Chimera letterhead. *Nada*. I looked through every scrap of paper, every Post-it note, the passwords taped to the bottom of one of his drawers. After committing that last one to memory, I moved on.

All I needed was a lead—the location of the main lab, the name of the project, Davis's contact at Chimera . . . *anything*.

A light flickered somewhere in the distance, and I glanced out through the thick, opaque window separating the office from the hallway on the other side.

Someone was coming.

I pressed myself back against a wall, willing my body flat, hiding my face in the shadows. I waited—and whoever it was walked right by. As the sound of footsteps became softer, more distant, I set back to work, all too aware that the next time, I might not be so lucky.

It didn't take me long to find the keys to the filing cabinet, but the files they contained weren't exactly what I would call helpful—more protocols, long printouts of data, medical information for the graduate assistants who worked in the Davis lab. Next, I turned my attention to the desk drawers, the credenza, the cushions in his black IKEA sofa.

And that's when I hit pay dirt: a cell phone, presumably Professor Davis's, was wedged in the crack between the cushions and the back of the sofa. I pried it loose and started scrolling through the recent calls.

BETHANY.

BETHANY.

BETHANY.

I tried not to feel guilty, seeing Beth's name, and forced myself onward.

ADELAIDE.

HOME.

And then, finally, a number that wasn't in his contacts. Two numbers. A third.

There had to be a way to trace the phone numbers to a location—and if I was lucky, that location might give me something: if not the actual lab where they were holding Zev, at least another name, another person whose office I could rifle through, more laws to break.

This time, the sound of footsteps treading through the exterior hallway was crisp and pert, and it stopped right outside the door. Pocketing the cell phone, I leapt for the door to the lab space, squeezing back through it and shutting it behind me an instant before the door to the hallway opened.

"Honestly, Paul, that's the third phone this month. You can hardly complain about Bethany's overage fees when you can't keep track of a BlackBerry to save your life."

In the time it took me to recognize that voice as belonging to Bethany's mother, her father was already speaking in reply. "What our daughter doesn't know won't hurt her—and the phone isn't lost. It's in here somewhere. Here, give me your phone."

It took me a second too long to realize why a person trying to locate their phone would ask to borrow one from someone else—and in that second, Paul Davis called his own cell.

It lit up a second before it rang. I didn't have time to figure out how to silence it, how to turn it off. Moving on instinct, I did the only thing a person like me knew how to do.

I killed it.

Snapped it in half like a twig, held my breath, waited.

"Did you hear something?" Through the thick metal door, Paul Davis's voice was muted, but I had no way of knowing how soft it would have sounded to a human. Maybe they wouldn't have been able to make out the words at all; maybe, on the other side of that metal door, the Davises wouldn't have heard that half of a ring, the crunching of plastic and metal, at all.

Or maybe this time, I'd get caught.

I thought of all the laws I'd ever broken: the trespassing, the slaughter, obstruction of justice, cruelty to creatures who'd died choking on my blood. I thought of Zev, caged in concrete, and of my father, lecturing in the building next door.

And then the door to the lab space opened, and a familiar woman with strawberry blonde hair peeked in. She met my eyes, and for a moment, hers glossed over, and I wondered if Bethany's mother was seeing things again: the boy her son had been, ghosts of everything he wouldn't ever be. For a moment, that faraway glint in her eye gave way to focus, clarity.

She saw me.

And then she closed the door. "Not so much as a ring," she said. "Are you sure you didn't leave it in the lecture hall?"

This time, I couldn't make out her husband's response, but a second later, it was punctuated with the sound of another door opening, closing. I started breathing again, a tightness in my chest reminding me that I'd stopped. I should have headed for the other exit—the one I'd entered through in the first place, but I didn't. Instead, I waited, and after a long moment, the door to Davis's office opened again.

"I know you," Bethany's mother said in a tone that would

have been more appropriate if we'd run into each other at some kind of country-club soiree. "You'll have to forgive me if I don't remember your name. I'm afraid I'm not much of a morning person."

I tried to form a connection between this polite woman, put together from head to toe and fully coherent, and the woman I'd met that morning, but came up blank. The difference was night and day, like there were two people occupying the same body—neither of whom was 100 percent there.

"And when I say I'm not a morning person, what I mean is that I don't know what you saw this morning. I can guess what you must think of me, but I love my children, and I love my husband, and I think it would be best if we both agreed that whatever you saw this morning never happened, and whatever I saw—here, with you—well, that never happened, either."

I had no response, no words. She was supposed to be crazy. She wasn't supposed to be bargaining with me.

"You learn," she said. "After a while, you learn how to pretend—to see what you want to see, and ignore everything else."

Listening to her speak, her cadence and tone an exact match for Bethany at her oh-so-popular iciest, I wondered which Adelaide Davis was the real one, and which was pretend. Was she crazy? Sane? Did she know her son was gone? Was what I'd seen this morning just an elaborate game? Or was this Adelaide—calm and cool, negotiating with me to keep her secret—just a cover, a mask constructed to hide the broken, jagged mind that lurked underneath?

"You're a very pretty girl," the woman in question said, tilting her head to the side. "Did you know that? Once upon a time, I had a pretty, pretty boy." She reached forward and touched my cheek with one manicured hand.

And just like that, it was like I wasn't even standing there any more. She took her own cell phone out of her purse and started tapping impatiently on its keys.

"Mrs. Davis?" I said her name, unsure if I should leave her here, if I should call Bethany to bring her home.

She looked up. "Don't slouch, Kali. It's unbecoming."

Her use of my given name nailed me to the floor. She turned her attention back to the phone, and finally, I coerced my feet into moving, made my way to the door.

"Don't let them hurt her." This time, Adelaide Davis's voice was quiet, steady. "It's not safe in that house. It's never safe."

She might as well have been rattling off a cookie recipe, for all the emphasis she placed on those words. I waited to see if she'd say anything else, but she didn't.

I opened the door.

I slipped back into the hallway.

And as the door closed behind me, I heard a light and airy sigh.

I'd come here with a lead, and I was leaving with a broken cell phone and a ball of nausea expanding in my stomach. Leaving Bethany's mother there, with her father, felt wrong— and it made me wonder. If Adelaide was here—alone—where was Bethany?

Why had Bethany just placed three calls to her father's cell phone?

And what did Adelaide mean about it never being safe in their house?

It's not safe in that house. It's never safe.

I couldn't shake those words, no matter how hard I tried, so instead of slipping back into my father's classroom and returning his ID card, I dropped it in the hallway outside his class—someone would find it, and I had bigger fish to fry. Ducking out of the building, it took my eyes a moment to adjust to the sudden change in brightness. The sunlight felt like a pinprick in the center of each of my eyes, but I was only vaguely aware of the discomfort as it spread outward, leaving them bloodshot and dry.

Where we come from, there isn't much of a sun. The more like us you become, the less tolerance you'll have for direct sunlight—but you'll survive.

I didn't know which part of that statement was the most disturbing—the idea that whatever I was, whatever I was becoming, the transformation wasn't complete yet, or the suggestion that people like us came from somewhere else.

I could tell you all about it, Zev suggested.

I saw the ploy for what it was: he wanted me to forget about Chimera, forget about Bethany, forget about anything that might spur me into action. In his ideal world, I probably would have completely ignored the fact that he was caged, lying in wait for the moment he could tear off all of their heads.

Nice try, I said. *But no.*

I told you I could handle this, Kali, and I meant it.

For a split second, there was something else there, something he wasn't telling me. I could almost see it, almost pinpoint the reason he wanted me to stay away, but a second later, it was gone.

Frustrated, I replied to his silent sentence out loud. "Yeah, well, you also spent the first twenty-four hours of our acquaintance appearing to me in shadows and stalking my dreams. Forgive me if I'm skeptical."

His response came in images, not words, and I got the distinct sense that up until I'd shifted from my human form, he hadn't been able to make himself heard more clearly—which meant there was a good chance that as soon as I shifted back, I'd lose the connection. Lose *this*.

I'd lose the boost that being bitten had given my already unnatural abilities—and the thirst.

I was used to watching my abilities slip away, leaving me vulnerable and human and raw. I was used to missing things, people, having a purpose, but this time, it would be worse.

Because this time, when I shifted, I'd lose Zev *and* the ability to save him.

Eighteen hours and twenty-four minutes.

I was on the clock—but I still couldn't make myself focus only on Zev, not with Bethany's mother's words echoing in the recesses of my mind.

It's not safe in that house. It's never safe.

It was probably nothing. The woman had lost a child—how

could any place feel safe after something like that? Bethany was probably fine—or, at least, as fine as she'd been when I'd left her—but given that she was almost as embroiled in this mess as I was, I couldn't ignore the possibility that she might not be.

If her mother was here, Bethany was home alone—and I'd already had firsthand experience with the way the men in suits handled loose ends.

She's fine, I told myself. *If they were going to hurt her, they would have done it already.*

In my head, Zev sighed. You're going back there, aren't you?

I chewed lightly on my bottom lip. *Maybe.*

That was the problem with caring about people—you had too much to lose.

I glanced down at my watch again, more out of habit than anything else, and then made a split-second decision. Bethany's house was a good ten miles away, but there was nothing saying I had to run there on foot. I'd go by, eyeball the house, make sure that Chimera hadn't sent anyone to pay Beth a visit—and then I'd find a way to get what I needed out of the mangled remains of Paul Davis's phone.

Scanning the cars in the parking lot, my eyes came to rest on my father's.

Hey, Zev? I said, sounding—to me, at least—oddly like Skylar. *Any chance you know how to hot-wire a car?*

† † †

I might have felt bad about stealing my father's car, had he ever acknowledged the fact that I was old enough to drive—and had been for over a year. But sixteen and seventeen were just numbers to him, and we'd never been much for celebrating birthdays. Given that, I figured that just this once, *he* could rely on public transportation—or walk the five miles separating the university from our house.

All's fair in love and war—and black ops.

Ignoring the quiet trill of guilt trying to sound off in my brain, I parked the car a couple of blocks away from Bethany's house, figuring that if Chimera hadn't figured out who I was yet, the last thing I needed to do was hand them my father's license-plate number on a silver platter. Closing the car door behind me, I started jogging toward Bethany's house, making an effort at slowing the unnaturally fast pace my body wanted to take.

I wasn't used to having to hold back, and it took the strain of pretending to be human to an all-new level.

My body wanted to run.

It wanted to blur.

It wanted to *feed*—

But I most emphatically wasn't going to think about that. The last thing I needed was for the neighbors to see me running by at an inhuman blur.

So I held back. I paced myself. And then I heard the scream.

Go. Quickly.

I stopped holding back, stopped thinking. One second, I was running, and the next I was there, and everything in between was fuzzy and indefinite in my mind. This time, when I heard the scream, I recognized its owner.

Not Bethany. Skylar.

That, more than the whisper of Zev's own hunt-lust in the corners of my mind, pushed me forward. I didn't have many friends—I wasn't entirely sure I had *any*—but Skylar was the closest thing I'd had to one in a very long time.

She was screaming.

I catapulted my way over the gate, lost myself to the blur of the motion, hit the front porch, and breathed in through my nose.

Death, I thought, the word oddly dull in my mind. The dead and the dying had a smell—a bit like rusted metal, a bit like rotting food. The scent of it set the hairs on the back of my neck on end.

Walkers, Zev said. **Lots of them.**

It took me a moment to translate, to know that by Walkers, he meant the walking dead.

Homo mortis.

Zombies.

I had my knife in hand before I realized I'd reached for it, and I had kicked open the Davises' front door before it ever occurred to me that it might have been unlocked.

"Kali?" A familiar voice—tight with panic, tinged with disbelief—caught me off guard. The only thing that kept me from putting my knife straight through the top of Elliot's spine was a surge of interest from the chupacabra inside me.

A realization that Elliot smelled human.

He smelled good.

"Where are they?" I asked. My voice sounded different—gravelly and low, humming with power and need and want.

"Beth's down the hall, barricaded in. I can't find Skylar—"

"No," I said sharply. "The zombies. Where are *they*?"

On cue, one of the living dead dropped down from the stairway overhead. Its bones crunched as it landed, and when it stood, I realized that it was like me—it couldn't feel pain, couldn't tell that its legs were broken, the bones protruding through dead and rotting flesh.

Its mouth—or what was left of it—opened, revealing a cavernous hole. *No tongue.* I caught the faint whiff of sulfur in its blood and wondered how anyone could have ever thought that zombies started out human.

"Kali, look out!"

Elliot's words were lost on me, his presence a distraction I didn't need.

Kill it, I thought. *Kill it now.*

I flung the knife and a second later, I heard the sound it made cutting through flesh, lodging itself in rock-hard bone. I leapt forward, a wild thing, slamming the heel of my hand into the hilt of the blade. The creature's spine gave way; its head detached, and a second later, my knife was back in my hand.

"Kali?" Every muscle in Elliot's body was tense. His face was pale, but his eyes were hard.

I said nothing. Somewhere below us, Skylar screamed.

"Weapons," I said, my voice a foreign thing in a throat that wanted nothing more than to be coated in the blood of the thing I'd just slain. "Whatever you have, give it to me and get out."

Elliot didn't seem any more inclined to follow my instructions than I'd been to follow most of Zev's.

"Beth's dad collects guns," he said. "They're in the basement. That's where I was headed."

I didn't have time for this. Not with Skylar screaming, not with the hunt-lust exploding inside of me like there were a hundred zombies in this house, a thousand.

I left Elliot—left him standing there, light blue eyes, cheekbones sharp as any knife. Either he'd survive or he wouldn't. Either way, I knew without asking that if it came down to a choice, he would have sent me after Skylar, told me to save her, protect her—

Kill them. Kill them now.

I didn't know the halls of this house as well as the layout of the biology building, but this time, I didn't have to rely on memory or a mental map or anything other than an unerring sense of where *they* were.

The things I needed to kill.

The closer I got to the sound of Skylar's screaming, the more of them there were. I felt like I was swimming in corpses, cutting my way through one after another after another in my pursuit. Around number ten, I lost my knife, left it buried in a corpse still twitching with what was left of its mockery of life. Then all I had was my hands, nails as sharp as blades, and my blood.

I fought my way toward Skylar, my flesh shredded and bleeding, and when I found her, she was still screaming, but she didn't look scared. She didn't look hurt. She'd managed to crawl on top of what looked to be a very large safe—easily one and a half times her size—and she'd squished herself back against the wall, just out of range of the yellowed fingernails and white-gray hands groping for her body.

For her blood.

"You okay?" I asked her.

She nodded, then screamed again, the sound piercing the air like a siren—and for a moment, the horde of monsters in between us shrank back.

"Little Sisters' Survival Guide, rule number thirty-seven," Skylar said. "Scream *before* they hit you."

And then she screamed again.

I didn't have time to question her logic—or the existence of the little sisters' survival guide. "Close your eyes," I shouted, over her shrieks and the wet, gargling moans of the things that stood between us.

Skylar didn't question the command, and I didn't have time to think about why I'd given it. She closed her eyes, and I dragged one jagged fingernail across the length of my neck, drawing blood, waiting.

One by one, the horde turned their attention from Skylar to me. One by one, they stopped scrambling for her blood. One by one, their eyes—pupil-less and without color—focused in on the line of blood I'd drawn.

I noticed the red, blinking collars on their necks a second before they lunged—each moving in tandem with the one next to it, with coordination the walking dead should never have.

Zombies were stupid and slow and incapable of anything but eating—their own bodies, others'—but this set moved with purpose, like rats through a maze.

My last thought, in the second before they closed in, was that maybe you *could* train zombies as easily as Pavlov's dogs.

At the sound of the bell, circle your prey and eat her flesh.

I had no weapons. No plan. Nothing but my blood and my

hands. They were coming, and there were more of them than I'd realized. Despite their increased speed, there was no grace to their movements, no rhythm. Their mouths were open, their bodies jerking as they advanced on me.

I grabbed the closest one by the arm and wrenched it off with a sickening crack, but the monster didn't blink, didn't howl. Instead, it went to return the favor, evenly spaced triangular teeth going for the flesh in my arms.

I fought—kicked, punched, tore through whatever flesh I could lay a hand on, but no matter how many times I hit them, or how many of them I took down, there were always more.

I was drowning.

In sweat, in blood, in the smell of death and the mounting pressure of bodies on mine. Hands on mine. Teeth, mouths, flesh on mine.

They were above me and below me. They were everywhere, and I couldn't tell now where my body ended and theirs began. I couldn't tell how much of the blood coating my extremities was theirs and how much was mine.

Retreat.

In all the time I'd been a hunter, that was an instinct I'd never felt before. I'd never wanted to run from a fight, never doubted that I would come out on top.

I'd never cared that maybe I wouldn't.

But right now, in that second, gasping for breath and breathing in rot and raglike skin, I felt like I had to get out of there. Bracing my heels against the ground, I shot forward, lashing out with my elbows and putting enough space between my body and theirs that I could slam the back of my head into something else's jaw. I felt bones giving way, felt flesh tearing—I saw the opening, and I went for it.

I crossed the room in a heartbeat, and in a single, coordinated motion, the zombies reoriented. The ones I'd laid low climbed to their feet, bones jutting out every which way. They glanced at one another with those soulless, empty eyes, in a gesture far too human to be comforting for me, and then they spread out—half on my left, half on my right, ready to surround and mob me once more.

I could feel their saliva working its way through my system. To a human, it would have been fatal, with a brief detour through madness before the final bow—but even my body had its limits.

I wasn't losing it. Not yet. But the colors in the room seemed like they'd been dyed neon, and I felt like I was moving in slow motion, each limb weighed down by something soggy and wet.

I felt myself stumble, forced my body to stay upright.

"Kali!" Skylar's voice broke through my haze, and I realized that she wasn't squatting on top of the safe any more. She was standing beside it, and it was open.

I realized, belatedly, that it wasn't the kind of safe that held money or top secret biomedical plans. It was the type of safe that held *guns*.

The sight of weapons sent a familiar thrill up the length of my spine, and unconsciously, my body straightened, my fingers curving inward in anticipation of the way they'd feel against a trigger.

I'd always preferred knives to firearms, always felt that people like me were made for killing at close range, not at a distance, but beggars couldn't be choosers, and just seeing the weapons laid out before me, I knew them—inside and out, from safety to barrel.

I didn't have time to think. I had to move, had to keep moving, because the one thing I had on the zombies was that even though they were faster than any I'd ever seen, even though they appeared to be working as a team and their venom was slowing me down—

I was still faster than a human. And thanks to Skylar, I wasn't fighting alone.

I ducked and dodged, slammed my way through their onslaught, and got close enough to Skylar that she could shove something cool and metallic into my hand.

Six bullets. Six hits. None of my targets down.

I dropped the gun, and Skylar handed me another one—longer, heavier, possibly illegal. I didn't question why Bethany's father might have one. You don't look a gift horse in the mouth.

My skin sang with contact. My back arched as I shot. The sound was deafening, the splatter horrific.

Shot. Shot. Shot.

There was a rhythm to it, a beauty, and maybe it was sick that I could see that, that I felt each and every bullet like it was an extension of my own body, as they tore through flesh and bone, severing the spinal cord, blowing holes in heads.

With only a few bullets left, a suggestion flashed through my subconscious, Zev's mind melding with mine so completely that he didn't even have to speak. Without pause, I followed through on his unspoken suggestion, aiming at the collars around the zombies' necks.

In rapid fire, the glowing red lights went out. Like someone had doused a fire, the eerie human quality drained out of the zombies' eyes. Instead of focusing on me, they grappled with one another, undead teeth tearing through undead skin, nails making mincemeat of already shredded flesh.

Without thinking, I shoved Skylar back toward the safe, and with an empty shotgun still in my hand, I surged forward, driving the butt of the gun into a straggler's forehead as another ripped a chunk out of my right shoulder.

My right hand shot out backward, grabbed the biter by the neck, twisted, tore—and soon there was nothing.

Nothing left in my hands.

Nothing left to fight.

Nothing but corpses.

Don't look now, Zev said, **but you've got an audience.**

I looked up. Elliot and Bethany were standing in the doorway. Skylar had climbed back on top of the safe, and her legs were dangling over the front.

Absolute silence.

I knew how this must have looked, how *I* must have looked, drenched in blood with bodies spread like petals at my feet.

My heartbeat slowed. I followed Elliot's gaze—steady, intense—from my chest to my stomach, my stomach to my arms. There was a hole in my side, bits and pieces missing from the fleshy parts of my arms and legs. My jeans were tattered, my body bruised. Bite marks dotted the surface of my skin, like bloody flowers just beginning to bloom.

Swish. Swish. Swish.

The sound of my heart was deafening. The sound of their

silence was louder. Pressure built inside my head. The room closed in around me.

I stumbled and started to go down, but Elliot moved forward to catch me. He held me up, his gaze guarded, his eyes on Bethany's across the room.

Vaguely aware of the fact that one bite from a zombie was enough to drive a human mad, I looked down at my own body, at Elliot's hand on my arm.

At the gaping hole in my shoulder and the muscles just starting to knit themselves back together.

Bethany took a step toward us, her green eyes every bit as glassy and far away as her mother's. "You went through the windshield," she said shrilly. "You broke your neck. The chupacabra didn't kill you. And those things, they tore you to pieces . . ."

This wasn't the way I'd imagined telling them my secret—and I hadn't imagined telling Elliot at all. But all of a sudden, I couldn't hold the words back, couldn't deny the obvious for a second more. My brain was muddled from poison, my body numb, my eyes dry. Every safeguard that had once stood between me and the outside world crumpled and fell—useless, dead, gone. There was no hiding it, no denial, nowhere else to run.

"I'm not like other girls," I said, the words coming out in a whisper. "I'm not normal. I don't feel things, I don't fear things." I held out my bloodied hands, palms up. "I don't die."

Sometimes, the biggest truths were the simple ones—inescapable, undeniable, pure. I'd worn my secrets like a robe, and now I was naked. I was bleeding and visibly healing and utterly exposed.

Heat spread out from my torso. My head felt fuzzy, light. I blinked and my eyes wouldn't open. Elliot let go of me, and I went down.

I'd been bitten so many times. There was so much poison in my system.

"I don't die. I don't die. I don't die."

I heard the words, heard someone saying them over and over again. I didn't recognize my own voice, didn't realize until later that it was me.

I blinked and my eyes didn't open. I'd finally told someone the truth, and fate was conspiring to make me a liar.

I don't die, I'd said. *I don't die. I don't die. I don't die.*

But people like me? Sometimes, we did.

I'm in the room again—the room where it hurts. Sometimes it's loud and sometimes it's bright and sometimes I have to sit still. Mommy swabs my cheek. Daddy gets out the polka dots—dot, dot, dot all over my head. I make a face at him.

"EKG is clean," he says.

I know those letters. E! K! G! I know lots of letters. So does Mommy.

"DNA." She says other things, too, but they aren't letters, so I don't listen much.

EKG. DNA.

I don't think those are good letters. I want to go home.

"Almost done, baby." Mommy smiles, tickles my chin. I reach up to tickle hers.

And that's when it's time for my shot.

I blinked, but the world around me didn't settle into focus. Everything was bright and blurry and warped around the edges.

"I think she's awake. Kali? Can you hear me?"

I tried to separate the sounds into words, but couldn't do it. My body felt . . . heavy.

Without the Nibbler, you'd be dead.

Zev's voice was low and serious, and I wanted to tell him that he was wrong, that I'd lived through attack after attack, that I could have survived anything—but one bite from a zombie was enough to kill a regular person, and I'd been bitten, scratched, and clawed dozens of times.

Even *my* body had its limits.

"Dead," I repeated out loud. The word came out sounding garbled.

"Dead? *Dead?* Oh, no. You don't get to tell us something like that and then die." Bethany put her face right next to mine, and it came into focus.

More or less.

"That's not how this works, supergirl. You don't get to go to sleep. You don't get to pass out. You don't get to die. The only thing you get to do is wake up and tell us what the hell is going on." Beth's words were harsh, but her touch was gentle as she pressed something warm to my skin—a warm washcloth, damp and soft. "And then," she added, working the cloth across the surface of my body, "we're going to have a nice, long chat about lying to the Bethany. Surface wounds, my ass."

My last thought before I drifted back into darkness was that Bethany appeared to be referring to herself in the third person.

This could not possibly be good.

† † †

"Do you know what this is, Kali-Kay?"

Mommy is in a good mood. I think. I look at the object in her hand and then shake my head.

"Nuh-uh," I say. I stick my fingers in my mouth and give them a light chew. "What?"

Mommy gently takes my hand out of my mouth. "This is a gun. Can you say gun?"

"Gun," I repeat dutifully.

Mommy takes my still-damp hand, brushes it over the surface of the barrel. It is cold and hard. It feels like a doorknob. It looks funny, too.

"Do you want to play a game, Kali?"

Mommy and I play lots of games. Secret games. I am her secret girl.

"Close your eyes and count to ten," Mommy says. I close my eyes and count to four. I like four.

"Okay, now open your eyes." Mommy smiles, but it does not reach her eyes. It makes my tummy hurt. "Where's the gun, Kali?"

I can't see the gun any more. She hid it, and I don't know where it is. I wish I did. I wish I could tell her. I wish I could be good.

"Find the gun, baby."

I'm not good at this game, the secret game. I put my fingers back in my mouth. We have lots of secrets, Mommy, Mama, and me.

† † †

This time, when I woke up, the world was the right color and the right shape, and I recognized the person looking down at me instantly.

Vaughn.

It figured—the almost invincible girl gets hurt, and they

call a vet. Given that the others had seen me tearing through a zombie horde like a wild animal, it seemed highly appropriate—if a bit insulting.

You're not an animal. They're human. You're more.

Maybe I was just in a bit of a mood after being zombie chow, but instead of warming me from the inside out, Zev's words made me want to roll my eyes. I'd never asked to share my brain with a two-bit motivational speaker.

I hadn't asked for any of this.

"Your vitals are good. Your wounds are healing, and based on your body temperature, I'd guess your system is burning through the *mortis* bacteria instead of allowing it to shred your brain." Vaughn paused, his brown eyes searching mine. "How do you feel?"

I felt fine, naked, and thirsty—in that order. I remembered the looks on my friends' faces when I'd made my confession all too well. Physically, I was doing okay, but I couldn't remember the last time I felt so open to attack.

So vulnerable.

So much for keeping my back to the wall.

"I'm fine," I said, not meeting Vaughn's eyes. "Thirsty."

I very purposefully did not specify what, exactly, I was thirsting for.

Hunting without feeding is ill-advised, Zev told me, undeterred by my response to his last comment. Healing you makes the Nibbler that much hungrier. You'll have to feed it soon.

Well, forgive me for having been too busy being eaten by zombies and trying to kill them dead to stop and think about drinking their blood to keep the parasite inside me plump and well fed.

Anyone ever tell you you're cranky when you almost die?

There was a retort on the tip of my mental tongue, but I realized that Vaughn was giving me a very odd look, and I wondered if a bevy of emotions had passed over my face with Zev's words.

The last thing I needed was for the vet to think I'd caught some kind of zombie-induced insanity. He'd be forced to report me for quarantine, and I'd spend the rest of the day unable to do a thing to save Zev.

"I know this probably seems really weird to you," I told Vaughn, thinking *understatement* all the while, "but I'm okay. Nothing hurts. Nothing's broken. And I'm about as sane as I get."

I waited for Vaughn to ask me how my recovery was possible, but he didn't. He just nodded. "I'd tell you to take it easy," he said, "but based on the pile of bodies in the basement, I'm guessing that 'easy' isn't really your style."

There was a light note of censure in his voice—though I was pretty sure he disapproved more of my aversion to bed rest than to the fact that I'd dispatched a horde of zombies to the great beyond.

"What time is it?"

Giving voice to the question felt like showing my hand, but I wasn't used to not knowing, and today, more than any other day, each minute, each second, was crucial.

Every second I lay here was another second that Chimera Biomedical had Zev—another second that they could be coming for me.

"You were out for just over an hour," Vaughn said, "assuming Skylar's timeline of the 'you-know-what incident' is somewhere close to the mark."

My lips curved upward at the idea of Skylar referring to zombies as "you-know-whats," but the second my brain registered the fact that I was smiling, a wave of nausea passed through my body, bringing with it a kind of bleak hopelessness I recognized as regret.

Skylar.

Despite my best efforts to the contrary, I liked her. She was brave and openhearted and insane—and now she knew. She knew what I was, or—more to the point—what I wasn't.

I wasn't normal.

I wasn't human.

I was a liar.

I shouldn't have cared what she thought about me. I should have been more worried about whom she and the others might tell, but instead, all I could think about was the fact that they'd hate me now.

They'd have to.

"Hey." Vaughn's voice was soft as he chucked me under the chin. "None of that."

"None of what?" I said, wiping all trace of emotion from my face.

"Don't go working yourself up over nothing."

"Nothing?" I was incredulous.

"You should rest." With those words, Vaughn stood, and I followed his gaze to the doorway. Elliot was standing there, his face as unreadable as his brother's. Beside him, Bethany had both arms crossed over her chest. Her mascara was smeared, her clothes torn, and I knew just by the way she was holding her chin that she wasn't going to be giving in to tears again any time soon.

From somewhere behind them, Skylar pushed her way into the room. "You're okay," she said, her voice uncharacteristically low. "I was pretty sure you would be, but you never really know, and then when you wouldn't wake up . . ."

I tried to say something, but the words stayed in my throat, unspoken, unsure.

"I am so, so sorry, Kali. I swear, I didn't mean for you to have to save me. I heard a noise downstairs, and Bethany was all 'see yourself out,' and so I did . . . via, you know, the basement. I thought I was supposed to be there. I had a feeling, but maybe it was a bad feeling, because the next thing I knew, there was a zombie. And then there were two. And then there were three . . ."

"Skylar," Elliot interjected. "Breathe."

Obediently, she took a breath.

"So I climbed on top of the safe, because I knew I just had to wait. I knew you'd come back. I knew you'd . . . do something." Skylar frowned. "But I didn't know it would be like that. I didn't know they'd hurt you. I didn't!"

"Skylar." This time, I was the one who interrupted her babbling. "I'm fine." She didn't look convinced, and I felt compelled to elaborate. "It didn't even hurt." Realizing how close I was treading to the edge, to speaking words I'd never said out loud, I looked down and made a thorough study of the back of my hands. "I can't—when I'm like this, nothing hurts. I could take a bullet to the gut, and I wouldn't even feel it."

Elliot winced. Vaughn's expression never changed. Skylar's bottom lip trembled.

"You promise?"

This was not how I'd expected this conversation going. "I promise."

For a moment, you could have heard a pin drop in the room. Bethany broke the silence. "That's too bad," she said, "because right now, I'd kind of like to slap you, and it just won't be the same if you can't feel the pain."

This was closer to the reaction I'd expected.

"I'll go," I said, sitting up, finding my way to my feet.

"Go?" Bethany repeated incredulously. "You're not *going* anywhere. You are *going* to move your mouth, and words are *going* to come out, and you're *going* to explain how any of this is even remotely possible." She narrowed her eyes. "And . . . go."

"I don't know what you want me to say." My arms hugged my chest, like I could keep my emotions from the surface by sheer force of will. "I already told you guys. I'm not normal. I'm a freak. I showed you the *ouroboros*—that's not normal. Normal people die when they're bitten. I got stronger. Normal people go crazy if a zombie takes a chunk out of their arm. I took a little nap. I don't know why. I don't know how. All I know is that I'm not normal."

Skylar's babbling tendencies must have been contagious, because I couldn't stop myself from elaborating.

"I'm not even human."

If I'd felt naked before, I felt vivisected now—like someone had taken a knife and sliced my body open, like the others were getting ready to paw through my insides, chunk by chunk.

Skylar was the first to recover. "Oh," she said. "I thought maybe you were a little bit human."

Inside my mind, Zev snorted, and I pushed back the

insane urge to laugh. *A little bit human*, I thought. *Story of my life.*

"What are you?" Bethany's words didn't sound like an accusation, but she didn't sound curious, either. If anything, her voice was hesitant, guarded.

"I don't know," I replied. Her eyes flashed, but before she could say a word, I preempted it. "I think I'm some kind of hunter. When there's something preternatural around, I can feel it, and there's this desire, this *need*, to fight. I don't get tired. I don't feel pain. And as much as I'm capable of track-ing the beasties down, they can track me." I ran my fingertips gently over the length of my arm. The skin was puckered, still healing, and for the first time, I thought of what I must have looked like with pieces torn out of my flesh, my eyes bloodshot and feral.

"They like my blood," I said lightly. "If they smell it, they come for me, so I go for them first. It's illegal, and people think it's wrong, but I have to."

"So this is a regular thing for you?" Bethany asked, her eyebrows arched nearly into her hairline. "Killing zombies, playing cat and mouse with your friendly neighborhood dragon . . ."

"There was nothing normal about that dragon," I retorted. "But to answer your question, yes. I hunt. If something kills people, I kill it."

Bethany aimed her gaze heavenward. "This explains so, so much."

I thought she was thinking about all the little things I'd said and done in the past two days, but she disabused me of that notion pretty quickly.

"I mean, no wonder you've got a savior complex. You do this for a living."

I almost pointed out that nobody paid me, but Bethany was on a roll.

"And when you saw I had an *ouroboros*, you knew that if you could get it to swap, you could kill it."

I thought of the parasite feeding me strength and thirsting for blood in return. Killing it had been the plan, but now it was as much a part of my body as my skin or my lungs.

"In theory."

"So yesterday, when we were running all over the place trying to save you—that was all just a show?" Bethany's words were crisp, and her voice went up an octave or two. "You were just pretending to be sick?"

"No." The word burst out of my mouth with so much force that I realized that I really didn't want her to think that yesterday was something I'd faked, that it somehow didn't count.

"What I am," I said carefully, "the things I can do . . . I can't always do them."

"This is ridiculous," Elliot said, speaking up for the first time. "I can't believe we're even sitting here talking about this like it's not insane. If there were people out there who were born to hunt the preternatural, don't you think we'd know about them? Don't you think the government would know about them? It makes no sense."

"Yeah, well, take a time machine back to middle school and tell me that," I snapped, but the words came out wispy and small. "Because I was twelve when this started happening, and I didn't know why, or what was going on, or who I could tell, because it was crazy. It's *still* crazy. It makes no sense. Sometimes I'm human, and sometimes I'm not. If Bethany really wants to slap me, all she has to do is wait seventeen hours and change, and I'll feel it the same way anyone else would."

"Seventeen hours?" Elliot repeated. "That would be around seven a.m."

"Dawn," Skylar supplied helpfully. "You'll be human again at dawn."

I nodded. I'd already said enough. Too much, probably.

"So when you took the chupacabra, you didn't know if you could kill it?" Bethany was stuck on that one moment in time—though considering it had been life-or-death for her, I could understand the fixation.

"I thought if I made it to sunrise, the chupacabra would die, and I'd be fine." I shrugged. "It seemed like a good idea at the time."

"And none of this—the healing, the warrior-princess act, the crazy eyes . . . none of that is because of the chupacabra?"

Beth's face was guarded, but I found that I could get inside her head as easily as if I were the psychic one. She'd seen the way the *ouroboros* had spread out over my torso. She'd known her father was experimenting on chupacabras. And then she'd seen me do the impossible.

It made perfect sense that she'd wondered if the two were related. And, yeah, they kind of were—but not in the way she thought.

"It would have killed you," I said, keeping things simple. "Whoever injected you had no way of knowing it wouldn't."

I realized a second after saying it that for an hour, Bethany might have been able to tell herself that her father hadn't been playing around with her life—that he'd found a way to make her faster, stronger. That whatever cure he was after for Tyler, there might have been hope.

And there I was, telling her she was wrong.

"People like me"—it felt weird to say that phrase out loud, I'd spent so much time thinking it to myself—"we have a different reaction to chupacabras. When I was human, it was killing me, but when I switched . . ." I gestured to the newly healed skin on my arms. "I don't normally heal this fast. A couple of days ago, I might not have been able to bounce back from this at all. Whatever chupacabras do to humans, they do the opposite to me."

Don't tell them about the blood, Zev advised in what I'm sure he thought passed for a very sage tone. *Humans are remarkably queasy about our liquid diet.*

"Would you just shut up?" I didn't realize I'd said the words out loud until everyone else in the room started giving me the "she's losing it again" look in a single, synchronized motion.

"Not you guys," I clarified. "It's like this . . ."

If explaining the whole "every other day" thing was hard, trying to tell them that being bitten had given me a psychic bond with another person—who'd *also* been bitten—was darn near impossible, but I gave it my best shot.

Skylar was the first to recover. "So he's in your head, and you're in his? That's *significantly* psychic phenomena." She seemed enthused. "Can you guys actually speak, or is it just images? Do you feel what he feels? Can you swap bodies at will?"

I got the feeling she would have gone on indefinitely, but Bethany stopped her.

"We have bigger problems right now than the fact that if Kali makes out with someone, it might qualify as a ménage à trois," she said. "Do you have any idea what will happen if my father figures out what you can do? If the company he works for does? They'll want to take you apart piece by piece, just to see how it all works."

I could see Bethany wondering herself—how it worked, whether or not my cells really did hold the answer her father was looking for.

For Tyler.

"That can't happen," Bethany said finally, and I got the distinct feeling she was saying that as much for her own benefit as for mine. "They'd use you as a guinea-pig lab rat and bleed you dry. That can't happen."

Guinea-pig lab rat? Zev sounded either amused or insulted— I wasn't sure which.

"I know exactly what they'd do to me, Beth." For once, she didn't correct me on the use of the nickname. I took that as a good sign and plowed on. "I know because that's exactly what they're doing to Zev."

In the silence that followed, I realized that I was almost out of secrets. I hadn't meant to tell them about Zev. I hadn't meant to ask for help. Bethany had already told me no once today. Now that she knew what I was, I couldn't imagine that the answer would be any different. She still had her mother to think about, and if one thing was perfectly, crystal-line clear, it was that I could take care of myself.

I just kept coming and coming and coming.

I was what I was.

"You know Chimera has your psychic boy toy. You also

know that they'd probably love to add you to their collection, too." Bethany's hands snaked out to her hips. "Please tell me you're not planning a rescue mission."

The look on my face must have said it all.

Bethany rolled her eyes, and I wondered if I'd imagined the way she'd washed my body clean of blood, her touch light, her bedside manner gentle. "Right. You're Kali. Of course you're planning a rescue mission. Stupid self-sacrifice is kind of your thing."

Beside her, Elliot cleared his throat. At first, I thought he was trying to get her to show a little tact, but then I realized the throat-clearing was for my benefit, not hers.

"Yes?" I said, meeting his eyes, feeling his gaze on my body and not knowing whether that was a good sign or a bad one.

Elliot opened his mouth, a muscle in his jaw tensing and betraying the seemingly calm tone in his voice. "Forget rescue missions," he said. "Am I the only one here who thinks we should call the police?"

Elliot was indeed the only person present who thought we should call the police. Skylar closed her eyes, hummed for a moment, and declared that she didn't think that was a very good idea. Bethany was positive her phone and the landline were tapped and that Chimera would know the second we placed the call. And Vaughn had a different suggestion.

"Call Reid."

Skylar made a face, and even though Elliot wouldn't have admitted it, he did the same.

"Who's Reid?" I asked.

"The brother I would have to promote if Elliot doesn't stop treating me like I'm five," Skylar said. "He's . . . difficult."

"And by that, she means that he's a hard-ass." Elliot leaned back against the wall. "Black-and-white moral code, nobody else ever measures up."

I turned to Vaughn, expecting him to weigh in, but he just shrugged. "He's a Fed."

Right. Because the one thing that could make this situation better was the involvement of the federal government. Why didn't I just take out a billboard, volunteering to let the army play Dissect the Kali for fun?

"If we ask Reid not to tell, he won't," Skylar said. "You're a kid, Kali. Reid would die before he'd hurt a kid."

Vaughn took Skylar's statement as a stamp of approval. Without a word, he stepped out of the room, fishing his cell phone out of a pocket as he went.

"So Reid will come and get rid of the zombie carnage?" Bethany asked. "And then what? He'll start an investigation into Chimera on the down low?"

Elliot nodded. "Something like that. If your dad tries anything with your mom, we can bring in Nathan."

"Nathan?" I repeated, glancing over at Skylar. "Wasn't that the brother who taught you to hot-wire cars?"

Skylar shrugged. "When he's not stealing cars, he's a lawyer."

I was beginning to think that there weren't any bases the Hayden family *didn't* have covered—but none of this changed my situation. Chimera still had Zev, and even if Reid could keep me out of the investigation, there was no guarantee that Chimera's operation would be shut down, or that Zev wouldn't be absorbed into some government lab once it was.

"Exactly," Skylar said, nodding her head to emphasize the point—though I don't think any of us were entirely sure what she was saying *exactly* to. "The good news is that Reid will handle it. The bad news is that Reid will handle it. He won't want our help. He won't accept our help, and if he thinks, even for a second, that any of us might be inclined to engage in helping of any kind, he will have us shipped off to a convent in Switzerland."

"He wasn't serious about the convent thing," Elliot said

with a roll of those icy, pale eyes. "And besides, Mom and Dad would never let him."

"He's Reid," Skylar retorted. "Mom and Dad won't even realize he's talking them into it. I'll end up sipping tea with the nuns, and you'll be dropping and giving some drill sergeant twenty at military school. Kali and Beth will probably end up in convents, too, and he doesn't even know them."

"Don't call me Beth."

Before Bethany and Skylar could get into it, I intervened. "If your brother wants you to stay out of it," I said, "maybe you should." I paused, letting the suggestion sink in before adding the caveat. "That's not an option for me."

You don't have to do this, Zev told me. *You shouldn't.*

"I have to do this," I said out loud, half for Zev's benefit and half for theirs. "I don't expect the rest of you to help me."

"Of course you don't," Bethany replied. "Because you're the hero, and we're the ones who walk away."

I didn't know how to respond to that, because she was right. I did expect them to walk away. They didn't owe me anything. We barely knew each other.

What reason could I possibly give them to stay?

"If we're going to break into Bethany's dad's lab," Skylar interjected, with no segue whatsoever, "we should probably do it before Reid gets here for zombie cleanup."

"Or," Elliot suggested, "we could not."

He crossed the room, so that he was standing next to me. Bethany tracked his progression with her eyes, but the expression on her face never changed.

"I get wanting to know what you are, where you come from," Elliot told me, his voice even and sweet. "I get wanting to help someone who can't help himself. But this is big, Kali, and you could get hurt." He paused. "Seventeen hours from now, you could die."

Sixteen hours and fifty-nine minutes, I corrected silently, but I didn't say the words out loud.

I wanted to tell Elliot that this was more or less my life. That I'd known from the time I was twelve years old that I'd die hunting monsters—that the only thing different this time was that the monsters were human. But what came out of my mouth was something else.

"You don't get it. You won't ever get it, Elliot, because you have a family. You have friends, and you have a future—you don't have to worry that tomorrow or a year from now or five years, someone will figure out what you are. You don't have to wake up every morning wondering why, and you don't have to go through the motions, pretending that someday it will stop, because it will never stop."

Never, never, never.

"I can't just walk away and forget about this—I *am* this, and the only person in the world who could 'get' that, the only one who might actually understand or, God forbid, have some answers—that person is the one you want me to walk away from."

Protecting other people was what I was born for. I had to believe that, believe that I had a purpose, because otherwise, I was just a killer. I was sharp edges and violence and making myself bleed. Either I did it to make the world a safer place, or I really was a monster, less human than I was willing to believe.

"I'm doing this," I said, shrugging off Elliot's touch before I even realized that he'd lifted his hand to my shoulder. "I'm not asking for your help, and I'm certainly not asking for permission—"

"I don't know the code." Bethany said the words like she hadn't just interrupted me, like she really couldn't have cared less about what I was saying. "I have no idea how to get the door to my dad's lab open, but I can show you where it is. Maybe the 'psychic' can intuit a few little bitty numbers for you."

Bethany did a good job of coating that last sentence with sarcasm and pretending not to care—but I'd mastered that particular art when I was nine, and I saw straight through it. If Bethany had known the code, she would have given it to me.

"I'm not sure about the numbers," Skylar said brightly, "but I can try."

"For the last time, Skylar," Elliot interjected. "You're not psychic."

"And Kali isn't supergirl," Skylar cooed back. "Your brotherly wisdom has been absorbed. On a related note, your job is distracting Reid."

Without waiting for a reply, Skylar darted across the room, grabbed me by the arm, and dragged me out. Bethany followed on our heels.

"Why are you doing this?" I asked her. A few hours earlier, she'd refused to let us anywhere near the lab.

"Kali, a horde of zombies attacked my house. Vaughn said they were wearing some kind of high-tech collars, and I'm pretty sure that normal zombies aren't supposed to coordinate their flesh-eating efforts. I may not be the sharpest eyeliner in the box, but even I can read in between those lines." She paused. "Besides, I'm getting really tired of you being the hero. When people bite me, I bite back."

"Boyfriend's little sister's in the room," Skylar reminded her. "If you could avoid talking about biting people, I'd really appreciate it."

Bethany rolled her eyes. "There." She brought us down an extra set of steps and gestured to a thick, metal door. "If you can crack the code, be my guest."

Skylar nodded and bit her bottom lip, but before she could place her hands on the door, I reached out and stopped her.

"Let me try something first."

Skylar may have been a little bit psychic, but I'd spent the morning rifling through Dr. Davis's desk. I'd almost forgotten that his cell phone hadn't been the only thing I'd taken away from my little recon trip.

I'd also memorized the passwords taped to the bottom of his desk.

I don't know what I expected to see in Paul Davis's home lab, but what I saw was . . . nothing.

The walls were made of chrome. The floors were tile. The sound of my footsteps echoed through the room, and I could see the colors in my clothes reflected in the walls—blurry, indecipherable shapes.

Skylar and Bethany stepped into the room behind me. Besides the three of us, the only things in this entire room were a computer monitor built into the wall and stacks and stacks of hard drives, lining the floor like Lego.

"Got any more passwords?" Bethany said, gesturing to the computer.

"Got a keyboard?" I returned.

It took us five minutes to find it—hidden beneath a panel in the wall. I ran through every password I'd seen taped to Dr. Davis's desk and came up empty.

In unison, Bethany and I turned toward Skylar.

"I got nothing," she said.

I resisted the urge to send my fist into the shiny chrome walls. If I let myself hit something, let myself want to . . .

I could feel the need rising inside of me, except this

time, it wasn't hunt-lust. It was an ache, an emptiness.

Blood.

The thought was overwhelming, all-consuming, and suddenly, I could smell the scents of the room so clearly.

I could smell Bethany—Skylar—

I could smell their blood.

"What?" Bethany said defensively. "Do I have something on my face?"

I tore my eyes away from her neck, but I could still hear the beating of her heart.

Thirsty. Thirsty. Thirsty.

Suddenly, Zev's warning about needing to feed when I hunted seemed a lot more reasonable. In retrospect, pushing my healing ability to the limit and then locking myself in a small room with two walking bags of blood probably wasn't my finest idea ever.

Stop it, I thought firmly. *They're my friends.*

The word might not have meant anything to the mindless, senseless parasite inside of me, but it meant something to me.

"What are you doing?" Bethany asked.

I'm trying not to tear out your jugular, I thought in response. *When I told you I didn't know what I was, it's possible that I was not being 100 percent honest.*

Then I realized that Bethany hadn't addressed her acerbic comment to me. She was talking to Skylar, who was down on all fours, investigating the hard drives.

"I'm looking for a USB port," she said like it was the most obvious thing in the world. "Move your foot."

Bethany didn't move. "Why are you looking for a USB port?"

"Because I thought it might annoy you," Skylar answered, the picture of innocence. "And also because Darryl gave me this."

She held up a USB drive.

"Darryl?" Bethany repeated, utterly lost. "Who's Darryl?"

"Big guy? Sits with me at lunch?" Skylar continued running her hands over the various drives, looking for a port. "Sound familiar?"

"Mute?" Bethany said finally. "You're crawling all over the floor because of something you got from Mute?"

If the popular crowd called Darryl "Mute," I really didn't want to know what they called the rest of us.

"Darryl *does* talk," Skylar said. "If you listen. And FYI, I have a really strong feeling that he's going to be the next Bill Gates, so you might want to be a little nicer to him."

"I have a really strong feeling," Bethany deadpanned, "that if you don't tell me what's on that USB drive, I will end you."

"Aha!" Skylar brandished the hard drive like she was getting ready to embark on a three-gun salute. Without answering Bethany's question, she plugged it in, and the blank screen on the monitor gave way to a matrix of letters and numbers, rotating through the screen in multiple directions.

"Darryl likes codes," Skylar explained. "A few weeks ago, I asked him what someone might hypothetically need to break into a supercomputer. He hypothetically made me this."

Suddenly, the walls all around us gave way to images. Apparently, the monitor wasn't just built into the wall. The monitor *was* the wall.

Glancing at Beth and Skylar out of the side of my eyes, I moved toward the keyboard and then double clicked on the first folder I saw. It was password protected, but Darryl's program made mincemeat of that protection, and a few seconds later, the three of us were staring at gibberish.

Scientific gibberish.

There were Excel files, full of data—numbers and columns and dates that were more or less Greek to me. Then there were documents—each labeled with a serial number.

HB-42. LOS-129. MC-407.

Something about that last one sent a niggling feeling into my brain. I opened it, and a single word caught my eye.

Draco.

I wasn't the world's best student, and I'd never been particularly fond of science—for obvious reasons. But I knew enough to recognize the genus of almost any preternatural creature.

Genus *Draco* referred to dragons. As I read through the document—which was laced with references to nucleotides and alleles and oxytocin knockout mice—I caught a few other terms I recognized.

Terms like *Equus aqua mysticalis* and *Pan yeti gigantea.*

There was also a figure, with a bunch of millimeter-long bars on it.

"Does that look like one of those DNA gel things to anyone else?" Skylar asked.

Bethany shook her head. "It looks like a pregnancy test on crack."

"No," Skylar said slowly. "I skipped a year in science, so I'm taking bio this year. That's definitely one of those gel things."

As the two of them bickered back and forth, I stared at the words on the screen, willing them to make sense—and then willing them not to, because if I was reading this correctly, then Skylar was right.

That was a DNA sequencing gel.

Nucleotides.

Alleles.

DNA.

Before I was old enough to walk and talk, modern science had already uncovered the secret to cloning sheep. The entire human genome had been catalogued. And researchers had discovered that preternatural creatures had triple helix DNA.

Pan yeti gigantea. Equus aqua mysticalis. Those were the scientific classifications for the yeti—also known as the abominable snowman—and kelpies—also known as a pain in my ass.

It was like the beginning of some horrific joke—a kelpie, a yeti, and a fire-breathing dragon walk into a bar—but I already knew the punch line.

Kelpies could literally disappear into water.

Yetis were man-eating primates with an affinity for ice.

What do you get if you mix a kelpie, a yeti, and a dragon?

"That thing from the skating rink," I said. "The ice dragon."

Twenty-four hours earlier, Skylar's psychic senses had led us straight to the ice rink—and the woman who appeared to be calling the shots at Chimera had shown up once the furor had started to die down. At the time, my mind had been a jumbled mess, and I hadn't been able to put the pieces together.

I hadn't been able to think.

And since I'd shifted, I hadn't spared more than a thought or two for the dragon, so it hadn't occurred to me that Chimera might have their fingers in more than one pot—that the chupacabra might not be the only creature they were studying.

Altering.

Experimenting with.

I felt sick—so sick that I brought my right hand to my mouth, for fear I might throw up.

There were thirty-nine varieties of preternatural creatures. They'd been documented, studied, protected by law. Some lived in locations so remote I'd never actually seen one; some hunted humans right in my backyard. I'd probably never be able to kill them all—for every monster I slew, there would always be a new one to take its place—but there was still some comfort in knowing that there was a limit to just how bad things could get.

Thirty-nine species, some of them endangered.

Thirty-nine was doable.

"They're making more." The words came out in a whisper, and for a second, I thought I might actually start crying. I did what I did because I had to. I fought every night I could and hated myself the nights I couldn't. It wouldn't ever stop, and they were making more.

More monsters.

Stronger ones. *Unnatural* ones.

That was the word Zev had used to describe the dragon at the ice rink, and I could see it now. As horrible as the rest of the preternatural world was, there was some rhyme or reason to it. There were limits.

But this?

There could be a thousand of me, and it still might not be enough to fight them back if Chimera had one too many successes, if those successes got out into the population the way the dragon had. Without meaning to, I thought of all the beasties I'd fought in the past few weeks. The hellhounds were just hellhounds. The zombies—aside from working as a team—were just zombies. And the basilisk . . .

Bigger.

Stronger.

Harder to kill.

This time, I really did punch the wall.

Beside me, Skylar scrolled through more files on the computer. I couldn't even look at them—I didn't want to know, until she came upon the file for chupacabras.

Until I saw the photo of Zev.

His hair was onyx—darker than mine and so black it was nearly reflective. His skin was pale, and I wondered at the fact that in my mind, I'd always seen him tinged in shadow.

Beside me, Skylar seemed to realize that the photo had caught my attention—and why. She opened her mouth to say something, and then her eyes lit on Zev's scientific classification.

Homo vampirus.

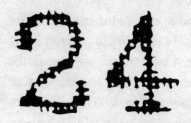

Skylar closed the file so quickly that you would have thought it had bit her. She glanced guiltily at me and then looked back at Bethany.

"How old do you think he is?" Bethany asked, tilting her head to the side. "Like, twenty?"

I hadn't noticed Zev's age in the picture, but I doubted he was twenty. He'd been in Chimera's captivity for two years, and he talked about that length of time like it was nothing.

I'm older than I look, Zev said helpfully. We don't age the way humans do. Not once we've taken on a Nibbler.

I didn't ask him to clarify, because I was still staring at the space on the screen where that one word had been a moment before.

Vampirus.

I lived in a world where the mythological was real. We all did—and had for a very long time. The old stories about super-natural creatures were the kind of thing we saw as funny or quaint or just downright ridiculous—the equivalent of thinking that putting a leech on someone could rid them of the flu. But even taking into account everything we knew about the preternatural world, there were still some things that fell outside the realm of possibility, things that were nothing more than the product of overactive imaginations.

Things like vampires.

And werewolves.

And psychics.

The sarcastic half of my brain couldn't help but wonder if Bethany went furry on the full moon, because if she did, we'd be batting three for three.

I'm a vampire, I thought. *I'm part vampire.*

We prefer the term Lonely Ones, Zev said. Because we're meant to come in pairs.

If that wasn't a loaded statement, I wasn't sure what was. I'd spent so much time on the outside looking in that the idea of being half of a pair—yin to his yang—made my eyes sting with tears I'd never shed. I had tried so hard not to let loneliness overwhelm me, had never thought that a person like me could be anything else.

And then I'd been bitten.

And then there was Zev.

"What are they doing to him?" Bethany did a good job of inspecting her nails as she asked the question. "Mr. Tall, Dark, and Gorgeous—what are they doing to him? Skylar closed the document before I could see."

Skylar met my eyes, and I knew that she'd closed it for my benefit—to keep Bethany from reading those two little words and figuring out what Skylar now knew.

What I was.

"They're cutting him," Skylar said. "Burning him, taking samples, injecting him with drugs. Sometimes, they cut off parts to see if they'll grow back." She paused. "They take a lot of blood."

Somehow, I doubted she'd gotten that information from the scientific document she'd just read. I was beginning to suspect that Skylar might have undersold her psychic ability.

"We can't leave him there, and we can't let them capture you." Skylar grimaced, like she was staring at the core of something physically painful to see. "This is bad—not just bad for Zev. Bad for . . . it's just bad, okay?"

Now I was also beginning to suspect that she knew something that I didn't. About Chimera. About Zev. About me. I couldn't explain the feeling, but I couldn't shake it, either, and this time, when I met Skylar's eyes, she looked away.

I guess we all have our secrets, I thought. Since Skylar didn't seem inclined to tell anyone mine, I could hardly hold her own against her. When she felt like telling me, she would. Until then—

Click. Click. Click.

My breath caught in my throat. I knew that sound. For a second, I thought that maybe it was in my head, but then I heard it again, loud and clear and just down the hall.

Click. Click. Click.

"What I don't understand, Ms. Malik, is how, precisely, the test subjects who escaped from your facility made their way here."

I recognized Bethany's father's voice a second before he rounded the corner. In a fraction of that time, I hit the POWER button on the computer, hooked an arm around Skylar, and pulled her into a corner, hugging the shadows and flattening both of our bodies against the wall.

The hard drives offered scant cover, but in this room, there was nothing else. As Bethany's father came into view, I realized that I'd left Beth there, out in the open. I flexed my fingers, razor-sharp nails ready to tear through human flesh if he gave me even half a reason to think that she was in danger.

I shouldn't have worried.

Bethany leaned back against the wall and crossed one ankle over the other. She looked down at her watch as if she'd been waiting for him to arrive. And when her father and the woman he was talking to—the woman from the school, the one from the ice rink—stepped into the room, Beth reoriented herself so that she was standing between them and us, giving us what little cover she could.

I lowered myself into a crouch, bringing Skylar with me, pushing back into the cover of the hard drives as far as I could.

"Well," a female voice said. "What have we here?"

I'd heard her voice before, at the school, but we were closer this time, and for some reason, the sound of it filled me with dread, the hairs on the back of my neck standing straight up, my stomach churning with . . . *something*.

"Here," Bethany said, responding to the woman's rhetorical question, "we have a teenager. And she's pissed."

Leave it to Bethany to play the queen-bee card with a woman who had, in all likelihood, ordered my killing. A woman who might have sent zombies to Bethany's house with the intention of cleaning up loose ends.

"Here I was, minding my own business, and my house— where my father left me alone, I might add—was overrun with zombies. Excuse me, *test subjects*."

From the tone of her voice, you would have thought

Bethany was talking to the populace back at school. She was the queen, and they had displeased her.

From the cover of the hard drives, I couldn't quite make out her father's response, or that of the woman who'd accompanied him, but I was going to go out on a limb and guess that it wasn't good.

"Bethany," Dr. Davis said calmly, "what are you doing in my lab?"

"Are you kidding me?" Bethany spat. "This is the most secure place in the entire house. Where would you go if the place was overrun with zombies?"

I could practically hear the woman in heels smiling. "So you've been here the whole time? You have no idea how the subjects' transmitters malfunctioned or, say, where their bodies are now?"

I registered the woman's words and drew the logical conclusion: Skylar's brothers worked fast. Either Chimera didn't know they'd been here, or Ms. Malik was playing dumb—either way, Reid had taken care of the bodies exactly the way Vaughn had said he would.

"Do I look like a zombie slayer to you?" Bethany asked. "This has been, like, the worst day ever."

"Yes," the woman said, a measuring tone in her voice. "I understand you had an accident this morning."

Skylar made a face that I interpreted to mean *I'll show you accident, lady.* Unfortunately, she looked more like a puppy than a pit bull, so even if the object of her glare had been able to see it, I didn't think it would have done much good.

"Look, you guys asked me not to call the police, I didn't call the police. You told me to stay home from school, and then zombies attacked. There had better be a Christmas trip to Saint Barts in my future, or else I'm going to get cranky, and you seriously do not want to see me cranky."

"Bethany," her father said, "calm down. Ms. Malik assures me they had nothing to do with this unfortunate incident with the zombies, and I'm assuring her that you know the meaning of the word *discretion*. Now, if you could go upstairs and check on your mother, she's had a really taxing day."

That was a low blow, and everyone in this room knew it. Bethany weathered it like a pro and flounced off, without once breaking her cover. If I hadn't known better, I would have sworn she was a spoiled, shallow little princess who would forget all of this for a trip to St. Barts.

I just hoped the woman in heels bought it as well.

"She's charming," the woman in question told Bethany's father. "Really. I can see why you enrolled her in the protocol."

"She wasn't supposed to be there when we attempted inoculation," Dr. Davis said, a vein in his forehead bulging. "It was a mistake—very nearly a tragic mistake."

I didn't know whether it was comforting that Bethany's father hadn't specifically infected her, or whether it was disturbing that he thought infecting other teenagers was okay.

"Shall we proceed to round two?" he asked, moving on. "Or should I expect to be retired soon, like Dr. Vincent?"

"Dr. Vincent moved to Florida," the woman said, her voice crisp.

Bethany's father met her gaze. "Sure he did."

Listening to the sounds of the room—their words, their heartbeats, mine and Skylar's—it would have been so easy to give up my hiding spot and make myself known.

So easy to tear out their throats.

Fight it, Kali.

I absorbed Zev's words. I fought it. And then the woman in heels stepped directly into my line of sight. If she turned, even a bit, to the side, she'd be able to see me.

As it was, I could see her.

She had dark hair pulled into a tight ponytail at the nape of her neck. Her features were even and pretty; her eyes were soft and brown, just a shade darker then her perfect, glowing skin. She was wearing a suit.

I'd seen her before—at the ice rink. At the school. I'd seen her reflection. I'd seen her when I was on the verge of passing out, but I'd never been this close, never fully taken in her features, never looked straight at her, my mind completely my own.

I've seen her before, I realized. Not just at the school. Not just at the ice rink. *Seen her, seen her, seen her.*

The sense of déjà vu was so strong, so violent, that I couldn't move.

"We'll hold off on round two," she said, and her voice washed over me—far too familiar for comfort. "We still don't know what happened to the body. If one of our competitors has acquired it . . . ," she trailed off. "Well, then, you can look forward to your retirement."

"Rena." Dr. Davis said the woman's first name. I recognized the attempt at intimacy and might have read into it more, but for the fact that those four little letters—R-E-N-A—unlocked something incomprehensible and vast in the corridors of my mind.

She's just a child, Rena.

Almost finished, baby.

Can you say gun?

I'd seen this woman before—not just at the ice rink or at the school, but in my dreams, all of them, for as long as I could remember. I'd held her face—not this detailed, not this clear—in my mind for what seemed like forever.

She'd been the memory I'd least wanted to lose.

The woman in heels—Rena Malik—was my mother.

A lifetime of broken memories came crashing down around me—flashes of the past, things I'd seen in dreams, pretty pictures I'd painted for myself. The air was so thick with it, I couldn't breathe.

Beside me, Skylar squeezed my hand, and I looked down, concentrating on the way her fingers—delicate, pale—looked interwoven with mine.

Do you know what this is, Kali-Kay? Can you say gun?

I wanted to bring my knees to my chest and my hand to my mouth. I wanted to rock back on my heels. I wanted to throw up. But I couldn't do any of that, because Bethany's father was standing five feet away—right next to my mother.

"I don't like being threatened, Rena."

How could I have missed this? Even looking at a distorted reflection, even on the verge of passing out—I should have known.

"I don't like threatening you, Paul, but you knew the score when you signed up. You knew we were on the cutting edge. You, better than anyone, know that there's a cost to every scientific advance."

I hadn't realized it until that moment, but there was a part of me that had always thought she was dead. I'd thought—stupidly, naively—that if she was really still out there, she would have made some effort to see me.

To know me.

But in all of my imaginings, I'd never considered the possibility that she might be alive and well and playing around with the forces of nature, that she might be the kind of person capable of threatening to "retire" someone if his research fell into a competitor's hands.

That's not all she ordered, my insides whispered, and I thought about the view from Bethany's car, about the men in suits, about lying in pieces on the side of the road, waiting for my body to make the switch.

You don't know that she ordered that, I told myself. *You don't know that she's in charge.*

That was the problem—I didn't know anything.

"Costs are acceptable," Dr. Davis said. "But let me be very clear, with you and with your employers: my daughter is not collateral damage. We all have our limits. That's mine."

The woman who was my mother smiled. "So noted."

I wanted to ask her if she knew—who I was, what I was. I wanted to ask what her limits were and if I was collateral damage.

I wanted to scream—or maybe die.

It was one thing to think that your mother had left you when you were three years old, that she'd walked out the door and never even looked back.

It was another thing to think she'd never loved you in the first place.

Almost finished, baby.

We're going to play a game, Kali.

Mommy's secret girl.

The memories came faster and more violently into my mind. I choked on them. My eyes burned, worse than they had in the sun, and I realized that I was on the verge of tears.

They hung there, unshed, in my eyes, and I willed something calm and cool and animal to take over my body. I wasn't going to cry.

I wasn't going to remember.

You're all right, Kali. Zev's voice wasn't gentle; I couldn't have taken it if it were. He was matter-of-fact, and I accepted his words at face value. I'm here. You're all right. You're going to be all right.

"You do your job, Paul. Let me take care of mine. Keep your daughter on her leash, and we'll all be just fine."

The words rhymed, making the ultimatum sound like some kind of sick nursery rhyme and threatening to send me back in time—to lying on my bed, while she brushed my hair out of my face.

She sang me to sleep, I thought dully.

And then she was gone—not just gone from my memories, or gone from my life, but gone from this room. The woman in heels—Rena Malik, my *mother*—followed Paul Davis out of the room, leaving Skylar and me hidden behind the hard drives, neither one of us willing to say a word out loud.

Seconds crept into minutes, and finally, I let out a long and jagged breath.

"You okay?" Skylar asked quietly, and I realized I was still holding her hand, still squeezing it.

"Sorry," I said, letting go.

"Sorry you're not okay?" Skylar asked, eyeing me with concern.

"Sorry about your hand," I corrected. She looked down, surprised, as if she'd forgotten she even had a hand. Then she smiled.

"Don't worry," she said, wiggling her fingers. "I have two." To demonstrate, she held up her left hand, and I smiled—or at least, I tried to.

The simple motion—my lips curving upward—brought bile into my throat. How could I smile? How could I do anything except lie there and hurt?

"Kali?" Skylar's voice was very small. "If this is about what I saw, when we were looking at those files—I won't tell anyone. Ever. I mean, we all have our things, right? I talk too much, and I look like a third grader, and I'm only a little bit psychic." She blew a wisp of white-blonde hair out of her face. "I don't care if you're a you-know-what."

"A vampire?" I suggested. It was the first time I'd said the word out loud, but worrying about a thing like that seemed so stupid all of a sudden. It was just a word.

And that woman was just my mother.

"It's not about that," I told Skylar. "It's . . ."

I couldn't form the words, physically could not do it.

Skylar nodded. "It's okay, Kali. I may not be significantly psychic, but I know that it's going to be okay. Everything is going to work out, and you're going to be okay. I'm going to *make* you okay. Okay?"

The repetition of the word made me want to smile. Smiling made me want to puke. This wasn't okay. *I* wasn't okay.

Moving on autopilot, I dug something out of my pocket. The cell phone I'd stolen from Davis's office was in even worse shape now than it had been when I'd snapped it in two. The plastic casing was pulverized, assorted keys hanging off it like a loose tooth dangling by a single thread of gum. It looked like it had been run over by a semi.

I ran my thumb over the broken, jagged surface.

This phone looked how I felt.

"I'm going to go out on a limb and guess that isn't your phone," Skylar said, hooking her thumbs through the pocket of her jeans. "Am I right?"

I nodded, unable to take my eyes off the broken, mangled frame. "It used to be Bethany's dad's. Now, it's nothing."

Nothing.

Nothing.

Nothing.

I used to have a memory of my mother—smiling, soft.

Now I had nothing.

Nothing.

Nothing.

"Reid could probably pull some data off the phone," Skylar said, a look of comic concentration on her elfin features. "He's got guys. Lots of guys. One of them could reassemble the memory card, and then pull the incoming calls."

"There were some numbers on there," I said, like that mattered. Like anything mattered any more. "Incoming calls."

Quick as a whip, Skylar slipped her own cell phone out of her pocket and hit the speed dial. "Hey, Gen? It's Skylar. Quick question—if you have a cell phone number, can you track the location a call was placed from?" Skylar paused.

"Not you specifically, but like, somebody-you? With the right equipment?" Skylar fell into silence again, twirling a stray piece of blonde hair around her index finger. "Okay, and say I wanted to keep tabs on the person who was running the number. And say that this person totally wouldn't expect me to be doing that, because he still thinks I'm five years old. Do you think . . ."

Skylar trailed off again and then beamed. "Excellent! Tell John Michael he's never allowed to make fun of you for watching police procedurals again. See you in five."

Skylar hit the key to end the call with more flourish than was purely necessary. "That was Genevieve," she said needlessly. "She says that Reid and company should be able to track the incoming calls on this phone back to the locations from which they were placed even if they're not listed. Same goes for the calls made from this number, so if Bethany's dad has ever been to the facility where they're keeping Zev, or if he's ever gotten a call from them, we should be able to track it. Or technically, *Reid* should be able to track it, but Gen said she could loan me a couple of bugs, so we should be able to keep tabs on Reid."

I tried to process Skylar's babbles and came to an utterly ridiculous conclusion. "Are you actually suggesting we bug the FBI?"

Skylar held up her right hand, holding her index finger a centimeter or so above her thumb. "Just a little."

"This is never going to work."

"Kali, if I want pessimism and brooding foreheads, I'll talk to Elliot. At least try to think positively."

"Sure," I said, forcing my fingers to let loose of their grip on the cell phone. "I guess it's worth a try."

I wanted to laugh hysterically—or possibly throw up. Zev was a lab rat, my mother was evil, and Skylar and I were discussing bugging the FBI.

"Yeah," Skylar said, and she had the decency to sound a little sheepish. "It's crazy. But sometimes, crazy is all you've got."

She reached out to take the phone, and the moment her fingers touched mine, an odd gleam came into her eyes, like a candle bringing light to a jack-o'-lantern's. For a moment, there was an unnatural silence between us, and I wondered what she'd seen.

"It's going to get better." Skylar's voice was very quiet, very small. "But first, it's going to get worse." She played with the end of her T-shirt, avoiding my gaze. "And when it gets worse . . . well, just remember that it's going to get better, okay?" She brought her eyes up to mine, and I felt like she needed something from me—acceptance maybe, or absolution.

"Sometimes, there aren't any good choices. Sometimes, making the right one is hard." She blinked and then cleared her throat. "It's funny," she said, "but when you really think about it, we're all broken. That's just what life does. It knocks you down and it breaks you and you either get back up again, or you don't. You either do things on your terms, or you don't." She grabbed my hand, and I was surprised at the strength of her grip. "You let the bad things win, or you don't."

It would have been so easy to stay down, to deal myself out, to stop caring. There was a part of me that wanted to say that I'd been fighting since I was twelve, and look what it got me.

But I couldn't. And even though I had no idea what Skylar had seen in our future, what she was holding back, the one thing I knew for sure was that she couldn't, either.

Crazy, insane, impossible, broken—it didn't matter. Some people were born to fight back.

Skylar squeezed my hand and then dropped it. "You know what the worst part is about being psychic?" she asked. In typical Skylar fashion, she didn't wait for a response to continue. "You always know when it's going to get worse. I get up in the morning and get ready for school, and I know *that word* is going to be written on my locker. I know that given half a chance, they'd write it on my face. Last year, when it first started, I knew—I *knew* it was going to go on and on and on; every day, every single day, it was just going to get worse. But you know what? Screw that, Kali. Whatever it is, whatever hurts so bad you can't even unball your fists—you either let it break you, or you don't."

This was the first time I'd heard Skylar admit, even for a second, that she wasn't invincible—that the things people said and did to her at school hurt. And maybe, compared to what I was going through, it should have seemed little and petty and so very high school, but it didn't, because fighting, getting hurt, letting the baddies break my bones and tear my flesh—that was the easy part.

That had always been the easy part.

Letting people in, caring, wanting them to care about me—that was hard.

"That woman?" I said, my voice husky and low. "The one who was just here? I'm pretty sure she's my mom."

Skylar blinked. And then she blinked again. "Do you think

she knows?" Skylar said finally. "That you're involved in all of this? That you're . . . you?"

That was the question, wasn't it?

"I don't know. I'm not even sure I care." I brought the heel of my hand up to my face, wiped roughly at the tears as they fell from my bloodshot eyes. "If we're going to illegally bug the FBI, we should probably get on that."

I had fourteen hours and twenty-nine minutes until my next shift. Fourteen hours and twenty-nine minutes to fight back—but until I knew where Zev was, there wasn't anything else I could do.

Fourteen hours and twenty-nine minutes.

I wasn't going to waste even one second thinking about Rena Malik.

Skylar's house was half the size of Bethany's, but even from the outside, there was something distinctly comfortable about it, something comforting. There was a basketball hoop in the driveway and a scattering of brightly colored leaves on the lawn. In the summer, the beds were probably full of flowers, and there was a slope to the driveway that looked like it had been handcrafted for snow days and sledding.

A worn wooden fence sectioned off the backyard, and the second Skylar stepped out of my (stolen) car, she made a beeline for the gate.

I paused at the curb and hesitated. Under my feet, there was a line of handprints, pressed into the cement like a Hollywood star. Tiny handprints and chubby ones, gangly and nearly full grown.

It may as well have been a line in the sand, a barbed-wire fence at a border crossing.

You don't belong here, it seemed to say. *Family and happy memories and home—those things aren't for you.*

"You coming?" Skylar called.

From somewhere in the distance, darkness beckoned. If I

ran long enough, looked hard enough, I could follow the trail. I could hit the outskirts of town and find something to hunt. I could let the hunter take over and turn off all feelings, emotions, longing.

I could feed.

But instead, I stepped over the line of handprints and followed Skylar into the backyard, trying with every step not to think about all of the things I'd never had, would never have. I tried not to think about the bits and pieces of memory I'd held on to my entire life: my mother's face, the way she'd held me, the way she smelled.

Not for me. Lies.

If Skylar sensed my thoughts, she had the decency not to comment on them and instead just hooked an arm through mine. "Come on," she said. "Let's go make trouble."

"You know," I replied, half joking and half not, "that might be the nicest thing anyone's ever said to me."

Skylar smiled and shrugged. "Not for long." With eyes alight with mischief, she pulled a key chain out of her pocket with her free hand. "Remember," she said. "Let me do the talking."

She didn't even need to ask. I'd broken my share of laws, but none of them had involved facing off against *people*. They certainly hadn't involved giving an FBI agent a key chain in which we'd planted a listening device that one of Skylar's friends had just happened to have on hand.

"Don't you think he's going to be a little suspicious that we're giving him a mangled SIM Card *and* a 'Number One Brother' key chain?" I asked Skylar as the two of us closed in on the back door to her house.

"Definitely," Skylar agreed. "That's why I altered the key chain on the way over."

I took a closer look at it and realized that in addition to hiding the listening device, she'd also edited the slogan on the key chain.

"Number Four Brother?" I asked drily. "Isn't that kind of insulting?"

Skylar smiled angelically. "He won't suspect a thing."

The inside of the Haydens' house was even smaller than it had looked from the outside. The walls were lined with school pictures, and there was music blaring from the kitchen.

"My mom's cooking," Skylar explained. "She requires a soundtrack."

I tried not to feel a twinge at how easy it was for her to say those two little words—*my mom*—but I only succeeded partway.

Concentrate on something else, I told myself. *Anything else.*

And that was when I heard it: the steady, solid beating of Skylar's heart.

Thirsty.

The thing inside me needed blood. This time, Zev didn't say a single word to talk me down.

Thump. Thump. Thump.

Skylar's blood smelled like strawberries. Now I wasn't thinking about family or betrayal or anything other than the fact that it had been hours since the basilisk blood, hours of hunting and healing and—

"Heya, Reid. Have you met Kali?"

Skylar said the words like she genuinely thought there was a chance that her oldest brother *had* met me before, and if I hadn't known better, I would have sworn she was completely guileless.

Apparently, Reid knew her better than that, too.

"We haven't met," he told me, ignoring his sister and bringing the full force of a miss-nothing stare to bear on my face. "But I believe I'm acquainted with some friends of yours."

I tried to read in between the lines of his words. Beside me, Skylar helpfully made zombie motions, her head lolled to the side and her arms held out like claws.

"Right," I said, at a complete loss for words. "The zombies. In case you didn't notice, we didn't exactly part on friendly terms."

The strength of Reid's stare never wavered, never lessened. "You don't say."

I took a moment to study him, even though there was a part of my mind that was still locked on to the rhythm of Skylar's heartbeat, the smell of her blood. While Skylar and Elliot were blond, Reid's hair—buzzed close to his scalp—had a reddish tint to it. He was a full head taller than me—wiry, but strong. And beyond the smile, the expression on his face was . . . blank. Completely blank.

Clearly, he was reserving judgment. On me. On the zombies. Or maybe he was just hoping I'd crack and spill out the whole story, from start to finish.

I looked down and away. Somehow, after meeting Elliot and Vaughn, I'd expected Reid to be more talkative. I hadn't expected him to treat me like I was a suspect—or a criminal.

Even though I was.

Beside me, Skylar rolled her eyes. "He's this way with everyone," she told me. "You'd be getting the Death Stare Third Degree even if you'd just come over for dinner—which, by the way, should probably be ready soon."

Reminded of Skylar's presence, Reid fixed her with the same implacable stare he'd given me. "Are you okay?" he asked, clearly a man of few words.

She nodded. "Peachy keen."

His stone-hard face softened, just a little. Then he turned back to me. I braced myself, but all he did was repeat the question he'd asked Skylar. "Are you okay?"

I nodded, sure that if I spoke, the words would sound like a lie.

"We brought you something," Skylar said, before Reid could ask me anything else. "It's the SIM card from Bethany's dad's phone. Or at least, it's what's left of the SIM card."

Reid folded his arms over his chest. "Do I want to know how you got it?"

Skylar glanced at me.

Reid cast his eyes heavenward. "I'll take that as a no."

Skylar must have noticed her brother's exasperation, but she expertly ignored it. "Do you think you might be able to pull something useful off the card?"

Reid gave her A Look, capital A, capital L.

"Hey, we're the ones who—" Skylar didn't even get to finish that sentence. Reid bent down to her level, Look still in place.

"You're the ones who did what exactly?"

Skylar did a passing job of looking like she'd been caught with her hand in the cookie jar. "Vaughn probably told you everything, anyway," she grumbled, sounding all of five years old.

"Vaughn probably did," Reid agreed.

"Are you going to look into it?" Skylar asked.

Reid didn't answer. He just took the SIM card and pocketed it. "If either of you hears anything else, if you see anything—I want you to call me."

He handed me a business card and turned the full force of the Look on me. "Anything, any time, no matter how small. Do you understand?"

Actually, no. I didn't. He didn't know me. He had no reason to trust me. And if Vaughn had told him everything, he knew I wasn't human, not really.

"If there's something to take care of, I'll take care of it. You shouldn't have to." He turned his attention back to Skylar. "And you," he continued, "know better."

"I know a lot of things," Skylar said softly, and for the first time, I saw a familial resemblance between them. "More than I'd like to."

"This could be dangerous." Reid's tone never changed. The Look never wavered.

"This isn't just dangerous," Skylar retorted. "It's deadly."

Blood and bleeding and my body lying on the side of the road, I thought. *Poison tearing through my body, fangs through my chest.*

"I'll take care of it," Reid said. "And I'll be fine."

"I know you will be," Skylar said, rising on her tiptoes to give him a kiss on his cheek. "By the way, I got you a little something."

Suspicion flickered across his face—until she handed him the key chain.

"Number Four Brother," he said, trying very hard not to laugh. "Cute."

This time, I could hear both of their hearts beating. I could smell strawberries and blood. There was warmth on my skin, and deep inside of me—hunger.

Thirst.

"You want to stay for dinner?" Skylar asked me. I looked from her to Reid to the pictures on the wall. In the kitchen, Skylar's mother was singing along to the radio, and I heard the rumble of the garage door—her father, home from work.

"I have to go," I said.

Go hunting.

Go home.

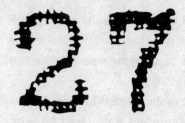

When I got home from hunting—*feeding*—my dad was in the kitchen. He seemed lost, like he'd forgotten where exactly the microwave was, and when I came in, he actually smiled.

"There you are."

I so didn't want to get into this—not now.

"I thought I might cook dinner tonight," he said. "Today was my sexual-selection lecture—the kids always love that one."

It took me a moment to realize that he was trying to make conversation. It seemed ironic that he'd picked today, of all days, to remember my existence.

"Your school called," he said suddenly. "They said you missed your classes."

Why did I get the distinct feeling that my father had run an Internet search for "what to do when your child plays hooky"? Hence the homemade dinner and his best attempt at a heart-to-heart.

Considering my own mother might have ordered someone to kill me, my dad's clumsy attempts to parent didn't seem as bad as they otherwise might have. Then again, on any other day, I might have actually let myself believe that things were going to change.

That we were capable of it.

"I stole your car," I said, because that seemed like as good a way as any to put an end to this father–daughter bonding session before it started.

"Oh," my father replied, blinking rapidly. "I thought maybe I forgot where I parked it."

That nearly startled a laugh out of me. It was comforting to know that the absentminded professor wasn't just forgetful when it came to pesky little details like my birthday, my age, and when and where he was supposed to pick me up.

"I got you a new phone." With an awkward little smile, my father turned back toward the counter and then handed me a new cell phone. "I remember you said you broke yours."

"A month ago. I broke that one a month ago." I hadn't meant to say that out loud, and when the smile faded from his face, I wanted to kick myself. My father was what he was, but at least he was trying.

At least he wasn't evil.

At least he'd stayed.

"I mean, thanks," I said, taking the phone. "And sorry about the car."

He raised an eyebrow. "Want to tell me where you were today?"

I tried to remember the last time he'd asked me a question that direct, but couldn't. "I actually went by the university," I said. "I saw part of your lecture."

The expression on his face wavered, and for a second, I thought he was going to laugh, or cry, or both. Instead, he shrugged.

"Nothing you haven't seen before, Kali."

He hesitated, ever so slightly, when he said my name, and I couldn't help hearing *her* say it.

Kali, baby. Kali-Kay.

I turned toward the sink and made a show of washing my hands. I waited for my father to say something else, and I told myself that if he asked, I'd tell him.

I'd tell him everything.

This was a game I played, one I always, always lost. *If he asks me why there's blood on my shirt, I'll tell him. If he asks me where I'm going, I'll tell him. If he asks why I don't have any friends, or if I want to go out to dinner, or if I'm doing okay—I'll tell him.*

In the past few years, I'd made those bargains with myself—and with the universe—a million times. If, if, if—and it never came to anything.

He never asked.

Until now.

"What's going on with you, Kali? You seem . . ." He trailed off, at a loss for words—clearly an unusual experience for a man known for giving eloquent lectures. "Are you okay?"

"No." I hadn't meant to say the word, but fair was fair. He'd asked. All those years, all those conditional statements, and now, he'd finally asked. "I saw my mother today."

For a moment, he was silent. He wrinkled his forehead, like whatever language I was speaking, it wasn't quite English. "Your mother?" he repeated finally.

"Contributor to half of my gene pool. About yea tall." I raised my hand to demonstrate. "Looks a little bit like me, only prettier."

"Kali, your mother—I'm sure it wasn't her."

If only that were true.

"This woman's name was Rena. Rena Malik."

I could tell by the look on his face that he knew that name, knew her.

"That was her name," I said softly. "Wasn't it?"

It was a funny thing not to know about your own mother, but since my father and I didn't talk about her, I'd never actually known her name.

"Rena," my father said, like she was standing right there in the kitchen with us, an ever-present ghost.

"Rena Malik," I said again. "I guess she never took your last name."

"We weren't married," my father said absently.

"You weren't?"

I don't know why that surprised me, but I guess I'd always just assumed that they were. My father wasn't the type of guy to have a kid out of wedlock.

"Kali, your mother and I weren't . . . *together*." My father chose his words very carefully. "She moved in with me after you were born, but the two of us were never . . . that is to say . . ."

If I hadn't wanted to hear my father give a lecture on sexual selection, I certainly didn't want to hear a play-by-play of my own conception, via a one-night stand.

"Where did you see her?" With that question, my father seemed to gain his composure—and an intensity that I hadn't heard anything but academia bring out in him in a very long time.

"She didn't see me." That wasn't exactly what he'd asked, but it wasn't like I could tell him that I'd seen my mother in Paul Davis's basement lab.

"Okay," he said. "Good."

"Good?" I repeated.

"Your mother," he said. "Rena—she . . . she's not the mother-
ly type, Kali."

"And you're the fatherly type?" I asked him. He blanched.

"Fair enough," he said after a moment. "I know I'm not
perfect, but—your mother didn't leave, Kali."

Of all the words he might have said, those were the last
ones I was expecting.

"What?"

She didn't want us, and she left. That was what he'd told
me for as long as I could remember.

"I left. I left her, and I took you with me."

I tried to imagine a world in which my father would have
volunteered to be a single parent. I tried to imagine what
could possibly have compelled him to do a thing like that.

The tests. The secrets. The games.

It was all hovering right out of reach, my memory hazy
and incomplete.

"What did she do?" I asked, my voice hoarse, my hands
shaking.

My father turned, busying himself with something at the
counter. "It was a long time ago, Kali."

Can you say gun? a voice whispered from somewhere in
my memory.

"What did she do to me?" I asked, my body running cold,
my muscles hardening to stone.

Sit still, Kali. Sit so still.

Time for my shot.

A possibility occurred to me, one I should have thought

of much, much sooner. One that made sense of the splinters I'd seen of my own past, one that answered every question I'd ever had about why I was the way I was.

Maybe they'd made me that way.

I'd spent my entire life thinking that maybe my mother was like me, that maybe my condition was hereditary, but what if it wasn't?

My father was a scientist.

My mother worked for Chimera.

Chimera specialized in making monsters.

Something snapped inside of me, and I walked over to the counter and opened the knife drawer. I pulled out a cutting knife, the largest of a set of five. I turned calmly back to my father. His brow wrinkled, and he realized what I was going to do a second before I did it.

He reached out to grab my hand, and I threw him off— threw him too hard, and he skidded across the floor, eyes wide. I took a step forward and brought the knife to my arm.

Slice, slice, slice.

Steel slid into my flesh. Blood welled up on the surface of my skin. I'd cut myself long and deep, and from his spot on the floor, my father made a choking, strangled sound.

I threw the knife down. With my right hand, I wiped the blood off my left. It smeared, and I turned to the sink and turned on the water. Mechanically, I washed off the cut.

I held my arm up, and my father watched in sick fascination as the skin began knitting itself back together.

"Am I even your daughter?" I asked. Maybe they'd just found me somewhere. Maybe I'd been their specimen, the way Zev was Chimera's.

"Yes," my father said, his voice shaking. "You're my daughter. And Rena's."

There were words then, so many words, coming out of my father's mouth. He'd been a junior professor. Rena had been a graduate student. She'd come to him with a mysterious blood sample.

"Get to the point." I meant to sound brisk. I didn't mean to beg. "Please."

He stammered. "Th-th-the idea that there might be preternatural humans, as similar to us as a yeti is to a gorilla . . . it was incredible, Kali. But we only had that one sample, and it wasn't enough."

I saw where this was going, saw it as clearly as the features on his face, but I didn't make it any easier for him. I just waited, the blood-covered knife gleaming on the counter.

"The DNA was close enough to human that Rena thought that we could splice it into the human genome, if the intervention happened early enough in development."

"How early?" I asked, wondering if I'd ever been normal. If I'd ever even had a chance.

"Conception," my father said, his voice hoarser even than mine.

Conception, I thought. So that was my answer. I hadn't ever been normal. I hadn't ever had a chance.

From his position on the floor, my father begged me with his eyes to understand. "My DNA, your mother's, our test subject's . . . we knew it probably wouldn't take. But it did, and suddenly, Rena was pregnant, and the two of us had to face the reality that this wasn't just some abstract thing. It wasn't just DNA. It was a baby." He paused and climbed to his feet. "It was you."

I'd spent the past five years wondering why I was the way I was, wondering what was wrong with me.

"Congratulations," I said. "Guess your experiment worked."

"But it didn't!" The words burst out of my father's mouth. "We ran the tests—ran them again and again, Kali, but they all came back human. You were human. And you were ours."

Their *experiment*.

"Things were fine, for a while. You were such a good baby, and Rena—she adored you, Kali. The way she used to look at you . . . I thought that maybe it was worth it. All of the risks we'd taken, the laws we'd broken, the lines we'd crossed—because at the end of the day, we had you. But then, when you were about two, Rena got a new job, in the private sector. She started hearing rumors about an undiscovered preternatural species. And the more she heard about what they could do, the more convinced she became that you might have inherited something."

It was all so clear in my mind now. The games. The trips to the lab. They'd taken my blood and hooked me up to machines and run every test known to man.

And when that hadn't worked, Mommy and I had started playing games at home.

"She quit her job to stay home with you full-time. I should have known, Kali, but I didn't. We were . . . *happy*. You adored her. And then one day, I came home, and you were holding a gun. You were playing with it, and she was just staring at you." His voice started catching in his throat. "We'd been told that alt-humans—that's what they were calling them then—that alt-humans had an affinity for weapons. But you didn't. You were just a three-year-old kid, and that gun was loaded."

I thought of the gun safe at Bethany's house, of the zombies mobbing me and the way the weapons sung in my hand.

"I'm not three years old any more," I said. "And I'm not human."

After all these years of keeping secrets, of dancing around even the simplest truths in our relationship, it was suddenly very easy to say.

"It started when I was twelve—right after my first period. I woke up really early one morning, and everything was different. I needed to get out of the house. To hunt." I looked back at the knife on the counter. "That's what we do, you know. People like me. We hunt the things that go bump in the night. We feel them like bugs crawling beneath our skin, and we hunt them down, and we keep them from killing anyone else."

My father didn't say a word—not a single word.

"Didn't you ever wonder?" I asked. "Didn't you ever see the clothes in the trash, the blood? Did you even notice when I wasn't in my bed at night? And in the papers, they were always talking about vigilantes and poachers and whatever else they call people who hunt the monsters instead of calling Preternatural Control. God, Dad, I broke into your lab."

"The zombies," he said dully. "My work. That was you?"

"It was always me," I said roughly. "Because that's what I am. That's what you made me—only I didn't know that. I never knew why. I didn't even know what."

"But that's impossible," my father said, shaking his head, as if that could make what I was saying any less true. "I tested you, every year, just to be sure. You took physicals. And your blood work always came up clean."

I shrugged. "Sometimes I'm human. Sometimes I'm not. It's not all that difficult to miss an appointment and reschedule it for a time when I'm just a girl."

Just an ordinary girl.

Yeah, right.

"Does your mother know?" His voice was honey-smooth and clear, like he'd recovered his composure, but his eyes were as dead as any zombie's. "If she does, we have to leave. Now. Tonight. It won't be easy, but I have some money set aside. We'll be fine for a while . . ."

"I have no idea what that woman knows," I said, "but I'm not going anywhere, and neither are you."

It shocked me that he wanted to, that he would pick up and leave everything behind—his career, our house, his friends . . .

He's done it before, I thought, and the reminder almost broke me all over again. The two of us had never been more than ships passing in the night. He had his life, and I had mine, and the only time the two coincided was when he needed a plus one.

"What Rena and I did was wrong, Kali. I know that. I've known it for a very long time, and when I look at you, when I think about what we did to you . . ."

I'd spent all of these years thinking he didn't care. And maybe he didn't, not the way fathers were supposed to, but there was something between us—something so powerful and awful and overwhelming that it hurt him to look at me.

"I was never good at this. She was, your mother. She

knew how to play with you and how to talk to you, and God, you adored her. You asked for her every night, every single night . . ." He trailed off. "She loved you, in her own way, but this—her being here, you being different . . . it's too much, Kali. It's a risk."

He didn't know the half of it.

"It's my risk to take," I said finally. "One way or another, it'll be over soon."

I waited for him to ask what I meant. *If he asks, I'll tell him . . .*

This time, he didn't.

There comes a moment in every kid's life when they look at their parents and realize that they're people—stupid and fallible and as breakable as the rest of us. Standing there, an ocean of space between me and my father, I realized that maybe he had tried. That maybe it hadn't been easy for him. That I'd never made it any easier.

I realized that maybe he did love me, just a little.

I hated him—for what he'd done to me and what he'd never done for me. I hated him because for years I'd been going through this alone, and if he'd told me, given me even a single hint about the way I'd come into this world, I wouldn't have had to.

I hated him, but I loved him, too. And when it came to family, I didn't have anyone else—I wouldn't ever have anyone else.

For better or worse, this was it.

"Don't worry about me," I told him, walking toward the door and pausing just long enough to press my lips to his temple. "I promise, Daddy—I can take care of myself."

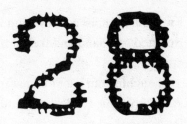

So now I knew—what I was, how I'd gotten that way, why my father had never been able to look me straight in the eyes.

I collapsed on the end of my bed and set the cell phone he'd bought me to the side.

My mother was a psychopath.

My father was the good parent.

And I was an experiment they'd whipped up in some test tube.

Kali?

Until I heard Zev's voice, I hadn't realized how much I'd missed it. Missed him. But right now, I didn't want someone else in my head. I didn't want anyone or anything. I wanted to be left alone.

Close your eyes.

What was the point in convincing myself that I didn't care if he could tell that I did? I wasn't okay. I might never be okay again.

Just close your eyes, Kali. It wasn't an order—just a request—and I let my eyelids get very heavy, let them close all on their own.

And just like that, I wasn't sitting on the edge of the bed.

I was standing in a forest, and Zev was standing next to me. He lifted one hand and trailed it over my cheek.

"Hello."

Laughter burst out of my mouth. We were having some kind of psychic rendezvous, and *that* was what he had to say for himself?

"Hello, Kali." His breath was warm on my skin, his presence coating my body, beckoning me forward as he repeated the first words he'd ever spoken to me, back when I was human and half afraid I was losing my mind. "I'm Zev."

"Hello, Zev," I said, leaning into his touch. "Have you been enjoying the show?" My voice was sharp, bordering on bitter. "Drama, revelations, betrayal . . . just another day in the D'Angelo household."

"You're hurting," he said.

"I'm an experiment," I countered. "What did you call that thing at the ice rink? 'Unnatural'? And what does that make me?"

Cooked up in a test tube. Manufactured so my parents could run tests on my blood. A *thing*.

"That makes you special," Zev said, bringing his free hand to the other side of my cheek and cupping my face. "It makes you unique."

He meant the words. I knew he did, but that didn't make me believe them. It didn't make them true.

"You're my other self," Zev said, sensing my refusal, pushing harder. "We're two halves of the same whole."

His hand trailed down my face, my neck. He lifted it off my skin, and my back arched, longing for the contact. His palm landed on my stomach, and I felt a burst of warmth under his touch. Suddenly, I was acutely aware of the parasite inside of me: I could feel it, like a tiny ball of light, and for the first time, I felt something from it other than *thirst*.

On instinct, I reached out my own hand, rested my palm on Zev's chest, just over his heart. Another burst of warmth, a realignment of the world, a *yes* overtook my body, my mind.

"Nibblers come in pairs," Zev said. "The one inside of you, the one inside of me—they're matched."

I thought through what Zev was saying and realized that it was his bad luck that the chupacabra matched to his had chosen someone like me. Not natural. Not normal. Not real.

"If given a choice," Zev said, "believe me, I'd choose you."

I closed my eyes, laid my head on his chest, listened to his beating heart.

"This isn't real," I murmured.

"No," he agreed. "It's all in my head. It's all in yours."

It didn't feel imaginary. It didn't feel fake. It felt safe and warm and like here, in our minds, we could make the world anything we wanted it to be.

"Now you know," Zev said, "why two years is nothing."

Two years. That was the amount of time he'd spent in Chimera's possession. I wondered if he came here, to this place in his mind, whenever they took their pound of flesh.

People like us couldn't feel pain.

We couldn't feel fear.

And once we'd been bitten, we were connected.

Brrrriiiinnggggg!

I came out of the trance suddenly, and it took me a moment to pinpoint the sound that had brought me back— the ringing of a phone. I spent one second wondering who could possibly be calling a number I didn't even know myself, but the answer became readily apparent the second I answered the phone.

"I have an address," Skylar said. "According to Reid, it's an old military base that hasn't belonged to the government since the fifties. It's supposed to be abandoned—something about radiation—but satellite scans suggest there's geothermal activity." She paused. "This *is* Kali, right?"

I made a face at the phone. "Did you just dial a number at random?"

I could practically hear her smiling. "Maybe."

I glanced down at my watch. *Twelve hours and two minutes.*

I wanted to see Zev—see him for real. I wanted to save him, and I didn't have much time.

"Hey, Skylar?" I said. "Can you send me that address?"

If I can't break out of here, what makes you think that you can break in?

Zev's question may have been rhetorical, but I did him the favor of answering, anyway.

Easy, I replied, slipping my cell into my pocket. *The bad guys* want *me in.*

For the first time since I'd recognized my mother, I smiled without feeling nauseous. I could do this.

I would do this.

I had to.

Shutting my mind against Zev's voice—velvet and smooth inside my head—I set to work. The moment I turned my mind to what needed to be done, I felt a slight vibration in the air, a song singing me closer, luring me in. The palms of my hands itched as I scanned the house for weapons.

I could do this.

I would do this.

I had to.

I started in my bedroom and worked my way quickly through the rest of the second floor. I didn't have as many weapons as another person might have had in my position, but I'd been hunting for five years, and during that time, the weapons I did have had been stashed all over the house. A knife here, a dagger there, the occasional sword.

My dad had a gun.

One by one, I tracked each of them down and tucked them into my clothing, heightened awareness of each blade bringing what I was about to do fully into focus. I saved the gun for last and tucked it into the waistband of my jeans, nestled against the small of my back.

Ready.

Armed to the teeth, I slipped out of the house, the way I had a thousand times before. This time, there was a chance my dad might actually miss me before I returned.

If I returned.

The thought gave me pause—but not nearly enough. I took one step away from the house, and then another. A moment later, I was walking, and a second after that, I broke into a run.

The address Skylar had given me was outside of town. Driving would have been easier and faster, but if things went well, I deeply suspected I wouldn't want to leave even a trace of evidence behind.

Getting Zev out of there wouldn't be enough. To end this, really end this, we'd have to make sure that there wasn't anyone left to chase us.

We'd have to crush Chimera—and everyone who worked there—to dust.

† † †

Running toward Zev felt better than anything had in a very long time. It felt like I was doing something.

Like I was going home.

I don't know how long it took me to get there. Time lost all meaning—a dangerous thing for someone like me—but by the time I came to a stop at a dead-end road, more desert than not, the sun was starting to set.

Prime hunting time, I thought, my body relishing the darkness as it slowly kissed the earth.

Go. Hunt. Just do it somewhere else.

The closer I got to Zev, the harder it was to brace myself against the sound of his voice—and the harder his words were to ignore.

Believe me, Kali, I'd rather be trapped here for another year—or two or three or thirty—than risk something happening to you. And if you come here, something *will*—

He broke off, like he couldn't bear to finish that sentence.

You can't ask me to just leave you there, I told him, and then, realizing that he could and had and probably was about to again, I clarified my words. *Don't.*

Why does it matter where my body is? Zev asked. It's just a body, Kali. They can't touch anything that matters.

All I heard was the word *body*, and all I could think of were the things they were doing to his. It was like living through an autopsy—over and over and over again.

I don't want you here, Zev said. I knew, in the pit of my stomach, that he was entirely aware how those words would sound to someone who'd never really felt wanted by anyone, until now.

Just go away.

That was what Zev said, but I was so close now that I could feel him thinking other things. I remembered the feel of my hand on his stomach, the feel of his on mine. Zev could tell me I wasn't wanted until my ears rang with the words, and it still wouldn't matter.

People like us were meant to come in pairs.

That thought fresh in my mind, I stopped running. I was close enough now that I could almost smell Zev's blood, could see the way they'd bled him again and again. The road itself wasn't abandoned, but the address Skylar had given me didn't exactly look commercial, either.

The entire complex was surrounded by a barbed-wire fence, rusted and rotting, like it hadn't been replaced in decades. There was a sign out front that warned would-be trespassers that the land beyond this fence had once been used to test explosives. Like the fence, the sign had seen better days: WARNING, it read, UNDE ONATED INES.

"Undetonated mines," I said, feeling like I'd solved the puzzle on *Wheel of Fortune*. "Isn't that convenient?"

I scanned the perimeter of the fence—there was only one access road. It led up to a single gate, with an abandoned guard post.

The gate was open. I took a step toward it, and Zev's voice echoed with bone-shaking vehemence through my entire body.

You don't have to do this.

I looked at the fence, the gate, the building in the distance. "Yeah," I said softly. "I do."

"Do what?"

My hand tightened over the handle of one of my knives,

but as my eyes adjusted to the newborn darkness, I saw the very last person I'd expected to see gracing a deserted road with her presence.

Bethany Davis.

"This is the place, right?" Bethany said. I looked past her—she'd parked her BMW just on the other side of the gate. "This is the address Skylar gave me."

"Skylar told you to come here?" I asked dumbly.

"No," Bethany said. "Skylar told me *not* to come here. Same dif."

"I knew you'd come if I told you not to." Skylar rounded the bend in the road a second after I heard her voice. "Reverse psychology. Behold my genius."

As Skylar walked fully into view, I realized she wasn't alone.

"Elliot?" Bethany said, sounding as surprised as I felt. "What are you doing here?"

"My little sister snuck out of the house carrying a circular-saw blade and a can of Mace." Elliot gave Skylar a look. "I couldn't exactly let her come alone."

A can of Mace? What did Skylar think she was going to do, pepper-spray the big, bad biomedical conglomerate into submission?

"Look," I said. "I appreciate the gesture, but whatever Chimera is keeping in there—" I gestured to the land that lay beyond the barbed wire—"I'm betting it's not pretty, and I can't do what I need to do if I have to worry about the three of you."

"You can't do it without us," Skylar corrected. "I've seen it, Kali—seen it for as long as I can remember. Most of the psychic stuff, it's pretty new, but this place, tonight, us—I've been dreaming it since I was twelve."

Elliot ground his teeth together. "For the last time, Skye, you aren't psychic."

She met his eyes, and I was reminded of the things she'd told me in Bethany's dad's lab—*It's going to get better. But first, it's going to get worse.*

"Yeah, El," Skylar said softly, "I am psychic. And you can pretend to be a skeptic, but if you hadn't believed me when I said we should come, you would have duct-taped me to a chair in the kitchen instead of coming with." Skylar must have seen the question in my eyes, because she clarified for me: "I've been duct-taped to chairs *a lot*."

Sensing that she'd gone off topic, Skylar smiled—a sad smile, the kind strangers exchange in cemeteries when they don't know what to say.

Sometimes there aren't any good choices, she'd told me. *Sometimes making the right one is hard.*

"You don't have to do this," I told her, unsure what it was that she thought she had to do, but feeling the weight of it in the air between us.

"Yeah," Skylar replied, responding to my assertion the exact same way I had replied to Zev's, "I do. If you go in there by yourself, they'll kill you. You'll die."

There was something about the way she said the words that made me believe her, absolutely and without reserve.

"If we don't go with you, you'll die, and a hundred thousand things that are supposed to happen—things that you could do—will die, too."

I wanted to ask her how I could do anything, how one

genetic freak of a girl could be of any importance at all, but before I could, Skylar switched from psychic proclamations to good old-fashioned logic. "Evidence has a way of disappearing when it implicates powerful people, Kali. You're evidence, and they've already tried to kill you once. They're obviously going to try again."

"As much as it pains me to admit this," Bethany interjected, "Skylar's right. One dead teenager in the middle of nowhere is easy enough to explain. Four dead teenagers, two of whom have a brother in the FBI? That gets tricky no matter who the CEO is bribing, blackmailing, or sleeping with."

In Bethany-ese, I took that to mean something along the line of "there's safety in numbers."

And maybe that would have been true—if there was any safety to be had. Glancing out over the dirt-dry land to the building in the distance, I got the feeling that there wasn't.

The sign in front of this complex might as well have been labeled POINT OF NO RETURN.

"I'm bulletproof." I countered Bethany's logic with fact. "You guys aren't. Worst-case scenario, they catch me. Worst-case scenario, you die."

I saw my words hit home with Elliot. Bethany pursed her lips. Sensing the chink in their armor, I turned the full force of my gaze on Skylar.

"You either let the bad things happen," she said softly. "Or you don't."

Her eyes shone—with certainty or tears, I wasn't sure which. "Everybody has choices. This is mine."

And then, before any of the rest of us could sort out

the exact meaning of her words, she turned on her heels and ran.

Right through the gate.

† † †

I caught up with Skylar quickly enough, but by the time I did, the gate that had separated the premises from the rest of the desert had clamped shut behind us.

Someone knew we were here.

"Stay behind me," I hissed. She melted into my back. The sound of footsteps told me that Elliot and Bethany weren't far behind. For better or worse now, the four of us were in this together—at least until I could find a way to get the three of them out.

"We get in, we get Zev, and we get out," I said, revising my earlier plan. Reducing this facility to ashes and dust would have to wait. I had more to think about now than just Zev.

"It's a search and rescue," Skylar said, nodding. "Got it. My brother Charlie is in the marines."

Of course he was. One of these days, Skylar and Elliot were going to run out of brothers. It was only a matter of time.

"Kali," Bethany said, her voice a ghost of a whisper, lost to the desert night, "we have visitors."

I expected to see the men in suits, or, worse, Rena, but instead, I saw eight pairs of blood-red eyes, glowing with hunger.

Hellhounds. Again.

"Seriously," I said. "These things are not endangered."

Automatically, my mind started playing out ways this fight

could go. I was faster and stronger than I'd been two days earlier, but there were eight of them this time. Three adults, five juveniles—all bigger, heavier, and uglier than me.

"Stay back," I told the others, keeping my voice low and praying that Skylar wouldn't get any more crazy ideas and that Beth wouldn't feel compelled to give a repeat belly-dancing performance.

I continued eyeing the beasts. "No sudden movements."

I'd bled enough in these clothes that if given the choice, the hellhounds would probably go for me and not my friends, but *probably* wasn't good enough—not when there was anyone's life at stake but my own.

"Stay back," I said again as I wracked my mind, trying to find a way that this didn't end in human bloodshed. "I can handle this."

Take out the adults first, Zev advised darkly. **Then go for the pups.**

Beside me, Skylar brandished her Mace. Bethany appeared to be holding a gun. As best I could tell, Elliot seemed to have come to this fight armed only with a pair of lawn shears.

This could not possibly end well.

Your humans are very strange, Zev said, as if that were the primary issue here. I could feel the hunt-lust rising in his body, the same as in mine.

Yeah, I replied, the world around me going very quiet and very still. *They are.*

A second before the largest male made its move, I made mine, flinging the knife in my hand and listening for the satisfying *thunk* it made as it tore through flesh and hit bone, knocking my target back and off its feet.

The remaining hellhounds growled and began circling. I kept my body between the others and the monsters, willing those beady red eyes to follow *my* movements, mark *my* scent.

The one I'd felled made a high-pitched gargling sound, and it stirred something inside of me.

Thirsty.

Now.

I leapt the moment I heard Zev's whisper, but this time, as my body collided with a hellhound's, I wasn't the one who went flying backward.

It did.

Its teeth tore into my flesh. My knife tore into its. The smell of sulfur and blood propelled me onward, as familiar and comforting as towels straight out of the dryer. Sword in one hand and a dagger in the other, I skewered the hound on top of me and was rewarded by its mate trying to detach my head from my body.

Behind me, one of the pups launched itself at Elliot. Skylar maced it.

I'd barely registered that fact before the beast I was fighting reared up, sending its massive skull directly into my chin. My head snapped back. I tasted blood in my mouth, but somehow, my dagger found its way to the beast's eye.

That was when I lost myself to the moment, the weapons, the fight. There was a rhythm to it, unbreakable and swift. I felt like I was dancing. It rained blood.

As I dispatched the one I'd stabbed in the eye, the largest juvenile—nearly full-grown—came at me from behind, snapping its massive jaw and nearly bisecting me at the waist. But I was too fast for it, and it only got a piece.

A tiny piece.

I thrust my sword arm backward, catching another one of the beasts straight through its heart. Black-red blood bubbled to the surface, but the sound of a human scream kept me from taking it—any of it—for myself.

Bethany.

I whirled around, expecting to see her impaled on razor-sharp teeth, but instead, I saw her staring in horror at Skylar.

She was lying on the ground—very still. She was bleeding.

One, two, three, four.

I couldn't remember how many I'd killed. However many it was, it wasn't enough. Elliot had managed to jam his shears back into the throat of the smallest pup, but it was still growling. I leapt for Skylar, but one of the remaining hounds took a swipe at my legs.

Inhuman rage bubbled up inside of me. In the bat of an eyelash, I had the beast's head—as broad as a truck tire—in my hands. I pressed them together, my muscles tensing to the point that I thought they might snap, the beast's bones cracking under the onslaught.

I met its eyes, and then, I tightened my grip and twisted.

A moment later, I flung its limp body to the side like a rag doll and eyed the remaining hellhounds.

There were two left—just two. They must have seen it in my eyes—the hunger, the rage—because they ran. With their tails between their legs, they lumbered off into the distance. I wanted to follow, but I didn't. I made my way back to Skylar instead.

Her head was lying to one side. She was pale, bleeding, deathly still, and I froze.

I'd known she was holding something back—about tonight, about this place, about coming here, helping me. Her eyes shining, she'd told me that *this* was her choice.

No, I thought. *Oh, God. No.*

I knelt next to her and felt for a pulse.

"Are they gone?" she asked, opening one eye.

Relief—bittersweet and warm—surged through my body, and I jerked my hand away from her neck. "You're okay?"

"I got clawed a little," she said. "Playing dead seemed like a really good idea at the time."

"Playing dead?" Elliot repeated, and I saw in his eyes that he'd bought her act as much as I had. From the moment I'd seen her lying there, I'd been sure that the worst had happened, that I'd killed her by not being fast enough, strong enough, smart enough.

"I'm fine," Skylar said. "And even if I wasn't—I chose this. I knew what it was going to be like, and it was my choice to make. Deal."

For a corpse, she was starting to get pretty mouthy.

"Come on," I said, wishing more than ever that I could send them back. "Let's go."

We moved forward, step by careful step, me on point and the others bringing up the rear. The world was silent, absolutely silent all around us, until I heard Skylar whisper a single word into the back of my head.

"Duck."

One word. Just one whispered word—but I did it. I fell to a crouching position the second before some kind of spear came whizzing by my head, close enough that I could feel the breeze it left in its wake. Close enough that if I hadn't ducked, it would have taken off my head.

I should have heard it coming. I should have smelled it: meat and day-old blood and something sickly sweet. Without thinking, I grabbed hold of the closest hellhound body. I dug my fingers into its hide and pulled, ripping off a chunk of flesh.

In one smooth motion, I stood, brandishing the hide as a shield.

"Okay, now that is disgusting," Bethany said.

I didn't reply. I was too busy waiting for the next shot— and tracing its trajectory back to the thing that had shot it.

I could see it in the distance, guarding the entrance to the building. It took me a moment to place it. Tail of a scorpion, body of a lion, three rows of razor-sharp teeth.

"Is that a manticore?" Skylar said. "Aren't they extinct?"

Apparently not. Of all the creatures in the preternatural world, this one most resembled the kind of hybrids that Chimera was trying to build. It looked like a dozen different creatures sewn together by the devil's seamstress. I catalogued its weapons: the teeth, the tail, the poisonous spines. A niggling sensation told me that I was forgetting—something that I'd read in a book.

Its voice, Zev said. Knowledge flooded my body—memories that weren't mine, fights that my body hadn't taken part in.

Lions roared. Harpies screamed. And manticores—with their human mouths and shark teeth—did something else, something unbearable and ungodly.

I processed the facts, but not fast enough, and the

manticore's cry reached my ears. It was like someone was taking a chainsaw to my eardrums, making mincemeat of my brain. For the first time ever in this form, I felt something that resembled pain.

Blood poured out of my ears.

The others went down beside me, hands clasped over their ears, writhing in pain. I felt the warmth of blood on my face, trickling out of my nose, as the beast fired—one spine after another digging into my makeshift shield.

Skylar shoved something into my hands—the saw blade—and without thinking, I threw it. It cut through the air, a ring of silver light in the darkness.

I saw the moment it made contact. There was another scream and then silence—just the sound of a heavy object dropping down onto sand.

The manticore's head.

"I thought that would come in handy," Skylar said, satisfaction lacing her tone.

She'd already saved my life once here tonight, when she'd told me to duck. Whether or not her choice of weapon had made a difference in this kill, she'd already made good on her word that having them there would make the difference between life and death for me.

"I'm glad," Skylar said fiercely. "I'd do it again."

Sometimes, I thought, sparing a smile for my small blonde friend, *crazy's all you've got.*

"Come on," I said, ready to put this night behind us. "Let's get this done."

We managed to close the space between us and the building without straying from the path. The tracker in me could see the places where wheels and feet had trodden before—safe places, in this rotting minefield.

Or at least, as safe as any place inside these gates could be.

How does the government not know about this place? I wondered. The simplest answer was probably that they did—or that they'd chosen not to. I consciously sidestepped that thought as we came up to the door. I was on the verge of kicking it in when it opened, and I found myself inches away from the one kind of adversary about whom my instincts had absolutely nothing to say.

Humans.

Even in the dim light of the evening, I recognized Rena's lackeys from the school, and they recognized me. The fact that I was walking around when they'd left me for dead on the side of the road seemed like the kind of thing their type would take as an insult, but their faces remained completely impassive.

They didn't draw their weapons.

They didn't say a word.

They just waited.

That was when I noticed the light glow to the air.

"Fireflies," Skylar said, thoroughly bewitched.

Not fireflies, I thought.

"Don't look at it," I ordered. Skylar smiled and tilted her head to the side. She walked right past me. I grabbed for her arm, but she pulled out of my grasp, following the tiny ball of light.

Beside me, I could feel Elliot and Bethany going slack, the tension melting out of their bodies as they took in the tiny dancing lights.

"They won't remember a thing tomorrow," one of the men in front of me commented. "Where they were, what happened . . . all they'll remember are the lights."

I cast my eyes downward, trying not to look directly at them myself.

Will-o'-the-wisps weren't deadly. They didn't feed on human flesh. They just confused people, led them off the path, made them feel like everything was all right, when it was anything but.

Even with my eyes cast downward, I could see Skylar tiptoeing farther and farther away.

"Skylar," I said sharply, lifting my eyes to hers.

She tilted her head to the side and smiled. "Pretty."

I could feel the magic working its way into my system, but I shook it off.

I wasn't safe.

These lights weren't pretty.

I shouldn't follow them . . .

"Well," one of the men said, "aren't you going to help your friend?"

Turning your back on an enemy was always a mistake. Always. But Skylar was getting farther and farther away. Making a split-second decision, I turned and was halfway to her, my body blurring with inhuman speed, when one of the men I'd left behind drew his gun.

He took aim and fired.

Not at me.

Not at Skylar.

At her feet. I was fast, but the bullet was faster. It hit the dirt. I ran toward Skylar, ran toward her with everything I had, but my mind was still gummy from the will-o'-the-wisps, and the man in the suit had known exactly where to aim.

Undetonated mines.

I heard the explosion before I saw it. Flames lit up the night sky, and the force of it sent me flying backward—away from Skylar.

From what was left of her.

As I lay there on the ground, the smell of charred flesh told me that this time, Skylar wasn't—couldn't—be playing. Tears stung my eyes until the only thing I could see was the memory of her face the second before the mine detonated, the expression on her childlike features.

Bliss.

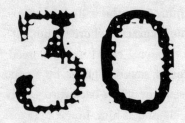

30

"Lay down your weapons, come with us, and no one else has to die." The man's voice was soulless and calm, as he aimed his gun at Elliot and Beth, and that was when I realized—

They'd killed Skylar to make a point. To make me malleable. To hurt me.

No.

Rage was a physical thing. It washed over my body until I was drowning in it, bubbled up from inside of me, like a volcano ready to explode. Inside and outside, hot and cold, it was everywhere, absolute.

I breathed it in, and I breathed it out. I swallowed the full force of it whole, because the alternative was giving into something else, that tiny voice in the back of my head that said that Skylar was . . .

No.

I tore my eyes away from the body that didn't even look like her, not any more, and I gave myself over to fury.

Blessed fury.

My eyes narrowed into slits. My fingers curled to claws. The man who'd killed Skylar must have sensed the danger, because he turned his gun from Bethany and Elliot to me.

I was on him in an instant.

He went down, hard, and his gun clattered down the hall-way like a rock skipping across water. I could have snapped his neck like a twig, a Popsicle stick, a toothpick.

But I didn't.

I straddled his body and backhanded him. I felt the crack of his cheekbone. I smelled his blood.

Beside us, his partner attempted to jab me with some sort of Taser. I reached back, grabbed him by the wrist and snapped it, angling the weapon back at his chest, his torso.

I smelled the scent of *his* charring flesh.

The second that Partner Guy went down, the lights in the air dissipated. Whatever I'd become, whatever I was on the verge of doing, even the will-o'-the-wisps seemed to know that now was the time to run.

I moved to toss the Taser to the side, but noticed a variety of controls across the bottom. Mechanically, I pressed each button. A blade popped out of the back end of the Taser. An alarm sounded.

And then, finally, the gate to the complex opened in the distance.

"Don't—," the man underneath me—still breathing, still alive, the way Skylar wouldn't ever be again—said. "You'll let them out."

"You killed her," I said, pinning him with my knees. "She never hurt anyone, and you killed her, just because you could." I looked him in the eye and dug my needle-sharp thumbnails into the balls of his shoulders, tearing through flesh until I hit bone.

He screamed.

"You killed her dead."

The voice that said those words didn't sound like my voice. It sounded old and angry, nearly feral.

"You're a killer."

I brought my face down near the man's. My lips nearly touching his face, I lifted my bloodied hands to his cheeks, painted them red.

Thirsty.

This time, I didn't fight it. I looked at the man. He looked at me. And then I buried my head in his neck.

Teeth met skin.

Skin broke.

And I fed.

Yes. Yes. Yes.

Yes to killing the man who'd killed Skylar.

Yes to the blood.

Yes to the red-hot fire and the feel of it against my throat and the living, breathing rage.

I could feel my pupils expanding, feel the man beneath me struggling, right up until the point when he didn't.

The phrase "go for the jugular" had always sounded merciless, but this—this was sweet.

I couldn't remember being human, couldn't fathom the fact that I ever would be again. And that was the way I liked it, because being human meant knowing, remembering . . . it meant looking back over my shoulder and seeing the girl I couldn't save.

The one who'd chosen to come here.

Chosen me.

You don't have to do this alone. You shouldn't have to.

Sometimes there are no good choices.

I'm glad.

Skylar's voice ringing in my mind, I let loose my prey and sat up. Power crackled through my body. I felt strong, like I could pinch a bone ever-so-lightly between my fingers and watch it crumble to dust.

A rustle of sound caught my ears, and I whirled around, catching the scent of sweat and human tears. Elliot was standing in the middle of the path, Bethany lying on the ground beside him. Her eyes locked on to my blood-smeared mouth, and she scrambled backward on all fours, like I might kill her next.

Like she was scared of me.

I'm scared of me, I thought. Blood on my face, my own heartbeat accelerating, I met Elliot's eyes.

"Skylar," he said roughly. "Where's Skylar?"

The name hurt. Just hearing it made me want to cling to the rage, the distance, the thirst . . . anything but this.

"Where is she?" Elliot said again, his voice echoing through darkness and desert, sharp as a whip.

I couldn't do this, couldn't think this, couldn't explain that the same creatures that had messed with his memories had led his sister off the path.

That she was dead.

Gone.

Just a body—and not much of one at that.

Without meaning to, my gaze flitted toward what remained of my first—only—

Friend, I thought dully. *The word is* friend.

Elliot followed my stare, and he flew to her side, no

questions, no hesitation. The few flames that hadn't burnt themselves out licked at his clothes and hands, but he ignored them.

Touching her would only burn him. I knew that. It wouldn't bring her back.

Moving slowly—for me, at least—I locked my hands around his shoulders and pulled him away from the fire, away from her. My eyes filled up with the things I couldn't say, but Elliot stared straight through me.

He pushed me away.

"I'll kill you," he said.

I closed my eyes, the night air cool against my blood-damp face. I wouldn't stop him. I wouldn't fight.

"Elliot," Bethany said, her voice breaking through the darkness. "This isn't . . . Kali wouldn't . . ."

She couldn't form the words—not when they'd seen me tear out a man's jugular with my teeth.

"Let's just go." Bethany's voice was little more than a whisper, but I heard her just the same.

Just like I heard Elliot let out a strangled breath.

Just like I heard the two of them walking, then running away.

† † †

I watched them go, and once they were gone, I watched the place where they had been. Then, finally, I moved back to the doorway, stepped over the guards' bodies, picked up the Taser, and pressed the button to open, then close the gate.

Nobody here but us monsters now, I thought.

I half expected Zev's voice to join the sound of my own, but if he was there, he was silent. Turning my attention from the inside of my head to what was going on outside it, I registered the ongoing ringing of alarms. I pressed another button on the Taser, and they stopped.

If anyone didn't know I was here before, they knew it now.

But as I tossed the Taser to one side and began walking down the single hallway, I couldn't shake the feeling that there wasn't anyone else.

Just me and the monsters.

I could feel them—close, but not too close, more of them than I could count. And yet, in this one, scant hallway, there was nothing but me and silence and the men I'd killed.

The ones who'd killed Skylar.

No. I wouldn't think her name. I wouldn't think anything—but no matter how hard I tried, I couldn't find my way back to that place of pure rage. I couldn't pretend that I wasn't frightened of the thing I'd done.

The thing I *was.*

Unarmed but for the gun at the small of my back and my smallest knife, I walked forward, my hands held out to the side, like I was some kind of dancer, like this was a tightrope instead of a hallway, and all eyes were on me.

I noticed a blinking red light in the corner. A camera.

"You wanted me," I said. "Now you've got me."

I waited for my words to sink in, then broke the camera.

My body warm with human blood, it took me two minutes to pace the entire length of the building.

Nothing.

No people.

No monsters.

No Zev.

There was, however, an elevator, and seeing it allowed me to make sense of the things I was sensing, feeling.

The hunter in me sensed prey, but no matter which direction I walked, the siren call of the preternatural stayed exactly the same.

I wasn't getting any closer or any farther away, because getting to the beasties wasn't a matter of turning right or left.

I went back to the entryway and snagged one of the guards' IDs.

"Going down."

† † †

The elevator door opened, feeding me out into another hallway. Unlike the first, however, this one boasted a light at the end of the tunnel—metaphorically speaking. Actually, the "light" was dark and shadowed, and the farther I walked through the hallway, the darker it got. As I rounded the corner, I realized that as ruined and rotting as this building looked from the outside, here, underground, it was immaculate. White walls lined a tile floor, and the room at the end of the tunnel wasn't just a room.

It's a mausoleum.

Or at least, that was what it looked like. The antiseptic white of the hallway gave way to walls made of marble and stone. I stepped forward, feeling like I'd invaded the sanctuary of the dead, and fluorescent lights flooded the room.

Almost immediately, I located a camera identical to the one I'd destroyed, and I wondered if they'd brought up the lights for my benefit, or if the cameras were attached to motion sensors. Either way, I could make out a door on the other side of this cavernous room.

I could also see the shadows on the floor, each one vaguely human in shape. I retrieved my lone remaining knife, and then I looked up.

The ceiling was twenty feet high, maybe not quite that, which meant that the creatures hanging upside down from the rafters were eight or nine feet above my head. There were dozens of them, each with a human head, human limbs, a human body.

Each put together wrong.

"They're called the Alan," a voice said. I looked up and saw that the door on the far side of the room had opened. "We didn't make them, if that's what you're thinking. We found them in the Philippines. They're hybrids, natural ones— between our kind and yours."

Overhead, one of the Alan opened its eyes. They were startlingly blue. It dropped down to the ground beside me, and my mind processed the reason its body had appeared nearly human, but not quite.

Its arms and legs were on backward, its neck so thin it could barely support its head.

"They die young and can't reproduce without assistance." Rena Malik leaned back against the doorway. "Two- and three-helixed organisms can't naturally crossbreed with anything approaching success."

The Alan stuttered toward me, heels first.

"Watch out," my mother said. "It bites."

The creature didn't bite me. It came right up to me and nuzzled me, its skin so thin I could feel the contours of its bones.

I stepped back.

"You can kill it if you like," Rena said. I wouldn't think of her as my mother, not ever, not now. "I won't mind."

Can you say gun?

I thought of all the games, all the tests, and I dropped my knife arm to my side.

"Go back to sleep," I told the thing in front of me, sidestepping it and closing the space between me and the real enemy here.

"You could kill me, too," Rena said. "But right now, I'm the closest thing you have to a friend."

Skylar's face flashed into my mind. "You aren't my friend," I said sharply.

"No," Rena agreed. "I suppose not. But I am your mother."

Hearing her say that was worse than the feel of the Alan's cheek against my own.

"It's good to see you, Kali. If you wanted to see this, see me—all you had to do was ask."

My fingers tightened around the blade in my hand, but I couldn't make my arm move, because her voice, the way she said my name, the soft smile on her face—it was all exactly the same.

Like nothing had changed.

Like she hadn't missed out on more than a decade of my life.

Like this was a house, not a laboratory.

Like her men hadn't just killed Skylar.

Like I hadn't killed her men.

"I didn't know it was you until today," she told me, like that made some kind of difference. "I didn't know that the host was you, and now I do."

Her words unlocked my frozen muscles. Claiming not to have ordered *my* death wasn't enough—not when Skylar was ashes on the wind. In a single, fluid motion, I brought my knife down on the back of her head—hilt first.

She crumpled to the ground, and something threatened to give inside me. I pushed back against it.

Later, I thought.

I could break down later.

I could miss her and hate her and wish I'd never heard her say my name later.

Right now, I had to find Zev.

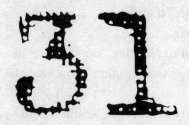

After the Alan, I'd expected Chimera's lab to be a little shop of horrors, but beyond the final door, it looked like any other research lab in any other facility in the country: clean, sterile, organized. Workstations lined a center island filled with enough equipment to give research types a geekgasm: electron microscopes and mass spectrometers and machinery I didn't even come close to recognizing. It was easy to picture the place bustling with men and women in white coats.

So why was it empty?

A company like Chimera had to have hundreds of employees, if not thousands. Even if most of those people worked on above-board projects, there had to be more people involved in this one than just She Who Shall Not Be Named and the men in suits.

Then again, I'd triggered some kind of alarm upstairs, and the only reason I'd been able to find this place was because the FBI had already gotten a lock on it.

They're already evacuating and shutting things down, I thought, the silence echoing all around me. *What if I'm too late?*

You're not. You need to leave, Kali. Please.

Zev had been silent for so long that the sound of his voice took me by surprise, and I clamped my lips into a straight line, refusing to show any external sign of weakness.

Where are you? I asked Zev silently, forcing myself to focus on the here and now.

Zev didn't answer, but I quickly realized that he didn't have to—hearing his voice had been enough, and now I could feel his presence like a beacon, calling me home. My inner compass guided me toward the far wall.

Another door.

This place was such a labyrinth. Each time I thought I'd reached my destination, another door popped up, and I had to venture farther and farther into the belly of the beast.

Luckily, the card I'd swiped to get down here worked for access on this door, too, and I let myself into another hallway: one lined with metal doors. A tiny slit-shaped window had been laid into each.

The smell of sulfur was overwhelming.

I walked down the hallway, trying not to look. I wasn't here to hunt, but still, I felt them.

Closer, closer, just a little closer . . .

"No," I said out loud, pushing down the urge to hunt. I was there for Zev. Everything else could wait. I forced myself to keep walking, and with each step, I felt a little warmer, a little more sure.

I caught sight of the clipboards hanging outside each door, but avoided reading the labels. I forcibly ignored the feeling of bugs crawling under my skin, the sound of scales scraping against concrete from behind one door, the near-human screams of some kind of primate, enraged, behind another.

Like clockwork, as I walked past each door, the beasts contained behind it came to life. They could smell me.

They wanted me dead.

My body quivered with the desire to return the favor, the *ouroboros* burning on my stomach, my chest, my back.

"Zev. Zev. Zev." I said his name out loud, focusing on the reason I'd come here—the reason I'd risked my life and others'.

Finally, at the end of the hallway, there was a door.

Unlike the rest, it didn't have a window. I couldn't peek in to see what it was hiding, but I knew. I tested the handle, then swiped the identification card. The lock gave, and a second later, I was standing in another hallway.

This place was a nightmare. An endless nightmare, with door after door after door, and I was never going to find him, never going to get out.

"Kali."

It took me a moment to realize that the voice wasn't in my head.

"Zev?" I rushed toward the end of this hallway. Toward the last door. I pressed my hands flat against the metal. My eyes were level with the viewing slit.

On the other side of the slit, there were eyes.

Dark eyes, light skin, lashes that belonged on a softer, more delicate face. They framed his eyes in a thick, ink-black fringe.

"Zev," I said, his name catching in my throat.

On the other side of the door, I could feel him placing his hands against the metal. I could almost feel his touch against mine, his breath against my skin.

I tried my card on this door, and the second I heard the lock give, the barrier holding back my emotions threatened to do the same.

I was so close now. So, so close.

Disbelief coloring his features, Zev pressed the door open, slowly, and stepped out into the hallway. He was taller than I'd thought he'd be, thinner than he'd looked in my dreams. He brought his hands to either side of my face, and I had one moment of utter peace, of feeling that this was how it was supposed to be.

He tilted his head to the side and looked at me like I was something precious. He ran his thumb over the skin of my cheek, and then he whispered, "I told you not to come here." His voice was tender, and then it broke. "You should have listened."

One second, his hands were on my cheeks. The next, they'd encircled my neck.

No.

My palms pressed back against his shoulders, but he didn't move.

I was fast. Strong. Inhuman. He was faster, stronger, older.

No matter how hard I fought, his hands stayed around my neck, like a metal collar. He squeezed, squeezed hard enough that a normal girl's head would have popped right off.

I can't breathe, I realized. *His hands are on my neck, and I can't breathe.*

This couldn't be happening. After everything, after *Skylar*—

Behind us, the animal screams of the other test subjects built to a crescendo, and I struggled against Zev's hold.

People like me didn't get scared, I reminded myself. We couldn't feel pain. But we could feel betrayal.

We needed to breathe.

"I told you not to come," Zev said, his voice wrapping its way around my body, steady and warm. "I tried."

The last thing I was conscious of before darkness claimed me—other than an incredible tightness in my lungs—was the sound of yet another door opening and closing. Footsteps crossing the hallway. And then, a pinch in my arm and a woman's voice.

"Hello, Kali. Welcome home."

I woke up inside a cell made of concrete—four feet by four feet, only about a head taller than me. My body was slumped against the wall. I checked my watch.

Four hours and fifteen minutes.

This was not good.

I fought back the haze that had descended over my body and belatedly remembered the pinching feeling of a needle being inserted into my flesh.

They'd drugged me.

They'd drugged me, and I was lying in a concrete prison, and Zev *knew.* He'd helped them hurt me.

I thought of Skylar, poor, stupid Skylar, who'd followed me here and died for her effort. She'd been so sure that she was supposed to, sure that whatever the cost, coming with me would be worth it, because if she didn't come, then I was going to die.

You made the wrong choice, I told her silently. *You should have let them kill me when you had the chance.*

But she hadn't. Skylar had chosen me, and now she was dead, and I was boxed in, the way Zev had been for years.

Zev. He was the one who'd done this to me. After everything—

I struggled to my feet, still dizzy from whatever they'd dosed me with.

"It was supposed to keep you out until sunrise," a female voice said. "I'm afraid we didn't anticipate your feeding on the guards upstairs. We would have altered the dose if we'd known you were taking human blood."

If the guards hadn't killed Skylar, I wouldn't have. Trying to rid my mind of that thought, I walked over to the thick metal door and stared out the slit, all too aware that this time, I was the one locked in. The eyes that stared back at me were a deep and mossy green. The eyelashes were light brown, the woman's skin the color of cream.

"Who are you?" I asked.

"I've had many names," the woman said. She smiled—even though I couldn't see her mouth, I could see it in her eyes. "You could say I've been around for a while."

She waited for her words to sink in, and I could see her eyes flicker with interest the exact moment I got it.

"You're a vampire." The word felt silly on my lips, even now, and the woman actually laughed at me.

"That word," she said, "never ceases to amuse me. I'm as human as you are. Though," she added with faux thoughtfulness, "I suppose that's a poor example—at least for another four hours or so."

Great. My captor knew about my shifting from one form to another—which meant that she knew that in another four hours, I'd be even more at their mercy than I was now.

"Why are you working for Chimera?" I asked her, my mind racing, trying to find a way out of this. "Do you have any idea what they're doing—to people like us? To the preternatural?"

"Kali," the woman said, thoroughly amused, "I don't work for Chimera. Chimera works for me."

One of these days, I was going to stop being caught off guard. I was going to be able to look down the road and see how the pieces of a puzzle fit together—but that day wasn't today.

"Chimera works for you," I repeated dumbly.

"Founder, president, and CEO," she said. "Guilty as charged."

"But why?" The question tore its way out of my mouth before I could stop it.

"Do you know, Kali, what we are?"

I knew. We were strong and fast, and once we'd been bitten, we were stronger, faster, and thirsty—for blood.

"We're hunters," I said, unwilling to say the v-word again.

"Hunters," the woman repeated. "Well, better predator than prey, I suppose." She smiled, thoroughly delighted with herself and with me. "There's a principle in evolutionary biology," she continued indulgently. "It's called the Red Queen's Hypothesis. It's taken from *Alice in Wonderland*—would you believe I actually knew Lewis Carroll? Tasty—but that's neither here nor there. In the book, the Red Queen comments that it takes all the running in the world just to stay in the same place. Evolution's like that, Kali. A species never reaches the point where it can stop evolving, because the rest of the world is always evolving, too. You can never stop, because the things you hunt will always be getting faster, stronger—and the same goes for the things that hunt you."

I thought of the creatures I'd hunted in the past five years—beasts that normal humans would never have stood a chance against.

"Natural, preternatural—they're just labels, Kali. If you took a giraffe and plopped it down in the middle of the Antarctic, it would look very strange, wouldn't it?"

The question was rhetorical, but my mind connected the dots and led me to the meaning behind her words. We were the giraffes in the Antarctic—freakish and unnatural because this wasn't the environment in which we'd evolved. My father's lecture at the university rang in my ears.

Are preternatural creatures really unnatural? Or are they simply the product of a different kind of evolution—one with a different starting point, a different progression?

"Zev said that people like us are from another place," I said slowly, my mind churning through the possibilities. "Another . . . planet?"

"Another planet?" the woman repeated, laughing gaily. "Little green men and life on Mars? How absolutely *precious*."

If she'd let me out of this cage, I'd show her "absolutely precious."

"We're from another *dimension*, dear. Hasn't that scientist father of yours taught you anything?" She held up her fist and then spread her fingers outward. "Big bang. Multiple earths. Flash forward forty million years, and all of those little differences from the beginning have yielded a very different environment—and very different creatures."

Her eyes sparkled, and I bit back nausea. There was something deadly there, something cold.

"There have always been people who catch momentary glimpses of the other side. Myths, legends, all those little stories that humans just love to tell each other—they had to come from somewhere, yes?" She sighed, a delicate, girlish sound. "Unfortunately, a few hundred years ago, through circumstances far above anything your pretty little head can grasp—some of *us* ended up stuck *here*. Permanently."

I got the feeling that she wasn't just talking about "us" as in vampires. She was talking about "us" as in the preternatural. Hellhounds and zombies, will-o'-the-wisps and basilisks, and everything else I'd hunted on my less-than-human days.

"Humans from our world are relatively good at blending. The other creatures . . . not so much. We kept them under wraps for as long as we could, but eventually, the cat got out of the bag."

Darwin. The hydra. My mind whirred with the implications. We'd always assumed that the preternatural had been here all along, that we'd only had to go looking to discover the truth, but if what my captor was saying was true . . .

She smiled, amused at the fact that she'd blown my mind. "Eventually, the existence of our kind will be common knowledge, too, and we're outnumbered here about ten million to one."

That meant there were others—like me, like Zev, like the crazy woman on the other side of the door.

"So you decided to, what? Join them in their scientific exploration?" I asked, but my voice came out more bewildered than sarcastic.

The woman's eyes crinkled—another smile that sent a wave of nausea straight to my gut. "They say knowledge is power." She leaned toward me, her eyelashes nearly brushing the glass. "Do you know what *I* say, Kali? Power is power. Pure, brute force. This world thinks they have the monsters our kind hunt under control. They *protect* them." She shrugged. "So I'm giving them new monsters. The less control they have, the more they'll need us. And the fewer humans there are . . ." She shrugged. "Well, evening up the numbers a bit can't hurt."

I thought of the scientists—my father and Dr. Davis and Rena and all the rest, who, at some point, had probably all told themselves that the things they were doing were justified by the greater good. Knowledge. Better medicine. Exploration.

And all they were doing was building better monsters.

"If you're concerned about the numbers," I said, my voice remarkably steady, "why am I locked up? Why is Zev?"

Saying his name hurt.

First Skylar. Then Zev. My mother.

Why did I ever bother letting anyone in? People only hurt you in the end.

"Oh, don't look like that, love," the vampire said. "It's not as if the poor boy had a choice. There's always a dominant partner in any pair—against someone like me, he never stood a chance."

People like us come in pairs. That was what Zev had said. I'd known it, deep down. It just hadn't ever occurred to me that Zev might already be part of a pair. That I might not be his other half. That there might be someone else out there who could take control of his body, his will, the way he'd occasionally taken over mine.

"If you and Zev are connected," I said, forcing myself to say it, forcing it not to matter, "why are you doing this to him?"

Assuming that Zev really was a lab rat—that everything I'd seen and felt from him hadn't been a lie.

"Not that it's any of your business, Kali, but I needed to see if it was possible for one of our kind to play host to more than one chupacabra." She seemed to find the scientific term amusing. "It took some tweaking, and some failures, and more than a little discomfort for poor Zev, but I have evidence now that it is possible. And if it's possible for our kind to host two, then someday, it might be possible for regular humans to hold one. In the long run, anything that makes humans less human will be better for us."

I digested what she was saying—the reason for the experiment that had resulted in Bethany being infected, the possibilities she'd discovered experimenting on Zev.

It was possible for Zev to have been bitten twice.

Possible for him to be connected to two others.

One who controlled him, and one he controlled.

No. Zev's voice was quiet in my mind, but it was still there. I wouldn't do that to you. Not unless you were in danger—and even then, I didn't do it on purpose.

I wanted to believe him, but he'd brought me here. He'd strangled me. He hadn't mentioned, even once, that this was a trap.

I couldn't. She wouldn't let me. I tried.

I could feel the hatred in his voice, loathing for himself, for her. I felt his emotions as intensely as my own and knew that he was wishing he'd killed himself before he could bring this kind of trouble to me.

I tried.

This was too much. It was just too much.

I'm sorry, Kali.

I wasn't sure that mattered. I also wasn't sure he had

anything to apologize for—he'd tried to warn me; he'd tried to fight. The only thing I *was* sure about was that in another four hours, I would be human again. I would be weak, defenseless.

I would hurt.

"You keep looking at your watch. I have to say, that surprised us. We hypothesized that a successful hybrid might have a portion of our skills, perhaps muted. Maybe it has something to do with the exact graft we used on your DNA, but the idea that you shift from form to form according to some circadian rhythm . . ." She trailed off.

"We?"

On the other side of the door, the woman smiled and turned her head to the side. "Didn't you tell her, Rena?"

The woman's use of my mother's name was like a knife, straight to my heart.

"I didn't exactly have the chance, Colette."

Colette. So now the psychotic woman had a name. I tried to concentrate on that—and not on the sound of my mother's voice.

"How rude of me," Colette said. "I haven't even introduced myself. You may call me Colette, if you wish, Kali. Or," she added, stepping back from the glass so that I could see her lips twisting into a smile, "you could always call me *Mama*."

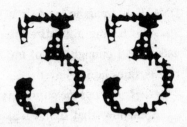

Mama. The word rolled off her tongue, ugly and sickly sweet.

I stared, uncomprehending, through the slit in the door at those delicately fringed eyelashes, and something gave way inside of me.

Mommy.

Mama.

Sit still, Kali. Sit so still.

"You remember," the woman who'd told me to call her "Mama" said approvingly. "I thought you might."

I didn't, not really. I was three when my mother left—*No,* I corrected myself. *I was three when my father left her.*

"He didn't know about you." I thought my way through it out loud, my eyes on the vampire's.

"Your father?" Colette said. "No, he did not. I was your little secret—and Rena's."

We had lots of secrets. Mommy, Mama, and me.

"Colette—" Behind her, Rena started to say something, but Colette waved it away with a delicate swish of her hand.

"She's as much mine as she is yours, darling." Even through the slit in the door, I could see Colette's eyes sparkle. "I donated the, shall we say, extraordinary portion of your

DNA, Kali. Imagine my dismay when you were born human."

As if having my entire life rewritten once in a single day wasn't bad enough. All of my father's revelations were half-truths, ones he'd believed.

Guess I'm not the only one who was lied to.

Somehow, that didn't make me feel much better. In the past twelve hours, I'd gone from having no mother to having two—and if there was anything worse than Rena, it was Colette.

"Well, enough chitchat, I suppose. It's been lovely, Kali, but there's much to be done in the next few hours." Colette wriggled her eyebrows. "I hear the FBI is planning a raid."

She didn't seem worried—and that terrified me.

"I'm afraid it would be easier if you weren't conscious for this next part," she continued. "Rena, did you remember to double the dose?"

Without thinking, I took a step back from the door, but there was nowhere to go.

I was trapped.

I'm sorry, Kali, Zev said, his sorrow bleeding over into my fear. I am so, so sorry.

He wanted to help me, but couldn't.

Wanted to fight her. Couldn't.

The door opened, and I stumbled backward until I hit the concrete wall. I'd expected to see Colette, but to my surprise, it was Rena standing there. She had a pair of syringes in one hand, each filled with an amber-colored liquid.

"A triple dose," Rena said. She met my eyes, and for a second, a split second, I thought I saw something else there.

A question.

A plea.

"Stay away from me," I said, and the words left my mouth as a growl. Drowsy or not, drugged or not, I was stronger than this woman who used to be my mother.

Much stronger.

"It's going to be okay," she said, moving toward me slowly. "I promise, Kali. It's all going to be okay."

The words set off an explosion of memory in my mind. *Everything is going to work out okay. You're going to be okay. I'm going to make you okay. Okay?*

Skylar was dead. Rena was coming toward me, needle in hand. Nothing was okay.

Nothing would ever be okay again.

"What Rena means," Colette said helpfully, "is that if you so much as move a muscle, I'll dose you myself—and I won't make it pleasant."

Now that the door was open, I could see that Colette's hair was a shade lighter than her eyelashes—a light honey brown. There was a dusting of freckles across her nose and an unadulterated cruelness to the set of her features.

She was a hunter. I was her prey.

"Please, Kali." Rena took my arm. I flinched, but she met my eyes again.

Let me do this.

That was what her eyes said to me, and I bit back the impulse to hit her again—harder, this time, than before. Hard enough to do some actual damage—but for better or for worse, I couldn't kill someone I remembered loving as much as I'd once loved her.

"I hate you," I said instead, feeling little and powerless and like nothing I'd ever said or done had mattered in the least. "I really, really hate you."

Rena pursed her lips. The needle pierced my skin.

"I know," she said.

At those words, Colette smiled and turned away. Rena pulled the needle out, putting her thumb over its tip. Then she pressed down on the back of the syringe.

The liquid dribbled harmlessly down my arm.

She did the same thing with a second syringe.

Then she reached into her white lab coat and withdrew a third, pressing it into my palm.

"Go to sleep, Kali-Kay." She closed her eyes, and I realized her hands were trembling.

Realized that Colette would kill her if she knew.

My fingers closed around the third syringe. I held Rena's gaze for another few seconds, and then I nodded. I closed my eyes and slumped against the concrete wall, like she'd knocked me unconscious.

And I waited.

I lay in my cell, feigning unconsciousness, for what felt like an eternity.

Three hours and forty-seven minutes.

Three hours and seventeen minutes.

Two hours and twelve minutes.

One hour.

And the longer I sat there, pretending that Rena had knocked me out, the more I wondered what the plan was, if she even had one.

I heard doors being opened and closed. Screams and calls and growls reminded me that I was surrounded on all sides by other creatures that didn't belong on this earth.

Experiments, like me.

Maybe in another hour, I'd feel for them, feel connected to them, but for now, I was still a hunter, and every instinct I had was saying to claw my way through this prison and *put the monsters down.*

Instead, I focused on diagnosing the meaning behind their screeches and howls and realized that someone was moving them. Evacuating them. Colette must have called in the cavalry, and by the time Reid and his team got here—

if they got here at all—they'd probably find the place empty.

Fifty-five minutes.

Forty.

Thirty-five.

Ten.

I couldn't lie there any longer. I couldn't afford to wait. In just a few minutes, I'd be human again. I could already feel it creeping up on me, the way other people could tell they were coming down with a cold.

Ten minutes.

Nine.

I was seconds away from standing and giving up my cover when the door to my cell opened. The smell of perfume told me it was a woman.

A knowing in the pit of my stomach told me she wasn't human.

Colette.

"The pièce de résistance," she said. "Pretty, isn't she? I can see why you got attached."

At first, I wasn't sure who she was talking to, but as he came closer, warmth washed over my body, and each and every one of my nerve cells stood on end.

Zev.

If I'd been capable of feeling pain, being this close to him and knowing what he'd done to me would have hurt. Even if he hadn't meant to. Even if he'd tried to stop it.

"Here," Zev said. "Let me."

"No." Colette spoke sharply, and I felt Zev's body freeze, felt her taking him over the way he'd taken control of my body at the ice rink, or in the car with Eddie.

His silver eyes went wild, every muscle in his body tensing at once as he fought her hold. I could feel my chupacabra, feel his, feel the sweat pouring down his temples and the pain that came with disobeying.

I felt him fight. And lose.

His muscles relaxed, and Colette smiled.

She's too strong, Kali. Too old. I should have killed myself when I had the chance.

I thought of his hands closing around my throat and couldn't push down the part of me that said that maybe he should have.

"Zev." Colette said his name in a way that sounded intimate and familiar. Too familiar. "Go check on Rena. Make sure she's got the A-level subjects evacuated. Anything else can stay here—we might as well give the Feds something to sink their teeth into."

The irony of hearing a vampire say those particular words did not escape me, but right now I had bigger things to worry about—like Zev walking silently away.

She doesn't know you're awake. She doesn't know what Rena gave you. That much, I can keep from her. That much, little Kali, I can do.

I pushed down the desire to open my eyes as I digested that statement. Zev knew I was holding a syringe. Colette did not.

Seven minutes.

This was it. Whatever drug they'd used to knock me out, I prayed that it would work on someone as old and powerful as Colette—because, if not, I didn't stand a chance.

Closer. Prey getting closer. Kill it dead.

I told myself that this was just like any other hunt. My heartbeat didn't accelerate. I didn't hold my breath. My muscles were loose and relaxed. Colette bent down to grab me, lifting me like I weighed nothing.

I let my body hang limp like a rag doll. She threw me over one shoulder and turned.

Six minutes.

With every ounce of strength and speed I had, I drove the tip of the needle into Colette's neck. Her grip on my body tightened—I heard bones pop and knew I'd be feeling it soon, but that didn't stop me from pressing down on the syringe.

Like a horse bucking its rider, she threw me across the room. I hit the concrete wall, hard. The back of my head warmed with blood. I could taste it in my mouth.

But somehow, I stood up.

I met her eyes.

She took a step forward, then stopped. "What have you done?" she asked, frowning, like I was just a naughty child, and she wasn't about to kill me dead.

"Triple dose," I said, wishing I had a knife, a sword, a gun—anything other than my fists.

She wobbled on her feet, but didn't fall. "Oh, I am going to kill that—"

She never got to finish that sentence, because a second later, she went down.

It took me a moment to process the sound of gunfire echoing in the chamber and to see the tiny hole in the back of her head, the blood dying her light hair red.

Someone shot her, I thought dully. *I drugged Colette, and someone shot her.*

I lifted my eyes to the open doorway—toward Rena and her smoking gun. All business, she walked forward and knelt next to Colette's prone body.

She put the gun to the vampire's temple and pulled the trigger.

Again. And again. And again.

"She won't stay down long," she said finally. "An hour or two at most. We have to get you out of here. Now."

"You shot her. In the head. Five times." I processed those facts. "I couldn't heal from that."

Rena dropped the gun onto the floor, her creamy brown skin tinged gray and pale. "She can."

I heard a scream—human, this time—and took a step toward the door.

"Anything we couldn't transport, Colette ordered let loose," Rena said. "The paperwork shows this facility as belonging to one of Chimera's competitors. They'll be faced with the fallout, and if the Feds get anyone from Chimera, it will be Paul or me."

Poor you, I thought, but after everything that had happened, I still wasn't the kind of person who could say something like that out loud. It must have shown on my face, though, because Rena responded like I'd slapped her.

"You have no idea what I just risked for you, Kali."

"I do know," I said, my voice soft. What I didn't say was that it wasn't enough, might not ever be enough.

"We have to get out of here." Rena reached to steady me, and she frowned. "You're bleeding."

Out of habit, I surveyed the damage. "Two broken ribs. A concussion. And I'm pretty sure she snapped my wrist."

Three minutes.

Not enough time to heal.

Rena latched her hand over my good arm and tugged gently. "There's a back way," she said. "We'll leave and seal it off. The Feds could be here any minute."

Realizing the implication of her words, I pulled back away from her grasp. "Where's Zev?"

"I don't know," she said. "Does it matter?"

I considered her question. I saw Zev in my mind's eye. I felt his fingers closing around my neck, felt him cutting off the flow of air. I saw him, wild-eyed and fighting vainly against Colette's hold.

He'd betrayed me, but he hadn't meant to. Hadn't wanted to. And Rena was just going to leave him here—with the place in chaos and Colette a ticking time bomb, waiting to wake up on the floor. And once Colette woke up, she'd be able to control Zev again. She'd stick him in another cage—if the FBI didn't beat her to it first.

He'd still be in my head. I'd still be in his. Eventually, someone would use him to find me, and the whole thing would start all over again.

"No."

"No, what?" Rena's voice was tinged with desperation, and the din in the background rose to new heights; a man's screams melding in with inhuman ones, as an alarm—jarring and violent—pierced the air.

"The Feds are here. This place is coming down, Kali. As your mother, I am telling you to move."

I looked at her, and my stomach lurched. She'd saved my life. That didn't make her my mother.

Without a word, I sat down next to Colette's body. Almost on cue, a bullet fell from her skull. She was already healing, faster than I ever had.

It's the Nibbler. You feed it. It heals you.

The words Zev had once spoken came back to me with a vengeance, and I did the math. Colette probably kept her parasite very well fed.

"Kali, I have to go. Please don't make me leave you here." Rena's voice broke. *"Please."*

"Knife," I said.

Apparently, that wasn't what she'd expected as a response.

"You have my knife," I said, lifting my eyes to hers, falling back on my senses while I still had them. "I'd like it back."

"Kali, the FBI is going to find you here. Eventually, Colette is going to wake up. You can't—"

"Give me the knife," I said. "And then go."

There was a long moment, an elongated silence, and then she nodded, her face going as blank and calm as mine. She reached down to her boot and pulled out my knife, the motion eerily similar to one I'd made myself a million times.

She handed it to me, hilt first. She brushed one hand over my cheek. And then she turned and walked—no, ran— away.

One minute.

I had sixty seconds—no time to heal, no time to think, no time to process the sounds of animal screams and gunshots in the distance.

All I had time to do was act.

Kneeling next to Colette's body, I cut open her shirt. The swirling pattern laid into her skin was complicated, and my eyes traced the interweaving circles and lines back to a central point, just over her collarbone.

An *ouroboros*.

"You don't want her," I said, my voice shaking as I brought the tip of my knife to my left arm.

Cut. Cut. Cut.

"You want me," I said. "I'm smarter. I'm younger. And I'm one of a kind."

Now *that* was the truth.

"You don't want her." I painted Colette's body with my blood, flashing back to that moment in the hallway with Bethany. "You want me."

I willed it to be true.

Ten seconds.

Nine.

Nine seconds, and I would be human.

I couldn't do this.

Darkness lapped at the edges of my mind. My temples pounded. My breath came fast and short—and then there was a sound like a gun going off, and a smell like rotten eggs.

I stumbled backward, hit the wall, and sank to the floor.

Four seconds.

Three seconds.

Colette's body twitched, the lines on her skin disappearing like sidewalk chalk under the force of a hose. For one horrifying moment, I thought she might wake up.

But she didn't. Her limbs stopped twitching. Her mouth went slack. And that feeling in my stomach, the one that told me that something preternatural was close, flickered like a lightbulb and died.

One.

The second I shifted, the pain was blinding, overwhelming, everywhere. I was little and human and bleeding.

I hurt.

"Kali." Suddenly, Zev was beside me, holding my head in his hands. "You're going to be okay," he said, checking me for injuries, staring into my pupils. "You're going to be just fine."

In his words, I heard an echo of Skylar's. *You're going to be okay. I'm going to make you okay. Okay?*

I gave myself over to the pain. Searing, blinding pain. I could get through this. I could.

The warmth of my skin built to an incredible, cleansing heat. I felt like I was wearing my body for the first time, like it was wearing me.

Here we go again, I thought.

I tried to smile, but it came out a sob. "Look," I said, tears dripping down my cheeks, my breath catching raggedly in burning lungs. "Now we both have two."

Zev followed my gaze to the *ouroboros* on my shoulder. His eyes went to Colette, lying still on the floor.

"You . . ."

He couldn't finish the sentence. I laid my head back against the cement, insane laughter bubbling up inside of me.

There were two chupacabras inside my body. My very human body.

"Guess I do have a savior complex," I said.

And then I laughed. It was a crazy, pitiful sound, like the mewling of kittens, but I couldn't make myself stop.

It hurt.

Everything hurt.

"The Feds are here," Zev said. "Colette moved some of her pet projects out, but the ones she left are . . . unpleasant. They'll keep our friends occupied while we duck out, but if the Feds are lucky, they'll survive." He ran his hand lightly over my hair. "We should go."

Before, when Rena had asked me to go, I'd said no because I didn't want to leave Zev, didn't want to spend the rest of my life looking over my shoulder for the woman who'd been pulling his strings. But now . . .

"Come with me," Zev said. "We'll leave, Kali. You and me. There's nothing here for you. We'll slip out of here, and we'll leave town, and we'll disappear."

I could see it—the two of us, spending our days in this world and our nights together in dreams. We'd hunt together, and we'd live together, and it would be so easy.

So right.

"I—" It was there, on the tip of my tongue, to say yes, but a volley of images flashed through my brain.

Faces.

One after another after another.

Bethany and Elliot.

Skylar.

My father.

If I left, he'd never know what happened to me. Even if I managed to say goodbye, he'd be alone.

Bethany and Elliot would never know what really happened to Skylar.

I'd never get to make this—any of this—right.

That was the second I realized that I had a choice. I could

run and run, farther and farther away. I could make myself forget. I could be what Zev was, do what he did.

Or I could stop running.

Stop trying to be something I wasn't.

Because at the end of the day, I wasn't like Zev. I wasn't like anyone. I was one of a kind. That wasn't going to change—it wasn't ever going to change.

"Go," I told Zev as the sound of footsteps echoed through the hallway and orders, shouted by men, reached my ears. "I can't."

Why—not? He spoke the words silently, and they came to me in pieces, like a radio signal interrupted by static, a reminder that I wasn't what I'd been an hour before.

Two chupacabras. Human body.

Twenty-three hours and fifty-four minutes.

"I'm tired of running," I told Zev, forcing the words across my lips, rather than speaking them mind to mind. "I have to do this. You have to let me."

Whatever Skylar had seen of my future, whatever had convinced her I was worth saving—I had a feeling I wouldn't find it on the road.

I owed it to her to stay and fight—no matter how broken I was, no matter how lonely.

"I will come back for you," Zev said.

I nodded, smiling and sobbing and hurting so badly I could have screamed.

"What if they hurt you?" Zev whispered.

I met his eyes, then pushed him away. "They won't do anything to me," I said, remembering Skylar's words about Reid. "Why would they? I'm just a kid."

Just a girl.

A battered, broken human girl.

Zev pressed his lips to mine. He kissed me. And then he was gone.

I hugged my knees to my chest, folding myself into a tiny ball, and that was how Skylar's oldest brother found me.

Just a girl—for now.

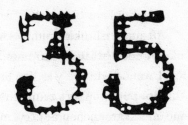

"Kali." Reid crouched to my level, and in his eyes, I saw the Haydens' house. The handprints on the driveway. The pictures on the walls.

"Skylar." That was all I was able to say—just her name, nothing else.

He closed his eyes, head bowed. "I know."

Another person might have looked at Reid and seen a complete lack of emotion. He might have looked like the consummate warrior, a blank slate. But I saw deeper, saw more.

I saw Skylar.

Gone.

I may have been the one bleeding, but the man in front of me was gutted.

"We have to get you out of here," Reid said, opening his eyes to fix me with a familiar stare. "This place is going down."

On some level, I was aware of the cacophony echoing all around us. Men fighting monsters. Monsters killing men. And even though I'd stayed for a reason, even though that had been *my* choice, I couldn't help the whisper in the back of my mind that asked why it mattered.

What did any of it matter, when Skylar was dead?

"It matters," Reid said, his voice cutting through the air like a knife, "because you're not."

I wondered if he was like Skylar—if he saw things, knew things—but I couldn't bring myself to ask. Gingerly, he lifted me off the ground, and I drew in a sharp breath.

"First we get out of here. Then we get you to the hospital."

I wanted to tell Reid that I could walk out on my own two feet, that I hated hospitals, that I wouldn't have blamed him if he'd left me there to die. But I didn't say any of that.

I said, "They killed her."

And Reid said, "I know."

He pulled a gun from his side and shouted something down the hallway. A shout came back, and a second later, the hallway was filled with men in bulletproof vests.

It figured the government would send the FBI into a facility filled with genetically enhanced monsters and expect *bulletproof vests* to do the trick.

A man who might have been Reid's boss spared a glance for me. "Preternatural Control has the first level secured. We've planted the explosives. Get her out of here. We detonate in three."

Three minutes, I thought, and the insane urge to laugh bubbled up in me again. I'd intended to burn this place to ash, and in three minutes, that was exactly what it would be. But as Reid carried me to safety, and I left the closest thing I'd ever seen to a war zone behind, all I could think about was the bodies we passed.

A miniature griffin with broken wings and a blood-smeared mouth.

A reptile whose eyes looked all too human.

The Alan.

All dead.

"They're going to want to ask you some questions," Reid said quietly, once we'd made it out and to the road.

I watched the building go up in flames. Watched the windows explode outward and the structure collapse. I thought of the will-o'-the-wisps, of Skylar, of Colette's body in the basement cell.

"I know."

The doctors patched me up. The FBI asked their questions, and I did my best to answer them quickly and efficiently—and most important, *before* the sun came up the next morning.

No, I didn't know the details of Chimera's operations.

No, I couldn't tell them what—if anything—had escaped before the facility had gone down.

No, I hadn't been in on this plan from the beginning.

Yes, I was just a kid.

No, I shouldn't have been there.

Yes, they'd killed my friend.

It was only after I'd told the agents that the woman whose remains they had found in the basement was the one calling the shots that they left me alone for a few blessed hours. When they came back, they had more questions.

No, those weren't real *ouroboroi* on my stomach.

No, I had no idea *what* the woman in question was, or why her remains weren't testing positive for human DNA.

Sure, they could take a sample of *my* blood.

Everyone but Reid must have been scratching their heads when the results came back human.

Three hours and fourteen minutes.

I could feel dawn coming, more strongly now than ever before. Soon, the doctors would come in and sign my release papers. Like the Feds, they must have suspected I was holding something back, but since—as far as modern science was concerned—it was impossible to play host to multiple chupacabras at the same time, they didn't have any reason to believe that I needed to be quarantined.

They just thought I had really tacky taste in tattoos.

Three hours and twelve minutes.

The stitches in my scalp itched. My wrist throbbed inside its cast. Each breath I took sent a sharp and jarring pain straight to my rib cage, and I was starving.

"That is a truly unfortunate haircut."

They'd had to shave a patch of hair to treat my head wounds. It figured that Bethany would comment on it. What didn't figure was that she was here. Pale, with her hair pulled into a messy ponytail, she stood in the doorway of my hospital room. Her hands were clasped together, and the thumb of her right hand worried at the palm on her left.

I couldn't bring myself to meet her eyes. I didn't want to know what I would see there.

"I might be able to fix it," Bethany said, and I glanced up long enough to see that she was looking down at her feet as well. "Your hair."

That didn't sound like the kind of thing you would offer a murderer, but the last time she'd seen me, she and Elliot had woken from a trance to find Skylar dead. The last time she'd seen me, my face had been covered in the guard's blood.

"Bethany—"

She interrupted me before I could say anything else.

"Don't make me tell you that I'm glad you're not dead."

"But I—"

Bethany held up a hand. "Don't want to hear it," she said. "And I really don't need to know." Without another word, she held up her keys and cocked an eyebrow in invitation.

I thought of the doctors, who were supposed to sign my release forms this morning.

I thought of the three hours left until dawn.

"Let's go."

† † †

We drove in silence for a long time. It occurred to me that my dad might return to my hospital room and wonder where I'd gone, but I'd lost my phone in the scuffle, and old habits died hard.

"The FBI came to talk to me," Bethany said finally. "I'm pretty sure they're going to arrest my dad."

Two days ago, I would have asked her what she'd told them—about me, about what I could do. But I didn't.

Didn't have to.

"If it makes you feel any better," I replied, "they'll probably arrest my mom." I paused and let myself picture Rena's face in my mind. "If they can find her."

"Are they going to arrest you?" Bethany never was one to beat around the bush.

"I didn't kill Skylar." That wasn't what she'd asked, but I had to say it. Hearing the words hurt. Meaning them hurt more.

"Kali. You *did not* kill Skylar." Bethany took her eyes off the road and looked at me. "You didn't."

This wasn't how I'd expected the conversation to go. She sounded like she was trying to convince me, instead of the reverse.

"I brought her there," I said, looking down at my hands, down at my stomach.

Two hours and twenty minutes.

"She brought herself there."

"If she hadn't met me," I said, my voice hard, "she'd still be alive."

"And if I hadn't let my little brother play in a friend's backyard, he wouldn't be brain-dead." Bethany's voice was matter-of-fact, but I knew the words cost her. "Hell, Kali, if Tyler were alive and well, my father never would have gone off the deep end, I wouldn't have been infected in the first place, and none of us would have ever even heard of Chimera."

If Bethany hadn't been bitten by the chupacabra . . .

If I hadn't saved her . . .

If I'd never met Zev . . .

If, if, if—and at the end of the day, none of it mattered.

"How long until sunrise?" Beth's abrupt change of subject did not go unnoticed. I didn't question it, or her, or the fact that the two of us were in this car together.

I just answered the question. "Two hours and fourteen minutes."

Two hours and fourteen minutes, as human as the next girl.

Bethany smiled. "Good," she said. "That might actually be enough time to do something about that hair."

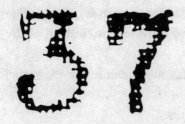

"Ashes to ashes, dust to dust."

The sky was dark and gray overhead, but as I watched them lower Skylar's coffin into the ground, a tiny stream of light broke through the clouds. To my left, Bethany stood as immobile as I was.

Maybe we didn't have a right to be here. Maybe the Haydens didn't want us here.

Maybe, maybe, maybe—and none of it mattered.

Across the lawn, Elliot didn't look at Bethany, didn't look at me. I found myself trying to match Skylar's many brothers to their descriptions and realized that I'd never hear her talk about them again.

They'd never see her again.

Handprints on the concrete, pictures on the walls—that's what she was now.

There were words spoken and hymns sung and none of it made her any less dead. I stood there, thinking of those last moments, the expression of pure and unadulterated bliss on her face.

I could have saved her.

I should have.

And nothing Bethany said could change that. Nothing I said or did or didn't do for as long as I lived would bring her back.

Beside me, my father reached out and put one hand on my shoulder, pulled me closer. On instinct, I stiffened at the physical contact, but after the moment of first contact passed, I leaned into his shoulder and watched them bury her.

I said goodbye.

And then I went home, cut the cast off my arm with a handsaw, and cried.

† † †

A week after we buried Skylar, I went back to school and found myself at the very center of the rumor radar. The investigation of Chimera's facility had been all over the news. Arrests were still being made. And though the Feds had kept my name out of it, everyone knew.

They knew that Skylar had died.

They knew that I was there.

And they knew that Elliot couldn't stand to look at me. That he wasn't talking to Bethany. That she'd started eating her lunch at the "freak table."

Suffice it to say, I was as surprised as anyone when Elliot approached me before school one morning and stiffly handed me an envelope bearing my name.

He didn't say a word. He just stood there and waited. After a moment, I forced myself to open it. Hot-pink letters danced across the page.

She'd dotted the *i* in my name with a little pink heart.

Dear Kali,

I don't know you yet, but I will. I'm going to say hi, and you're going to say hi, and we're going to be friends. At some point, I'm probably going to tell you that I'm a little bit psychic, and you probably won't believe me.

And the truth, Kali, is that you shouldn't believe me. Because, honest to God, I'm psychic <u>a lot</u>.

I don't even remember when it started, but there it is. So when I tell you that everything that's going to happen—that it's worth it—I need you to believe me, because it is. Maybe it doesn't seem that way right now—but five years from now or ten or twenty, it all works out.

This is how it's supposed to go.

That's why I'm going to do what I'm going to do, and that's why you're reading this, and why I'm not there to say anything myself. Don't be mad at yourself, and please don't be mad at me.

We're going to be friends.

So do me a favor, Kali, and watch out for Genevieve—once I'm gone, the other girls (but not Beth, of course!) are going to give her a really hard time. And make Darryl ask that cute freshman to the prom. And give yourself a break every now and then, because you deserve one.

XOXO,
Skylar Hayden
(School Slut)

P.S.: When they ask you what they're going to ask you, say yes.

P.P.S.: Tell Elliot I love him—and to stop being a tool.

I wasn't sure whether to laugh or cry, so I just handed the letter to Elliot and let him read.

"She wasn't psychic," he said. "She was just a kid."

She was both, I thought, but I didn't argue the point out loud. Instead, I thought of Bethany, whose father had been arrested. Bethany, who knew what it was like to carry someone else's death on your shoulders for the rest of your life.

Bethany, who'd lost almost everything in the past few days.

"Elliot," I said, surprised at how clear and steady my voice felt, "quit being a tool."

Eighteen
Months
Later . . .

The decision to take hellhounds off the endangered species list was a long time coming—whole lot of good that did me. Hunting them was still illegal; the only difference was now there were more to hunt.

"Here, puppy, puppy, puppy."

I really shouldn't have been doing this. If I got bloodstains on my graduation gown, Bethany was going to kill me, and Elliot was going to laugh. Adjusting the cap on my head, I spun my knife lazily in one hand.

Closer. You're getting closer.

If someone had seen me from a distance, all they would have seen was a normal girl, just graduated from high school.

A girl who lived bit by bit and day by day.

I closed my eyes, tasting sulfur on the wind and waiting. *Here, puppy, puppy, puppy.*

Catching a hint of something in the air, I jerked to a stop. This was the place, but there was something . . . off.

And that was when I realized that the hellhound was already dead.

"Hello, Kali."

I whirled around and found myself face-to-face with eyes I

would have recognized anywhere: silver eyes, fringed in black.

Eighteen months. It had been eighteen months of radio silence in my head. Eighteen months without a word, and now, he was here.

"Hey, Zev," I said. I nodded to the hellhound on the ground, noting the distance between its body and its head. "Just for the record, the next one's mine."

Zev smiled. "I think that can be arranged." He raked his gaze over my body, and then his eyes drifted slowly to the side. I turned and followed his gaze to two men standing at the edge of the park.

They were wearing suits.

I stopped twirling my knife and took a single step forward before I realized that one of the men looked very familiar.

"Reid?"

Skylar's brother nodded. He and the other man started walking toward us, and belatedly, I realized that the two of them—and Zev—moved like a team.

"Congratulations," Reid said, gesturing toward my cap and gown. "Got any plans for after graduation?"

I'd been entertaining the idea of taking a few classes at the University That Shall Not Be Named, but as I glanced from Zev to Reid, something clicked inside of me, and I started spinning the knife in my hands again.

Zev was a vampire. Reid was FBI. And according to something I'd once overheard the mother I hadn't seen in eighteen months saying, Chimera wasn't exactly one of a kind.

PS: When they ask you what they're going to ask you, say yes.

I brought my eyes to rest on Zev's. "What exactly did you guys have in mind?"